KEEP THIS TO YOURSELF

KEEP
THIS
TO
YOURSELF

TOM RYAN

Albert Whitman & Company
Chicago, Illinois

Library of Congress Cataloging-in-Publication
data is on file with the publisher.

Text copyright © 2019 by Tom Ryan
First published in the United States of America
in 2019 by Albert Whitman & Company
ISBN 978-0-8075-4151-7

Printed in the United States of America
10 9 8 7 6 5 4 3 2 1 LB 24 23 22 21 20 19

Cover images copyright © by Noel/Adobe Stock,
eugenesergeev/iStock, Artem Bali/Unsplash
Design by Aphee Messer

For more information about Albert Whitman & Company,
visit our website at www.albertwhitman.com.

100 Years of Albert Whitman & Company
Celebrate with us in 2019!

For Andrew.
How did I get so lucky?

ONE

TO BE HONEST, I'm not sure I was expecting anyone to show up, but when I come to the end of the overgrown path, pushing through a tangle of bayberry and wild roses into the clearing, Ben is already there.

He's still dressed in his graduation clothes: khakis and a button-down, his tie undone so that it hangs limp around his neck like a rope. His bike has been tossed onto the grass, and he's hoisted himself up onto one of the granite ledges that shelters the space, dangling his feet off the side. He raises a hand as I approach.

"Hey."

"Hey." I smile, trying to act normal, as if we still hang out here every day. As if we hang out at all, anymore.

"You managed to get away," he observes.

"Finally," I say. "My parents dragged me out to dinner with my grandparents. I thought it would never end."

He lets out a half laugh, one dead syllable that drops

straight to the ground.

"My parents can't even be in the same room together," Ben says. "They started arguing in the school parking lot over who would get to take me out to eat, so I slipped away and came here instead."

"You've been here that long?" I ask, surprised. It's been over two hours since our graduation ceremony ended.

He shrugs. "I like it here. It's nice."

I scramble awkwardly up onto the ledge to sit next to him, and we stare out at the water. He's right—it is nice. It's a beautiful June evening, still bright, although the sun is starting to drop toward a bank of thick clouds painted on the horizon.

From up here on the bluff we have a perfect bird's-eye view of Camera Cove: rows of brightly painted wooden houses; the commercial district, with its quaint shops and restaurants; the town hall's elegant brick clock tower; the boardwalk twisting along the stretch of sandy beach to the jagged, cave-riddled cliffs at its far end.

From a distance, you would never think that there was anything more to the town than the postcard prettiness that's always been its claim to fame; was its *only* claim to fame, before last summer.

"Hello, boys."

We both turn at the sound of the voice. Doris has materialized at the base of the path, as if from thin air. She's the kind of person who looks exactly the same now as she did when she was a little kid, and probably still will when she's eighty. Pin-straight, shoulder-length black hair, bangs sharp enough to slice your finger, tortoise framed glasses, wide strapped canvas shoulder bag. Every piece of clothing is perfectly clean and neat and pressed, every hair in place.

"Congratulations. Or should I say, 'congraduations?'" she says, in a pretty accurate impression of Anna Silver's perky valedictory speech. "Jesus, that was tough to get through. I was dying for a Xanax."

Something else that will never change about Doris: her sarcasm. She might be neat and tidy on the outside, but inside she's all barbs and sharp edges. I've known her since we were kids, but she's a tough nut to crack.

"It wasn't that bad," says Ben. "I thought she did an okay job."

"Are you kidding me? She actually used the phrase 'now it's time to spread our wings.' I thought she was going to break into song."

I don't say anything. Anna's speech might have been a bit chipper, but it would have been a hard job for anyone this year, under the circumstances.

"No family party for you?" I ask instead.

Doris rolls her eyes. "Fat chance of that. I'm surprised my parents even showed up at the ceremony." She points at the sun as it begins to dip behind the clouds. "Looks like I'm just in time. Let's get this show on the road."

We all turn to look at the ancient, gnarled oak, the only tree on this windswept bluff.

"Do you think we should wait for Carrie?" asks Ben.

"I was sure she'd be here," I say, which isn't really true. I *wanted* her to be here. The Carrie I grew up with wouldn't have missed it, but I've barely spoken to her since last summer.

He shrugs. "Maybe she'll still show. It's kind of important."

"Important," scoffs Doris. "Give me a break. Carrie's not coming, guys. She's done a better job of forgetting things than the rest of us."

"If it isn't important, why are you here?" Ben asks her, with an uncharacteristic flash of irritation.

I look back and forth between them as they bicker, vaguely aware that the sun has disappeared behind the clouds and the light has shifted. They look distant to me, as if I'm watching characters in a movie, rather than people who used to be my best friends.

"It seemed like a good way to wrap things up," says Doris. "I'm ready for this year to be over. I'm sick of thinking about it. I'm sick of knowing that everyone else is thinking about it. I'm ready to start thinking about something else."

"You make it sound easy," he says.

"No, it's not easy, Ben," and now Doris is the one who sounds irritated. "But it's necessary, so let's have our little ceremony or whatever and start getting the hell over it."

She walks over to the oak tree and crouches at the base, and Ben and I follow her.

"Why did you come, Mac?" Ben asks me as we kneel down beside her.

"Because we made a promise," I say.

They glance at each other. It's a quick, instinctive thing, almost imperceptible, but I notice it. It occurs to me for the first time that they might only be here for my benefit. Because they feel sorry for me, their weird friend.

Even though we're not friends. Not really. Not after last summer.

The three of us stare into the thick claw of roots at the base of the tree, muscular and knotted. It's easy to imagine them continuing down in a death grip beneath the surface. In front of us is a hollow, packed tight with rich, dark earth.

"How are we going to do this?" I ask. "I wasn't really thinking. I could run home and get a shovel or something."

But Doris has already unslung her bag and opened it in front of us. She pulls out a large Ziploc bag. Inside, cocooned like police evidence, is a gardener's trowel, caked with dirt.

"It's my mother's," she explains. She opens the bag and pulls out the trowel, then twists it forward into the hollow and starts to dig awkwardly.

"Let me do it," says Ben. "My arms are longer than yours."

Doris pulls back without protest and hands him the trowel. It's only a few seconds before Ben hits something, and after he clears away a bit more dirt, he reaches in and pulls out a metal tube.

"That was easier than I thought," I say.

"We didn't really bury it all that deep," says Doris. "It's not like anyone was going to think to look for it."

Ben carries the object out from the tree and puts it on the ground in the middle of the ledge. We sit in a circle, staring at it; an old stainless steel thermos.

"This was always your idea, Mac," says Doris. "You do the honors."

I reach over and grab the thermos. It's lighter than it looks. I hesitate, just for a moment, then use the sleeve of my hoodie to brush away some of the grime that covers it like a skin. The revealed metal dully reflects the sunset back at me. I glance up at Doris, to my left, and Ben, to my right. They're watching me, waiting, and in the weird, vivid light they look almost unreal—familiar faces seen through a blur of stained glass.

I twist the top of the thermos, and with a scrape of grit, it opens.

There's a piece of paper folded up inside, on top of everything else. I pull it out and open it, read aloud my pompous junior high handwriting.

"On this, our last day of school, in our eighth grade, we, the undersigned, do bury this time capsule."

"This must have been during your Ben Franklin phase," says Doris.

I ignore her and continue reading. *"Having spent our young years together as friends, the undersigned do solemnly declare that we will unearth this time capsule on the day of our high school graduation, four years hence."*

I stare at the signatures, frozen. For a moment, I feel like I can't breathe. But then Doris nudges me, and I manage to pull my eyes away and pass the paper along to her.

Once we've all had a chance to read it, I turn the thermos upside down and shake it. Envelopes, folded tightly and wrapped in rubber bands, fall out, followed by small school photos of each of us, floating like feathers to the ground.

I sift through the envelopes, reading the names and handing them around.

Doris opens hers, and Ben and I watch and wait. She taps it on her palm, and a small pendant falls out—a silver heart on a chain.

"I remember that thing," I say. "You always had it on."

"My aunt Marie gave it to me," she says, and for a moment, her cynicism fades away, and she smiles slightly, remembering. "It was a gift for my twelfth birthday. I told my mom I lost it. She was pissed."

"What was your prediction?" asks Ben.

She pulls a piece of paper out of the envelope and reads to herself. Her face reddens and she shoves the paper into her pocket.

"What is it?" I ask. "What did it say? You have to tell us."

"No," she says. "It's stupid."

"Come on, Doris," says Ben. "This is the thing. This is what we came here for."

He sounds genuinely disappointed in her, and she shakes her head at him, exasperated, but she pulls the paper back out.

"I'll get a full scholarship to Cornell," she reads, her voice flat.

Ben and I look at each other, confused.

"You did get a scholarship," I say. "You've been saying you wanted to go to Cornell since you were a kid."

"Yeah," she says. "I know that. I just…it seems conceited or something."

"You earned it, Doris," says Ben, quietly.

She looks to me, and I can tell from her expression that she wants to change the subject, so I rip open my envelope. Inside, there's a keychain—a memento from a trip I took to visit my cousins in Boston. Up to that point, it had been the best week of my life, but it seems cheap and insignificant now, compared to Doris's contribution.

"Lame," I say. Nobody disagrees. I unfold my prediction. "We will all still be best friends on graduation day."

There's another long pause, and the air around us grows thick.

"Wow, Mac," says Doris, finally, with forced sarcasm. "You should really get a job writing greeting cards."

Ben doesn't even smile. He's lost in thought.

"Ben," I say, and he snaps back to the present. He rips open his envelope, pulls out some hockey cards, and flips through them quickly. "Garbage," he says, tossing them onto the ground. He unfolds his paper and reads. "I'll be captain of the hockey team."

"Sad trombone," says Doris.

"Whatever," he says, crumpling up the paper and tossing it over the hill. He might pretend he doesn't care, but I still feel bad for Ben. As long as I've known him, he's been obsessed with sports, and although he's played pretty much everything—basketball, soccer, and his beloved hockey—he's only ever been good, never great. After everything that happened last year, he went into a bit of a nosedive. Not only did he not make captain, he didn't even make the team for our senior year. But that's not something I've ever talked to him about, and I'm not about to start now.

Instead, I say, "We haven't opened all the envelopes."

We all look at the pile in the middle of the circle.

"It doesn't really seem right to open Carrie's without her here," says Ben. "Maybe one of you guys can give it to her?"

Doris throws her hands up. "Don't look at me. We're not what you'd call 'close' these days. Anyway, you live right next door to her, Mac."

"Fine," I say. "I'll do it." I grab Carrie's envelope and shove it into the pocket of my hoodie.

My eyes drift back to the center of the circle. To the envelope still sitting there.

"We have to," I say, after a moment.

"I don't know if it's such a good idea," says Ben. "That's not really why we came here, is it?"

"Then why did we come here?" I ask. "If we don't remember him, who will?"

At the first mention of him, the air becomes charged with an unsettled energy, as if we've released the unanswered questions that we've all tried so hard to put behind us.

Ben and I turn to look at Doris. Tiebreaker.

She reaches out and picks up the envelope, stares at the signature scrawled across the paper.

"He would have wanted us to," she says finally, handing me the envelope.

"How can you know that?" asks Ben. "I wouldn't want you to open mine if—"

"Yeah well, he was a different person than you, Ben," I snap. I realize that I'm glaring at him and drop my eyes, not sure where this wave of anger came from.

Ben shakes his head at me, pissed, then sighs. "To hell with it," he says. "What do I care?"

I rip open the envelope and tilt it. Something slides out and bounces off my hand and onto the ground. Ben reaches over and picks it up. It's a dog tag, a flat piece of blue aluminum, shaped like a bone. A registration number is punched into one side, *Prince* engraved on the other.

Doris turns away, with a harsh, ragged exhalation. It's the first real display of emotion I've seen from her today.

"Prince," I whisper. "The Andersons' old dog. He died right around the time we buried the time capsule. He loved that dog, remember?"

I look up, smiling at the memory, and realize that Ben is crying. He turns away from us, pulling the back of his hand up to his face.

"Ben," I say, tentatively, reaching out but not quite putting my hand on his shoulder. "Are you going to be okay, man?"

"I'm fine," he says, his voice muffled but aggressive.

"Are you sure?" I ask.

Doris stands up and steps back from us, scowling. "There's no sense crying about it, Ben. It's done. He's dead."

"Jesus, Doris," I say, feeling like the wind has been knocked out of me.

"We should be thinking about his parents," she says, her voice tight with anger. "What they're going through. What all this must feel like to them."

"Yeah," I say. "Of course, but—"

"She's right, Mac," says Ben, turning back to face us. He wipes his eyes with the back of his hand and takes a couple of deep breaths, pulling himself together. "All that matters is that it hasn't happened again."

"It won't happen again," says Doris, decisively. "It's over. It's been a year, and the cops say it's done. Whoever did it has moved on."

"Yeah," says Ben, although he doesn't sound convinced.

Doris turns to me. "What about his prediction?"

I realize I'm still holding the envelope tight in my hand. I dig inside and pull out a folded piece of paper. My fingers tremble, and for a brief unhinged instant, I'm sure that I'm going to open it and find the whole thing written out, a clear and horrible prediction of his own shocking death.

But when I unfold the paper, there's no prediction at all. No words, even. Just a sketch.

Even at thirteen, his talent was obvious. His hands were never still, constantly doodling and drawing and sketching.

The portrait in front of me takes my breath away. It's the five of us, still just kids, smiling into the future. There's only one word on the page, the perfect block letters that I could probably forge from memory if I had to. A signature.

CONNOR.

TWO

LAST SUMMER, a serial killer paid a visit to Camera Cove.

By the time the dust had settled, four people were dead. George Smith, forty-four, who had only just moved to Camera Cove with his wife and kids. Maria Brindle, twenty-eight, a new mother and the wife of a popular town council member. Joanna "Joey" Standish, a sixteen-year-old girl from a trailer park outside the town limits. The so-called "Catalog Killer" always left a calling card: a page ripped from an old catalog, pinned to the victim's clothes. All of his victims had been overpowered, tied up, poisoned, and posed...with one notable exception.

Connor.

Seventeen. Tall and good-looking. Always smiling. Loved by everyone. The kind of guy that adults liked to say had "a bright and promising future ahead of him."

One of my very best friends since childhood. One of my *only* friends, if I'm being honest.

The last person to die before the Catalog Killer disappeared without a trace.

Connor Williams.

Gone forever.

× × ×

With the time capsule opened and all mysteries solved, things get awkward. There's nothing more to say to one another. It's time to go home.

When Ben stands up, he's smiling. It's like his breakdown didn't even happen.

"I'm going to head out," he says. "I need to grab a shower before the grad party. Maybe I'll see you guys there."

Before Doris or I even have a chance to respond, he's grabbed his bike and is pushing it through the shrubs back toward the road.

"Did you see that?" Doris asks. "He couldn't get away from us fast enough. He's such a pussy."

"He's upset," I say, a bit surprised. I'm used to Doris's sarcasm, but this is harsh even for her.

"He's a mess," she says. "He keeps breaking down in public. It was an awful, terrible thing that happened, and everyone is shook up, but he's still acting like chief mourner, when the rest of the universe is trying to move on. I mean, suck it up, right?"

"Come on, Doris," I say. "They were really close."

"Yeah, I know," she says. "But so were the rest of us, and you don't see us having emotional breakdowns in the grocery store. You don't even see Connor's mother doing it, for that matter."

"You don't see his mother anywhere," I counter.

Her face softens, conceding. "Yeah, well, that's to be expected, I guess. It's just…it drives me crazy that Ben wants to drag all of this on and on for some reason. I just want to put it behind me and get out of here."

"Maybe we all just deal with things differently," I say.

"I guess so." She sounds unconvinced. After a moment, she asks, "What do you want?"

"What do you mean?"

"Well," she says, "Ben wants to keep reopening old wounds, and I just want to forget all about it. How do you want this to end?"

I pause, considering. "I think I just want Connor to be recognized, somehow. Not just for how he died, but for what he was going to do with his life. His art."

"You think he would have been remembered for his art?"

"Absolutely," I say, picking up the sketch he put in the time capsule. "He was the most talented person I've ever known."

We both stare down at the drawing. The sketch is simple, obviously drawn quickly, but despite its simplicity, he'd managed to capture who we were better than any photograph ever could. The way one of Doris's eyebrows is slightly raised, a subtle hint of her default skepticism; Ben's easygoing athletic posture, his twitching mouth ready to laugh at any moment; Carrie's effortless cool, her arms crossed confidently in front of her chest, a perfect section of hair falling loose from her ponytail to half hide one eye; me, a half step away from the rest of them, my hands shoved awkwardly into my pockets. There's a slight slouch to my shoulders, but a shy smile on a handsome-enough face. I'm happy with the way he drew me.

Then there's Connor himself, crouched down in front of the rest of us, smack dab in the middle, ready to pounce. With his thick, wavy hair, square jaw, and muscular arms bulging from beneath his T-shirt, it's clear that he's the team leader, the captain of our squad.

We look like a gang of teenage superheroes, the way I sometimes imagined us when were still close.

"He sure did have a hell of an eye," she says.

I carefully fold the sketch and tuck it away in my backpack, then Doris helps me gather everything else. We shove it all back into the thermos.

I pick up the dog tag and roll it over in my fingers.

"Maybe I'll bring this back to Mr. Anderson," I say, tucking it into my pocket as we begin the short hike back to the road. "He'll probably be happy to get it back."

Doris shudders. "You're on your own. I hate going there since Mrs. Anderson died. It's so quiet and sad. To be honest, he creeps me out."

"He's not creepy," I say. "He's just lonely."

"Whatever you say."

The path winds up from the bluff, a narrow twist of packed gravel and an occasional chunk of granite. Both sides are edged with thick clusters of juniper and bay and wild roses, and pushing through them involves careful maneuvering to avoid getting scratched. The path ends at a low barrier: a rusted wave of steel bolted to two heavy wooden posts. On the other side is the dead end of Anderson Lane.

There are six houses on Anderson Lane. To our immediate right is Anderson Farm, a simple white farmhouse surrounded by a barn and various outbuildings, all with a full, high view of the coastline and the town far below. The other five houses are newer, built on lots that were carved from Anderson Farm in the early 90s, when Joe and Margaret Anderson subdivided a few acres to make some quick cash. My parents built here first, before I was even born, and by the time I was old enough for school, Carrie's parents had built. A year later, Connor's family moved in across the street, and by the end of second grade, Ben's parents and Doris's had also settled into the neighborhood.

It was a happy coincidence that there was a kid my age in every house on the street, and because we were so far out of town, we automatically fell into a friendship. At the time, it seemed natural, as if we would have found each other even if we'd been scattered all over the county. It wasn't until I was much older that I realized how untrue that was. Friendship is random, and there are no guarantees, even when you've known each other your whole lives.

We arrive at Doris's house first and stop at the end of her driveway.

"Are you going to the party?" I ask her.

She gives me a withering look. "Are you kidding me? I can't think of anything I'd rather do less."

"What are you going to do instead?"

She shrugs. "I don't know. Read. Go online and stare at pictures of the Cornell campus on their website. Pray for September to come earlier than scheduled. Why? Are you going?"

"I doubt it," I say. "I'm not really in the mood for a party. Besides, I'm starting my new job in the morning."

"Ah, yes," she says. "The library. A thrilling way to spend the summer."

I shrug. "It's a job."

She unfolds her hand and I realize she's been clutching her heart pendant the whole time. She looks at it and lets out a deep sigh, her sarcasm and bravado seeming to leave with it. Now she just seems sad and exhausted.

"We were so stupid," she says. "Anyone who tells you that high school is the best time in your life didn't grow up in Camera Cove. Even without the Catalog Killer."

Without warning, she leans in and envelops me in an awkward hug. I hug her back and pat her on the shoulder, and when we pull away, I see that she has tears in her eyes.

"This year has really fucked us all up, hasn't it?" she asks, wiping her eyes with the back of her hand. For a moment, I feel like she's going to say something else, but then she turns away and blinks hard a couple of times, and when she turns back to me, her expression is closed off again. "Congratulations Mac," she says. "I'll see you around." Then she flips her bag back over her shoulder and hurries up the driveway to her house.

If Connor were alive, the graduation party would have been a no-brainer. The five of us would have gone together. Ben would have scored some booze for us from somewhere. Doris would have had something sarcastic and hilarious to say about everyone else at the party. Carrie would have told all the same, awesome old stories about back when we were stupid kids. Connor would have been at the center of everything, toasting our group, making some cheesy, perfect speech meant to convince us that we would be friends for the rest of our lives.

And I would have been happy, like I always was when the five of us were together.

But Connor isn't here to hold us together anymore, and there's nothing I can do to change that.

I cross the street, passing Ben's old house, still empty with a faded *For Sale* sign stapled to the mailbox. Carrie's is next, then mine. My parents are in the TV room, watching a movie. I holler to let them know I'm home, then go upstairs into my room.

My room, as always, is a disaster. The bed isn't just un-made—blankets and sheets tumble off it and onto the floor. Clothes and books and old homework lay tossed in piles, and the surface of my desk is barely visible under a school year's worth of random debris.

My parents used to make an effort to get me to tidy up after myself, but after the murders, they gave up. I don't know if it's because they didn't feel right about nagging me after what happened, or if they just truly stopped caring. Whatever the reason, things are more out of control now than they ever were, but I really don't care. What difference does a messy room make when your life has been thrown completely off the tracks?

Connor, whose room was as obsessively tidy and organized as mine is messy, used to joke about the difference.

"I thought gay guys were supposed to be super neat and clean, Mac," he'd say, lightly punching my arm to make sure I knew he was just joking. "What the hell happened to you?"

If Connor had one flaw, this was it: the way he labelled people, placed them in little boxes.

It was hard to be too annoyed at him about it, because the thing is, he *liked* us that way. We were his crew, filling in the same roles we always had. I was the shy gay kid. Doris was the uptight nerd. Ben was the jock sidekick. Carrie was the cool girl.

I think sometimes he saw the world in simple terms, like we were just real-life versions of his sketches. If I'm being honest, I found it reassuring, knowing that in Connor's eyes, I had a part to play.

But there was more to me than that. There still is.

At least, I think there is. Before last summer, before the murders, I was starting to imagine my life after Camera Cove. I didn't have an air-tight plan, but I could picture myself heading to college, taking interesting classes, meeting boys, maybe even starting to date. I didn't have Connor's talent, or Doris's brains, but I was confident that something would work out for me, that eventually, a future would come into focus.

But then the shit hit the fan, and like everyone else in town, my plans took a back seat to the reality unfolding around us. The problem is that even now, a year later, whatever motivation I once had seems to be gone forever. How can I just up and leave when so much remains unsettled?

I shove the old thermos onto the top shelf inside my closet, wedging it behind a pile of sweaters and tattered magazines. An empty chip bag flutters down to the floor, and I kick it beneath the pile of clothes that's spilling out of my hamper, shoving the door closed.

I unzip my backpack and pull out Connor's sketch, unfolding it and then staring at the walls around my room, considering where to put it. My wall art is as undisciplined as the rest of the room. Every square inch is covered: band posters, pictures of hot shirtless guys, cool houses, and expensive watches that I've ripped out of magazines, maps of places I want to visit, a scattering of old photos, and many, many drawings done by Connor.

In the years before he died, Connor had become a lot more serious about his art, even studying with a private teacher. But he started out by copying superheroes. These are the most prominent of his pictures on my walls: confident, dramatically posed images of Batman and Rogue and Silver Surfer done in markers and colored pencils and even ballpoint pen. He may have been talented enough to move on to more serious stuff, but he never stopped reading comics.

Using a thumbtack, I stick Connor's group portrait to the wall, dead center above my desk, then I shove a pile of clothes off my chair and sink into it. I stare across the room at my bookshelf, at the cluttered stacks and rows of comics. Unlike every other surface in my room, the top of the bookshelf is empty, except for one thing. An old plastic grocery bag—a grocery bag I haven't been able to bring myself to open since the day I got it. Since the day Connor died.

Connor and I might not have seemed like the most likely of friends, but we bonded over an obsession with comics. As kids, we spent every spare cent on them, swapping titles back and forth and getting into endless conversations about them while Ben and Carrie and Doris rolled their eyes.

We were nine when Connor had the brilliant idea of pooling our resources and divvying up titles. Connor bought every new issue of *Spider-Man*, *Iron Man*, and *X-Men*, and

I was responsible for *Superman*, *Batman*, and *Justice League*. Every week, like clockwork, we swapped. Right up until the day he died.

Inside the grocery bag is the final stack of comics Connor ever bought. After reading them, he'd tucked them neatly into the bag in methodical, alphabetical order, then walked across the street to drop them off for me. The exact same way we'd been doing it for years. There was nobody home, so he'd left them hanging on my front door, where my mother had found them. She'd tossed the bag on my desk and had forgotten to mention it.

Later that day, the Catalog Killer had caught up with him.

It wasn't until after his body was discovered and the world came crashing down around us that I found the bag. I couldn't bring myself to open it then, and I haven't been able to do it since. It just doesn't seem right. As if by opening this final thing from him, I'm leaving Connor behind.

I get out of the chair and walk to the bookshelf, reaching up to put my hand on the bag. I press my index finger to its edge, running it up and down the thin hard spines inside.

Connor held these, the day that he died.

I pull the bag of comics off of the shelf and grip it tight along the sides. Still holding the bag, I walk to the window and stare across the street. Connor's house is dark, except for a light on in the side porch that leads to the kitchen. There are two dormer windows upstairs, and the one on the right stares directly across the road at my bedroom. Connor's room. We used to sit and look across at each other as kids, flashing elaborate signals with flashlights.

The weight of the bag is heavy in my hands. I sink back into my chair, surprised to realize that my lower jaw is trembling and my eyes are flooding.

Connor isn't alive. All of this is irrelevant to him now.

I rub the back of my hand across my eyes, take a deep breath, and open the bag. I pull out the stack of neatly bound, glossy papered comics. They're year-old issues, with storylines long since wrapped up.

I flip open the comic on the top of the stack. *The Avengers*, Connor's favorite. I catch my breath when I realize that there's a piece of looseleaf, folded crisply in half, sitting inside the cover.

I reach for it, my hand trembling as I unfold it. It's a note, in Connor's crisp, perfect block letters.

MAC, CAN YOU MEET ME TONIGHT? I'VE FIGURED SOME-THING OUT—SOMETHING IMPORTANT—AND I REALLY NEED YOUR HELP. MEET ME AT THE BEACH AT MID-NIGHT, AND KEEP THIS TO YOURSELF.

THREE

I STARE AT THE NOTE, shaking. My stomach begins to twist in on itself, and somehow, I end up on the floor, on my knees, my hands on the ground, worried that I'm going to throw up. The nausea passes, and the ringing in my head finally calms. I manage to get myself into a sitting position, my back against my bed.

The note is on the floor, just a few feet away from me. Such a small, unimportant looking thing, a piece of loose-leaf. But it's so much more than that. It's a message from beyond the grave, a year too late.

Why did Connor need my help? What did he know?

And if I hadn't missed this message from him, on the day he died…would things have been different? Could I have stopped it?

I bury my head in my hands, cursing quietly to myself. I can't stay here. I need to talk to someone. Someone who knew Connor; someone who can help me figure out what to do next.

Doris is home, just down the street from me, but I can't deal with her sarcasm right now. Carrie might actually take it seriously, but she's never around anymore. I consider texting her, but I know she'll be out somewhere with her boyfriend, and I can't be sure she won't tell him. That leaves Ben. I have to talk to Ben.

I turn and push out of my room, bound down the stairs, and stick my head into the family room.

"Can I borrow the car?" I ask, trying to sound normal, hoping my voice doesn't betray the inner turmoil that's threatening to spill out.

My parents, sitting on the couch, twist their heads to look at me. They try to conceal it, but I can see the alarm on their faces—the knee-jerk response to last year's events.

It's hard to blame them. Last year, there was a police curfew, which meant they had an excuse to keep me inside. The curfew ended months ago, though, and we've been told repeatedly that the murders are done, that we're safe, but nobody, least of all parents, can swallow that so easily.

"Where are you going, honey?" my mother asks.

"There's a grad party on the beach," I say. "I figured I'd make an appearance."

"The beach," repeats my father. I know what he's picturing—it's the same thing I've had on my mind every day for almost a year.

"It's cool, guys," I say. "There's going to be a cop in the parking lot all night. Nothing's going to happen."

"Of course," says my mom. She gets up from the couch and comes over to give me a hug. "You've earned a little bit of fun. Everyone has."

"Thanks," I say. "I won't be too late."

"Don't forget that you start work in the morning!" my father yells after me.

× × ×

Sure enough, there's a police car sitting near the entrance to the beach parking lot. As I drive past, I catch a glimpse of Chief of Police Patricia Parnatsky in the driver's seat, looking exhausted—like she has since she failed to catch the killer last year. I know she could have put another police officer in charge of the parking lot, but Trish Parnatsky feels responsible, I think. Responsible for everything that happened, and everything that might still happen if the killer surfaces again, somewhere else.

Before last summer, a cop at a party would have sent people scattering, grabbing their jackets and backpacks, hiding their booze, climbing in cars, relocating. Now the car is ignored, and although nobody comes out and says it, the security it represents is probably welcomed. There's an understanding now. There are things far more terrible than some drunken teenagers.

People can pretend all they like that things are back to normal, but deep down, we all know they aren't.

Instinctively, I reach down to touch my pocket, feeling the note I've folded into a tight bundle. I could walk across the parking lot right now, show Parnatsky the note, and ask her what to do, but something holds me back. What if she confirms what I've already started to suspect—that Connor's note could have saved him, if only I'd seen it in time? I don't think I can handle that. Not tonight. I know I'll have to come forward with the note eventually, but another day or two won't make a difference.

I cross the parking lot to the boardwalk, following it to the first set of steps down onto the beach. The night is bright and clear, and I can see people moving along the beach toward the cliffs at the far end.

Toward the caves.

A chill works its way up my spine when I realize where they're going, and I stop dead in my tracks. There's no way I'm going to the caves. Not now, not ever.

"Mac!" a shrill voice calls out, and I turn to see Anna Silver skipping down the boardwalk steps. Anna Silver: valedictorian, prom queen, captain of the volleyball team, and student council president.

"Congratulations!" she says, throwing her arms around me. "Can you believe it? We're finished!"

I smile at her, surprised and kind of pleased that someone actually seems happy to see me. "Yeah," I say. "It's hard to believe. Hey, I liked your speech today."

She smiles humbly, a practiced move after a day full of compliments. "I'm glad you came," she says. "You never come to parties."

"I wasn't planning on it," I say, "but I was out driving around and thought I'd stop and see what was up." I turn back toward the parking lot, suddenly anxious. I want to see Ben, but now that I'm faced with entering the caves, my determination wavers. Maybe I should wait and talk to him tomorrow. "I think I'm probably going to head out now, though."

"You can't!" she protests. "It's your graduation day, Mac!

You have to celebrate! You've earned it, just like the rest of us."

She grabs my hand, and I realize I'm not going to escape that easily. Anna pulls me back to where her boyfriend, Jeremy, is lugging a cooler down the stairs.

"Hey, Jeremy," I say. In response, he grunts and tilts his chin at me. A man of few words.

"Where's the bonfire?" Anna asks, turning to look down the length of the beach.

"I think it's in the caves," I say, trying to keep my voice even.

Her eyes widen. "What? I thought there was going to be a bonfire on the beach! Nobody said anything about the caves!"

"It's always at the caves," says Jeremy.

"Not last year," she argues.

"There wasn't any grad party at all last year," I say.

"Well, I think it's tasteless," she says. "People should show some respect. Things aren't the same since…well, you know."

"Since Connor died," I say. "We're not talking about Voldemort. You can say his name."

"I just don't like it," says Anna, ignoring my comment. "It's a bad place. Bad things go on in there."

"You listen to too much gossip, Anna," says Jeremy.

"Oh, come on, you've heard it too," she persists. "You know they say Junior Merlin runs drugs in and out of those caves."

"Well, Junior Merlin isn't here tonight," says Jeremy. "He's not going to drop into a high school party with a sack of weed when the cops are sitting up there in the parking lot."

"You know very well that I'm not talking about marijuana," says Anna. She turns to me. "Is it true that Carrie is dating his brother?"

I shrug. "Yeah, I think so."

"Is she crazy?" She shudders with distaste. "Ant Merlin. What is she thinking?"

I shrug. "I don't really talk to her much anymore."

"Are we going or not?" asks Jeremy, obviously losing his patience. He drops the cooler on the sand and stretches his arms over his head. I try not to look at the stretch of tight muscular stomach that appears between his shorts and T-shirt. Difficult.

"What do you think, Mac?" asks Anna. "You were friends with him. Is it disrespectful?"

"Everyone was friends with him," I say. The note pulses in my pocket.

"Yes, but you were his neighbor. You knew him forever."

I shrug. I don't want to admit that going into the caves terrifies me. I had enough "poor Mac" looks from Ben and Doris earlier this evening. "I don't know. I guess a bonfire in the caves isn't that different from a bonfire on the beach."

"Well, if you feel so strongly about it," she says, "let's go."

Somehow, I find myself walking along the beach with them, listening to Anna chatter.

"Jeremy and I are trying to spend as much time together as possible this summer," says Anna. "Aren't we, babe?"

Jeremy just grunts, stopping briefly to readjust the cooler on his shoulder.

Anna reaches over to give him a playful squeeze on the arm. "Jeremy has a full scholarship to Northeastern, and I've got one to Amherst. It'll be hard being at different schools in the fall, but they're just a few hours away by car. We'll see each other on weekends."

"You're going to Amherst?" I ask. "Me too."

She stops and her mouth drops open. "Shut up! That's awesome! I didn't think I'd know anyone else!"

"Yeah, that's cool," I say. "Makes it a little less scary."

"We totally have to hang out. What are you majoring in?"

"I don't know for sure," I say. "We don't have to pick till the end of sophomore year. I'm thinking maybe English."

"That's cool," she says. "I'm double majoring in chemistry and biology. Both programs are supposed to be really great, and it was just too hard to choose." She says it as if she's apologizing for something. "Besides, it'll look really good when I apply for med school."

"You really have things figured out," I say. "I barely got my application in on time." I don't tell her that I'm not even a hundred percent sure I want to go to college. How can we be expected to just leave and start new lives elsewhere, as if nothing has happened?

We arrive at the cliffs on the far end of the beach. The sea caves, a series of chambers deep inside the granite cliffs, are one of the trademarks of Camera Cove, tailor-made for stories of hidden treasure and rum-running. A couple of feet above the sand, a wide gaping hole flickers with a hidden light, evidence of the bonfire deep inside. This opening, at the far end of the beach, is the only way to enter the caves from dry land. The rest of the cave mouths are further along, where the cliffs drop straight into the waves.

The stories about the caves go way back. If you believe the legends, pirates hid treasure in them hundreds of years ago. It's more documented that they were used for rum-running during Prohibition in the 1920s, rowboats shuttling booze back and forth from the caves to sailboats that ran it up and down the coastline.

I've also heard the more recent stories—the ones Anna is talking about. Stories about Junior Merlin, the town's most notorious drug dealer and low-level criminal, stashing large quantities of narcotics deep within the caves, bringing them in by water in the dead of night and redistributing them by boat, much the same way the rumrunners did, years ago.

Jeremy's right that Merlin isn't stupid enough to be anywhere near the caves during a high school party. If he *is* hiding drugs in the sea caves, he's probably doing it farther down the coast, not here in the main chamber.

The red glow makes the cave opening appear like a door to hell. Nothing about this appeals to me in any way, and it has nothing to do with the stories of hidden drug stashes.

"I still think this is completely unnecessary," says Anna. "I can't believe anyone thinks this is a good idea."

"Come on," says Jeremy, "there's at least a hundred people in there. Don't be such a chicken shit."

She gives him a dirty look but steps primly around him and up the rough stone steps into the cave. Jeremy follows and together they disappear into the tunnel.

I could leave now. I could leave and nobody would blame me, or even notice. I look back at the beach. It's empty now, just a moonlit stretch of sand. My eyes scan the dunes; seagrass moves gently in the light breeze, and deep shadows slip down into the hollows. The hairs on the back of my neck stand up. I know there's no one there, but suddenly the thought of walking back alone is worse than the thought of going into the caves.

I reach into my pocket and rub my fingers over the folded square of loose-leaf paper. If I want to talk to someone tonight, Ben is the only real option.

Reluctantly, I step up into the mouth of the cave.

FOUR

AS I ENTER THE TUNNEL, there's a wave of hollow, disembodied screams and laughter from the chamber at the cave's far end. The passageway is narrow, but high enough that I only have to crouch a little bit.

I turn sideways as a couple of sophomores scrape past me, squealing and chattering.

"I can't believe this is where he died!" one of them says, before they scurry away in an obvious rush to get out.

I stop, debating whether I should go on. The light shifts and flickers, red and white and soft. Erratic tendrils of smoke waft past me, smelling like weed and tobacco and the acrid scent of burning driftwood and beach debris.

I could turn back now, step back into the fresh air of the clear summer night. I could follow those girls back to the parking lot, so I wouldn't have to be alone on the beach. I could even take off my shoes, put my feet in the water, and take a minute to look up at the space between me and the stars.

I could find a bottle, stuff Connor's note inside it, and toss it into the sea. Let it become somebody else's problem.

Instead, I keep going.

The tunnel spits out into a large, high-ceilinged chamber, and I'm struck by how huge the space is. At least half the size of our school gym, and in some places just as high. In the middle of the chamber, people are throwing driftwood on a bonfire. Although you'd expect a fire in an enclosed space like this to create huge amounts of smoke, that's not the case. Like magic, it twists into a narrow rope and disappears into a hidden chamber in the ceiling.

Someone has set up a speaker in the corner and heavy bass reverberates through the space. It blends with a cacophony of human noise: laughter, shrieks, drunken arguments, and murmured conversations.

Underneath it all, filling in the background, is a hollow, rhythmic rumbling—a deep repetitive rush, in and out like a beating heart. The ocean, squeezing its way in and out of the low sea caves that maze their way beneath the cliffs. I don't really want to look, but my eyes are drawn to the low hole in the wall at the back of the chamber. Not surprisingly, it's been given a wide berth, and there's nobody sitting or standing near it.

For a long while, I stand in the entrance to the chamber, just watching the scene in front of me. I've known most of these people my whole life, but I've never really felt comfortable with them. My anxiety hums. Nobody is even glancing at me, but I can't shake the feeling that they're watching me from the corners of their eyes, wondering why I'm here. Judging me.

If Connor were around, I wouldn't be paranoid like this. Being around him always made me feel comfortable. His presence—at parties or in the busy hallways at school—calmed me down and made me feel like I was part of the group, a citizen of the world beyond Anderson Lane. I haven't felt that way since he died.

If it weren't for Connor, I wonder if a random group like ours ever would have ended up friends in the first place. When I think about how quickly the distance between us all has grown since he died, I seriously doubt it.

Connor knew everyone. Was friends with everyone. Garnet Fuller, who was on the debate team with Connor, is in the corner with his girlfriend, Meryl Brandt, whom Connor had had some kind of fling with between ninth and tenth grade. In fact, I realize as my eyes make their way around the room, Connor had flings with several of these girls, at one point or another.

I know he messed around on and off with Gina Kay, whom I spot tossing back a wine cooler in the corner.

Flossie McKenna is sitting cross-legged next to the fire, sharing a joint with Cliff Starling. She cheated on her boyfriend with Connor.

Then there's Taryn Watts, tucked into a corner with Anna and a few other girls, gossiping earnestly. Taryn and Connor actually dated for a few months, about a year before he died. She was the closest he ever got to having a real girlfriend.

She was furious when he broke up with her—completely freaked out at him in public. But I remember her at the funeral. She was a mess.

Nobody makes an effort to greet me. If Connor were here, he would have pulled me into the conversation, made me feel like I belonged. He made everyone feel that way, like he was their best friend.

"Mac!" I turn around at the sound of my name, registering the figure who stumbles toward me.

Ben. He shoves past some people to get to me, then does a stupid little end-zone dance before tossing his head back and laughing. He leans forward and throws his arms around me in a bear hug. Some people nearby turn and glance at the scene, smirking, and I get self-conscious. He pulls back and holds me out in front of him with his hands tightly gripping my shoulders, as if he's a long-lost uncle, giving me the once-over at a family wedding. He stinks of rum.

"Mac, Mac, Mac," he croons. "I am so happy that you made it. I didn't think you'd make it."

"Ta-da," I say, throwing my arms to the side and pulling away. He doesn't get the hint, but instead moves to my side and drapes an arm around my shoulders, buddy-style. I haven't been touched this much in my life, and it's making my skin crawl. Jolly Drunken Ben is a very different person from Tragic Weeping Ben.

"This is my main man, Mac," he tells the group of people sitting closest to us, some sophomores I don't really know. "My oldest friend. One of them, anyway. Are you guys being nice to my buddy Mac? Gay Mac, the gayest guy I know. The *bravest* fucking guy I know."

I cringe, and one of the guys snickers. His girlfriend punches him in the arm.

"I'm serious," says Ben, narrowing his eyes. "You guys had better be nice to him, or I'll kick your asses."

"Have another one," someone mutters, but Ben isn't paying any attention. He's turned back to me, and his eyes are wide, intense. I wonder if maybe he's had something stronger than just rum.

"Come on, buddy," he says, dragging me by the arm toward the low hole in the back of the chamber. When I realize where he's taking me, I pull back.

"Hang on, Ben," I say. "What's going on?"

"Don't you want to see?" he asks. "Have you even been here since it happened?"

"No," I say, shocked. "I don't want to see. What the hell is wrong with you?"

The jocularity in his face disappears, and he narrows his eyes at me. "You didn't come here for this? Really? Why the hell else would you come? It's not like you ever socialize."

I barely have time to react before his expression becomes pained. "Oh man, Mac, I don't know why I said that. I'm sorry. I've just been so messed up lately. I don't know what the hell is wrong with me."

"It's okay," I say, desperate to get out of here. "It doesn't matter."

"Will you please come with me?" he pleads. "I need to go in there and see it for myself."

I recoil. "Absolutely not. Come on, Ben, you don't need to do this."

Ben gives me a look that I can't read, then he turns and walks through the crowd and over to the opening of the hole. He crouches to sit, and then slips his legs through.

I realize that the noise has dropped off and that everyone in the chamber is staring at us. In the corner, I see Anna's group of friends surrounding Taryn, who has started crying. She has her hands over her face, and they're trying to comfort her.

"What the hell are you doing, Ben?" someone asks.

"Fuck you," he replies, and then he disappears into the hole. I realize with an uncomfortable start that I have to go after him—Ben is in no state to be by himself right now, and I'm worried about what will happen to him if he's down there alone.

I force myself to ignore the stares, then I crouch and follow him in, kicking feetfirst into the hole and sliding forward to shimmy down into the cavern. The ambient, flickering light from the main chamber only barely reveals the new space, but my eyes adjust, and I can soon make out enough to see the grotto.

In contrast to the massive main chamber, the sea caves are small and tight. I have to crouch to move around, and there's not much space between the ledge I'm standing on and the water.

I see Ben right away. He's sitting on the far end of the ledge, his feet hanging out over the tunnel that sucks water in and out of the chamber.

I walk over and join him. Across the grotto, shadows indicate entrances to other caves and tunnels. I lean forward a bit, running my gaze along the chamber opening. I can barely see the open water through the mouth, which is just wide and high enough to let a small boat in. I picture rowboats, back in the day, laden with wooden chests or rum barrels, navigating their way into the chamber. There's no question; it would be a good spot to hide treasure or booze…or drugs.

Ben pulls a flask from his coat and offers it to me, but I shake my head. "I'm driving," I say.

I want to talk to him, show him the note, but he's not in any shape to be thinking about this stuff. I should have gone to see Doris. She would have at least had some advice, sarcastic or not.

"I'm sorry I freaked out at the time capsule," he says. "It's just a lot, you know?"

"Yeah," I say. "Of course. Don't worry about it."

"Doris can be such a bitch sometimes," he says. "I don't understand it. I don't know how she can be so cold about it all."

"I guess we all just deal with things differently," I say. I realize as I say it that I told her the exact same thing about him. Funny.

He looks at me, and his eyes are wild. "Murder, Mac. Think about it. Our best friend was murdered. Right here. Right on this ledge."

I drop my eyes to the ledge and look around. In the dim light, all I can see is damp granite and corners crusted with grime. A few empty bottles have been shoved into niches, and the damp remains of a cigarette package sits pressed up against a wall.

Almost a year ago, this was a crime scene—the site of a struggle between Connor and his murderer. Blood spatter that turned out to be Connor's; one of his drawing pencils, snapped in half; trace amounts of rat poison, the same stuff that had been used on the other three victims; a catalog picture of a teenage boy.

Connor's body. Drowned. Retrieved from deep within the narrow passage that led from this grotto to the sea.

All of it pointed toward a terrible struggle, a failed attempt by Connor to fight back against the murderer who had lured him into this cave. But sitting here, at the scene of the crime with Connor's note burning a hole in my pocket, something about this scene strikes me as odd.

"Have you ever wondered…" I begin, then stop. Ben turns to look at me.

"Wondered what?" he asks. His eyes are suddenly clear and focused.

"I don't know," I say. "It's just…isn't it weird that he was found here? In the caves? I mean, all the other victims were found at or near their homes. Why would the killer change up his routine? Why would he risk bringing Connor here to the caves, where things would be so much more uncertain?"

Ben shrugs. "It was a fucking serial killer. I have no idea how that kind of twisted, fucked-up mind works."

I think about this, chewing on my lip. The killer might have been insane, but he was also methodical and followed a routine for the first three murders. It doesn't make sense to me that he'd switch things up so dramatically and leave this much to chance.

The assumption has always been that Connor was lured to the caves and then killed during a struggle, before the killer had the chance to use the poison. But Connor had wanted my help with something that day—something secret. What if, in this case, the killer wasn't the one setting the trap?

What if Connor had lured the killer, and not the other way around?

If this were true, then Connor might have known the killer personally. Or else there was another good reason to meet someone in the caves. I look at Ben. "Do you believe what they say about Junior Merlin? That he runs drugs through these caves?"

He shrugs. "I dunno. Probably. I mean, he's the most notorious dealer in three counties, and he's never been busted. He's hustling his shit somehow, and his place is right down on the water. Everyone says he moves the drugs around by boat, and the cops have never found anything when they've raided him. It just makes sense, I guess." He stops and narrows his eyes at me. "Why are you asking?"

"I'm not sure," I say. "I just can't stop wondering why Connor was here in the first place."

Ben laughs. "Well, I can promise you he wasn't here to meet Junior Merlin. Connor didn't do drugs. Nothing hard, anyway. It wasn't his style. Besides, Merlin's got enough on his plate without somehow finding the time to turn into a serial killer."

I nod, satisfied. I'm no closer to understanding why Connor ended up here that night, but at least one theory seems to be off the table.

"Anyway, Mac, if you want my advice, you'll stay away from drugs too. Stick to rum, just like the pirates. Y'arrrrrr." He stands up, waving his bottle, but then abruptly drops the charade, blowing out a frustrated breath. "This was stupid. I don't know why I came here. Can you drive me home?"

"Yeah," I say. "For sure. Now?"

"Yeah," Ben says, and he steps back to the opening and climbs back into the chamber without waiting for me.

I stop for a moment before following him, turning around to take in this weird, awful place one last time. If I hadn't missed Connor's note, would I have been here with him that night? Would I have helped him catch a killer?

Would I have saved Connor's life?

By the time I've clambered up, Ben is already leaving the cave, and I have to push through the crowd to catch up to him.

"Mac!" I turn to see Anna walking over to me, a worried expression on her face. "Are you okay?" she asks. "I knew this was a bad idea. What the hell is wrong with people?"

"I'll be okay," I say. "Everyone's just a bit messed up, is all."

She gives me a look of genuine sympathy, then reaches out to grab my arm.

"Text me if you want to hang out this summer," she says. "Grab a coffee or something. We can make plans to hang out at Amherst!"

"Yeah," I say, surprised at her offer. "I'll do that. Thanks."

I have to run to catch up to Ben, who is already halfway across the beach to the parking lot. We climb the steps in silence, and as we cross the lot, I sneak a glance at the police cruiser. Parnatsky is staring at us, expressionless, and I quickly look away.

In the car, Ben slumps into his seat and leans his head against the window. As I pull away from the beach parking lot, he lets out a long sigh. I'm having a hard time keeping up with his mood swings.

"Do you know that Connor could have been one of the best athletes this town has ever seen?" he asks, out of nowhere.

I look at him, surprised. "Connor didn't play sports."

"Not in high school he didn't," says Ben. "But when we were in middle school, he played on my soccer team and my softball team. He could run faster than anyone; made everything look easy. When he quit, his dad was pissed, and both coaches begged him to keep playing, but he just wasn't interested. Said he had more important things to do."

Ben shakes his head at the memory. Now that he's mentioning it, I vaguely remember it myself—both of them heading off to practices and games together while I stayed home, just thankful my parents didn't expect me to join any teams. Sports were the last thing on my mind; I guess it never occurred to me to wonder whether Connor was any good.

"I forgot all about that," I say.

"He was a total natural at everything he did," says Ben. "I would have killed to have his talent. And look how he ended up. Such a stupid, fucking waste."

I pull up outside Ben's new house, the one he shares with his mom and stepdad. He turns and glances out the window, but makes no move to get out of the car. "Man I hate this place," he says. "I miss the old house. The old street. I miss being a kid there, don't you?"

"Sure," I say. "Everyone misses being a kid."

He nods slowly, repeatedly, as if I've just said something incredibly profound.

"Do you think we could have stopped it?" he asks. "If we'd been paying attention?"

It's the same thing I've been asking myself since I found the note. "I really don't know."

"Maybe if we'd paid more attention," he says again. "Maybe we would have noticed something. I feel like we should have seen it coming."

Ben doesn't sound drunk anymore, just sad and helpless. I think again about the note, about how the only reason I came out tonight was to show it to him. I could show it to him now, let him know that he's not the only one who feels guilty about what happened. But when I look him in the eye, he looks so pained and confused that I hesitate.

"Ben," I say instead, "the entire town was on lockdown. Cops were everywhere. There's no way in a million years we could have known he'd be next."

"Yeah," he says. "You're right." He opens the door and slides out, then bends down and sticks his head back in. He's smiling again, a forced drunken grin, though his eyes still look miserable. "Thanks Mac. See you around, right?"

I wave and watch until he's made it up the front walk and unlocked his door, then I pull away from the curb. When I stop at the end of the block, I glance back in my rearview mirror. He's still standing there in the open doorway, watching me leave.

FIVE

I QUIETLY LET MYSELF IN, half expecting my parents
to be sitting up, waiting for me to get home. But the house is
quiet and dark.

My dog, Hobo, comes to greet me, yawning and stretching,
his little tail wagging sleepily. I crouch and pull him close,
scratching under his neck and on the top of his head at the
same time. As always, he melts into me, and when I stand up,
he's reinvigorated. He turns in a happy little circle at my feet
before trotting back to the family room to wait at the sliding
doors to the backyard, so I can let him out to pee.

"Okay, buddy," I whisper, as I follow to let him out. I step
out onto the patio, and as Hobo runs off into the shadows,
I drop into a lawn chair and pull my phone from my pocket.
After a few minutes, I realize that Hobo hasn't returned. I
glance up and let out a low whistle, but he doesn't reappear.

"Come on, dog," I mutter, getting up from the chair and
moving to the edge of the patio. "Hobo," I call quietly toward

the trees that back our property.

The only sound is the wind rustling through leaves, and I pull up my hood, realizing that it's actually getting kind of chilly. I walk to the edge of the woods and stare into the tangle of trees. Shadows on top of shadows. No telltale rustling of a dog in the bushes.

"Hobo?" I call out again, starting to worry. I'm about to step into the woods, when something moves in my periphery, and I turn in time to see something leaping toward me. My heart skips a beat, but it's just Hobo, bounding in my direction as if he hasn't seen me for months.

"Where the hell did you go?" I ask, bending down to scratch his chin again.

"He was spying on me," says a voice.

I turn and see Carrie, standing on the boundary of our yards, between the spirea hedge and my mom's compost bin.

"Spying, eh?" I ask, pointing a scolding finger down at Hobo, who sits obediently, a worried look on his face.

Carrie pushes past the spirea into my yard, as loose and comfortable in her own skin as she always has been, brushing her wild, light brown curls out of her face. "I can't remember the last time I took the secret passageway."

I smile. When we were really small, before any of the others moved to the neighborhood, Carrie and I were straight-up besties. The woods behind our houses were full of trails, and the short path between our yards was the "secret passageway," a route that nobody else ever took.

I realize with a pang that I can't remember the last time she's taken it either.

She steps up to sit at our picnic table. It's the saddest piece of furniture we own, sitting alone in the corner of the yard, paint peeling, never used. I join her, and Hobo comes and sits in front of us, his head tilted like he's waiting for instructions.

Carrie laughs. "He is such a good dog. How old is he?"

"He's eight," I say. "He was my tenth birthday present."

"Oh man, I remember that now," she says. "You totally freaked out. It was the best birthday party ever!" She puts a hand on each side of his face and kisses him on the head. "You're almost an old man, Hobo," she says, before letting him go to scamper around in the shadows. She sits back and lets out a long breath, and we sit quietly for a minute.

"So," she says finally. "Did you go?"

"To the grad party?"

She raises an eyebrow. "You know what I mean, Mac."

"Yeah," I say. "I went."

"I couldn't do it," she says. "I just…" She trails off.

"I know," I say.

"The three of you?" she asks. "What did Doris have to say?" She asks it with an edge to her voice. "I'm sure she was full of sarcastic comments to make everyone feel stupid."

"I don't understand what happened with you and Doris," I say. "You used to be so close."

"Used to be," she repeats. "Come on, Mac. There's no rule that says you have to stay friends with the people you were tight with as kids. There's a whole world of people out there; we don't have to stick with the ones who happened to live on our street."

"You wouldn't be saying that if Connor were still alive," I counter. "I bet you and Doris would still be tight as ever."

She shrugs. "Maybe, who knows? But the fact is, he's gone, and things aren't the same. I mean, you and Ben haven't been hanging out this past year, have you?"

"No," I admit. "I guess Connor really was the glue holding the five of us together."

"Not us, Mac," she says. "You and I were friends first, and we'll be friends forever. I swear."

She reaches over to ruffle my hair, and I swat her hand away, half annoyed, half amused. "Speaking of Ben," I say, "he's kind of gone off the deep end."

She closes her eyes and pinches the bridge of her nose as if she has a headache. "Shit. Ben. What did he do now?"

I tell her about his behavior at the beach.

"Holy shit," she says. "He needs to pull himself together. He's not the only one having a hard time with the whole Connor thing."

"Are you?" I ask. "Having a hard time?"

She looks at me, obviously angry, and for a second I think she's going to stand up and leave. Then her expression wilts, and she stares down at her hands. "Of course I am. How could you ask that?"

"Sorry," I say.

She lets out a long sigh. "I think about Connor all the time," she says, then looks at me, a weird expression on her face, like she's trying to decide whether to tell me something. "Did you know that he and I hooked up last summer?"

My head snaps up to look at her. "What?"

She laughs, lightly. "I guess that's a no. Yeah, we had kind of a fling, just for a while."

"I can't believe you didn't tell me," I say. What I really mean—what I don't say—is that I can't believe Connor didn't tell me.

"Tell you?" she asks. "I didn't realize I was supposed to get your permission to hook up with a guy."

"It wasn't just some guy," I say. "It was *Connor*." To my horror, my voice cracks, and I have the sudden, shocking realization that my eyes are welling up.

"Oh, Mac," she says. Her voice is kinder now, and that makes me feel even more upset. Despite my best efforts, my eyes overflow.

"Fuck," I say.

"Yeah." She digs around in her bag and pulls out a wad of Kleenex.

I wipe at my eyes and pull myself together, still mortified. It's not like Carrie hasn't seen me cry a million times, but this is a different kind of embarrassing.

"The real reason I didn't mention it to you," she says, "is that it was all so quick. We hooked up one night, and then we decided to try making it into something more serious. I think mainly because we didn't want to hurt each others' feelings. Bad idea."

"Why?"

She shrugs. "Neither of us was really feeling it. It was weird, and we both knew it—we were too close of friends. I never expected it to turn into anything more serious."

"Did you break up with him because of Ant?" I ask.

She shakes her head. "Actually, Connor broke it off after a couple of weeks. He was really nice about it, but he didn't really explain. At first I thought maybe he'd started messing around with someone else, but it might have actually had something to do with Ben."

"Ben?" I ask, surprised.

"You know Ben always had a crush on me," she says. "Connor used to talk about it a lot, like 'Ben's going to be so upset if he learns about this.' I didn't think that mattered. As far as I was concerned, it was none of Ben's business, but I get it. Connor was just trying to be a good friend. Anyway, it ran its course, and after a while I started dating Ant, and that was the last I thought about it. Until…"

"Until he died."

She nods. "I went to the cops right away," she says. "I told them about us, and they were really interested. They asked a million questions."

"What did you tell them?" I ask.

"There wasn't much to tell them," she says. "We were together when George Smith got killed, and he and I talked about it a lot, about how crazy and creepy it was. By the time the second murder happened, that girl—"

"Joey," I say.

"Yeah, Joey Standish. We'd already broken up by then."

"Do you think he had any suspicions?" I ask. "About who the murderer was?"

She looks at me, her head tilted to one side, trying to figure me out. I want her to ask me why I think that. I want her to give me a reason to show her the note, because Connor's words—"keep this to yourself"—are making me hesitate. I want someone on my side. Instead, she looks at me with a sad, knowing expression and sighs.

"I don't think so," she says. "Why would he?"

"I'm just trying to figure out what happened."

She smiles sadly at me. "I want to know what happened too," she says, putting her hand out to touch my arm. "But it's been a year. Things are just starting to get back to normal. I don't think we will ever know."

"Carrie," I say, trying to figure out my words carefully. "How long after you and Connor broke up did you and Ant Merlin become a thing?"

"A couple of weeks," she says, suspiciously. "Why?"

"Did Ant know about you and Connor?"

Her reaction is so swift that I'm completely taken aback. She stands abruptly from her perch, her eyes blazing.

"Jesus, Mac," she says. "Yes, of course Ant knew about me and Connor. Are you seriously suggesting Ant had something to do with it? That he was the serial killer? I'm sick of people making stupid assumptions. Ant is the kindest, least judgmental guy I know."

"He's a drug dealer," I say.

"He sells a tiny bit of weed," she says, "and he only does it to keep his brother off his back. He doesn't touch the stuff himself. Doesn't drink. He even gives me a hard time about cigarettes."

"Sorry, I guess I let my mind get away with me," I say. "There are so many rumors about Junior Merlin running drugs in and out of those caves, right by where Connor's body was found. There's just something about it all that doesn't sit right."

"Ant had nothing to do with it," she says, firmly.

She sounds so sure of herself that I just nod. That seems to satisfy her, and she settles back onto the picnic table. We sit quietly for a long moment.

"I'm sorry I didn't come to the time capsule thing, Mac. I know it meant a lot to you. It was just too much for me right now."

"Hey, it wasn't a big deal," I say. "Just a thing to do. It was kind of a stupid idea, really."

I remember then and reach into my pocket, pulling out the small envelope with her name on it in her own fourteen-year-old handwriting.

She takes it and looks at it warily.

"You going to open it?" I ask.

She rips it open and pulls out a tiny square of something and smiles.

"What is it?"

She holds it up, and I see that it's a four-leaf clover, laminated into a tiny square. "I looked for a whole morning to find this. My mom took it to work with her and laminated it for me." She tucks it into her pocket. "Maybe it will bring me some good luck."

"What about your fortune?" I ask.

Carrie laughs. "I don't even have to read it. I know what it says." But she takes the paper out anyway, unfolds it, then looks at me with a sideways smile.

My first kiss will be with Mac.

"You've got to be kidding me," I say.

She laughs. "I had the biggest crush on you, Mac."

"What the hell?" I ask. "Do you have any gaydar at all?"

"Now I do," she says. "Back then, I just thought you were really sweet and gentle. Quieter than Connor and Ben."

"I was always really nice to your Barbie dolls," I admit. "You were barking up the wrong tree with the whole kissing thing, though."

"So have you found anyone more appropriate?" she asks.

I feel myself blushing. "What do you think?"

She shrugs. "You're so cute. There must be somebody around."

"I'll just have to wait until I'm out of here," I say.

She persists. "You haven't talked to guys online? I bet there are loads of nice guys in Portland."

"You don't know what it's like, Carrie," I say, more harshly than I intend. I take a deep breath to calm myself down. "Finding someone isn't really on my radar. Not now."

"I get that," she says, "but I hate to think of you as lonely." She starts say something else, but hesitates.

"What is it?" I ask.

When she continues, she speaks slowly, and it's obvious that she's treading carefully. "Do you ever think that you can't get over Connor's death because you haven't come to terms with your real feelings about him?"

I shake my head, desperate to get out of this conversation. "It isn't like that," I insist. "I just can't stand knowing that his killer is still out there. It's not fair."

She nods, accepting my explanation, but the truth—of course—is more complicated. When he was still alive, I didn't have to think about my feelings for Connor, because it wouldn't have mattered. He was out of reach in that way, and nothing I did was ever going to change that. But now that he's gone, the things I kept hidden for so long have expanded to fill the space he left behind, and the note in my pocket isn't making things easier.

"I'm sorry," she says again.

"It's fine," I say. "Seriously."

"No," she says. "I mean I'm sorry it didn't play out the way you wanted. That we didn't stay close, the way you wanted."

"I think we would have, if Connor hadn't died," I say. "But maybe I'm just dreaming."

"As far as dreams go, it's a nice one." She stands and steps down from the picnic table. "I'll see you around, Mac."

The note burns in my pocket, and I call out to her before she reaches the edge of my yard.

"Carrie."

She stops and turns back to look at me, waiting.

"Do you think Connor knew the person who killed him?"

She considers this. "It was a drifter, Mac. I don't think any of them knew the guy." She smiles sadly. "And I don't think we'll ever find out who he was." She turns and disappears back through the shadows, back to her own yard.

Hobo is sitting by the door when I turn around, ready to go back inside. I close the sliding door behind us, making sure to latch it tightly. In my room, I clear some space on my desk and flatten the note. I turn on my desk lamp and use my phone to take a photo of it, then I read it over and over, trying to understand.

But it's not just the note that has me feeling weirded out. Something's wrong. Something out of place. It takes me a minute to figure out what it is.

I'm being watched.

Across the street, the light in Connor's bedroom is on, and there's a figure sitting at his desk, looking across at me. I jerk back in my chair, my heart pounding, and I've half moved out of my seat when I realize who it is. His mother. I stand, pressing my fingers down on my desk. I watch as she rises slowly and turns toward Connor's door on the other side of the room. She opens it and steps out, flicking out a hand to shut off the light, plunging his room once again into darkness.

SIX

I BIKE INTO TOWN early the next morning, picking up speed as I leave Anderson Lane to descend the long hill into town, still blanketed with morning fog. The route flattens out when I hit the historic district, and I slow down and pedal comfortably along several streets of brightly painted Victorian houses.

I slow down as I turn onto Main Street, coasting gently past gift shops and galleries, the tourist-trap seafood joints that have been here forever, and the newer, hipper restaurants that advertise "locally sourced" ingredients. When I reach the town square, I hop off my bike and lock it to a light post, then I cross the perfect green expanse of lawn.

Town hall looms before me, a stately stone building that predates the town's founding. Out of superstition, I dig a quarter out of my pocket to toss into the stone fountain. Then I climb the wide steps and push through the heavy brass-trimmed wooden door into the lobby.

Camera Cove Police Department occupies the western wing of the building, down a hallway and through another heavy wooden door. A receptionist slumps behind an ancient beige computer monitor at a three-sided desk. Her hair, a tight blond perm, is crisply attentive, in sharp contrast to her face, which regards me with a mixture of boredom and irritation as I approach. Reading glasses are perched on the end of her nose, and I can see the glow of a Facebook timeline reflected in her lenses. She sighs as I reach the desk and raises an eyebrow.

"Can I help you?" she asks, in a tone of voice that tells me she'd rather do anything else.

"I'd like to speak to Chief Parnatsky," I say. "Is she here?"

"Reason for your visit?" she asks, ignoring my question.

"It's about the Connor Williams case."

"Catalog Killer," she mutters. "It's always about the Catalog Killer." She rummages in a drawer, pulls out a clipboard with a yellow form on it, and holds it out across the counter to me. "You can fill out the details and leave it with me."

I don't take the clipboard. "I think she'll want to talk to me," I persist. "Connor was a friend of mine. I was interviewed after the murder. I have some new information."

She considers me, eyes narrowed, chewing on her bottom lip.

"What's your name?" she asks.

"Mac Bell."

The receptionist swivels in her chair and grabs a phone. She punches in a code. I hear someone pick up on the other end of the line.

"I've got a young man here, says he's got information about

Connor Williams that you're going to want to see. Mac Bell. Says you interviewed—" She stops and listens, then nods. "Okay. Yes, I'll send him down."

She hangs up and points down the hallway. "Last door on the left."

Officer Patricia Parnatsky is leaning back in her chair when I enter. She's about forty, with short dark hair and a muscular build. I don't think I've ever seen her smile, although I can't really blame her. Nobody becomes a cop in a town as small as Camera Cove expecting to be a central figure in an unsolved serial killer investigation.

"Hi, Mac," she says. "Have a seat."

I unsling my backpack and sit down across from her, glancing around the room, which is a stark contrast to the busy space it was last year. When I was interviewed back then, a giant corkboard plastered with photos and maps and index cards covered the wall. The corkboard is still there, but it's mostly empty, except for photographs of the victims, thumbtacked neatly along the top edge. Beneath each one hangs a colored photocopy of the images that gave the Catalog Killer his nickname.

Many serial killers have a calling card. Jack the Ripper sent letters to police. The Night Stalker scrawled pentagrams onto walls and mirrors, and even onto one of his victim's legs, using lipstick. The Catalog Killer, as the name implies, left behind pages from old mail-order catalogs. Colorful vintage ads, originally from Sears, were found neatly folded in half and safety-pinned to the clothes of each victim. Each picture had been carefully chosen to include a model that corresponded to the victim, and an *X* had been drawn through each of those faces with a magic marker.

George Smith was first. I recognize his photo on the corkboard from news coverage. He was a short but well-built guy with a crew cut and a shirt and tie. Underneath his picture is a bright, saturated image of a mom and dad and their two kids—a son and daughter. It's a happy nuclear family enjoying a barbecue in their backyard...but an *X* is neatly drawn across the father's face.

Maria Brindle's wedding photo is also very familiar to me, tacked next to George's picture. The catalog image below it shows a mother and her two children: another boy and girl. This time, it's the mother's face that has been crossed out with an *X*.

By the time Joey Standish's body was found and details of her catalog image had begun to circulate, the press had figured out the calculated nature of the murderer's choice in victims. Joey's photo on the board looks like it was blown up from someone's Instagram; she's laughing, and her eyes are half closed. Her catalog picture, found nailed to the tree she was propped up in, shows a brother and sister, arm in arm, pointing to some unknown landmark in the distance, the sister's face marked with an *X*.

It became clear, then: the killer was picking off a de facto family, one by one. The father, the mother, the sister—all dead. Only the brother was left. And the inevitable, horrible question on everyone's mind was, Who's next? The fear that had drifted into Camera Cove like a fog quickly morphed into full-blown terror.

My parents refused to let me leave the house by myself. Police implemented a curfew. Tourists left in droves and were replaced by journalists. The town was filled with empty hotels, empty vacation cottages, unrented sailboats, and restaurants where bored waitstaff leaned against counters doing crossword puzzles.

An invisible clock counted down somewhere in the sky above all of us.

There was a boy left alive in those catalog pictures. But not for long.

I stare at Connor's class photo, beaming down at me from the bulletin board. Beneath it, a handsome teenager with a feathery 80s haircut and an X across his face is modeling a pair of acid-washed jeans and a matching jacket.

Connor's catalog image was stuck to the wall of the cavern, this time with letters neatly cut out from a magazine and pasted across the center of the picture, spelling out THE END.

It was true. The end. No more murders, as if the story had been brought to an inevitable conclusion. Two weeks after Connor's murder, the police found the culprit's campsite: a cellar underneath a rotting, abandoned farmhouse in the woods at the end of Abernathy Road, outside of town. Whoever had been sleeping there was long gone, but it was obvious right away that it had been the killer; they found an old duffle bag full of disassembled catalogs, and residue of the poison he'd used to kill the victims.

It was a drifter all along, now off to bring his sick choreography to another part of the world. The police believed the killer was done and gone, and it turned out they were right. There hasn't been another murder since. For the people of Camera Cove, desperate for an end to our summer of terror, it wasn't the resolution we'd wanted, but it was enough.

Besides, hadn't the murderer told us it was over?

Trish Parnatsky remains sitting, watching me examine the pictures on the board, patiently waiting for me to explain my visit.

"I found something," I finally say, turning back to unzip the backpack. I pull out the bag of comics and place it on her desk. I'd placed the note back inside the bag when I decided to come here, in case the whole thing was evidence.

She opens it, giving me a quizzical look when she realizes what's inside. She carefully pulls the stack of comics out and lays them on the desk in front of her.

"Inside the cover of the front comic," I tell her.

She finds the note, pulls it out, and reads it. Her expression goes slack, then she looks at me.

"Explain," she demands. She drags a notepad out from the pile of papers on her desk and holds a pen over it, waiting for me to speak.

"Connor and I—we traded comics," I begin. "We've been doing it since we were kids. He bought some titles, and I bought other ones, and we'd swap them back and forth. The day he was murdered, he dropped these off at my house, but I didn't find them until later."

She scribbles furiously. "You didn't look at them after you found them?"

"No. I didn't want to. At first I was just…I didn't care about comics. Why would I read comic books when my friend had just been murdered?"

She looks up from her pad. "You were interviewed that week, weren't you?"

I nod. I remember the interview well. Anyone who had anything to do with Connor—his teachers, girlfriends, teammates, co-workers, and friends—was summoned to the investigation center, which had taken over not only the police station, but most of the town hall's other offices and meeting rooms as well.

Parnatsky had been in the room, but the actual interviews were conducted by two federal cops who had been dispatched to run the investigation: an intense woman with a rushed way of speaking, who had asked all the questions, and an old man with glasses and an impassive face, who had sat next to her and stared at me, without saying a word.

"It didn't occur to you to tell us about the comic books then?" Parnatsky asks. "It didn't seem weird to you that he'd dropped them off on your doorstep the day he died?"

"No," I say, "because it wasn't weird. It was just what we did; the same thing we'd done for almost ten years. Even when life started to kind of get back to normal, I still couldn't bring myself to look at them. I just put them on the shelf, still in the bag."

Parnatsky sits calm and straight-backed across the desk as she grills me. She doesn't really react to my answers, but I find myself slowly shrinking down in my chair, reaching up to grab the back of my neck, and avoiding her steady gaze. Why do I feel so guilty?

"So let me try to understand," she says. "You got these comics, put them on a shelf, and promptly forgot about them? Even after Connor's body was discovered? Seems strange that the last thing your dead friend gave you just slipped your mind, doesn't it?"

I glance up at her, not sure how this conversation has gone in such an uncomfortable direction. I open my mouth to answer but can't figure out what to say. I shift in my seat and try again.

"It didn't slip my mind. I mean, I looked at the bag all the time, thought about taking the comics down and reading them." I struggle to explain. "I guess I kind of felt as if opening that bag was the same thing as closing a chapter, or something like that. So they just ended up staying there."

"Until last night," she says.

"Yeah."

"Why did you finally decide to open them last night?"

I explain about the time capsule, high school graduation, the feeling that things were finally coming to an end.

"It seemed like it was time," I say. "I've tried to get over Connor's murder for the better part of a year, and nothing's worked. I thought maybe opening the bag would help me get closure." To my embarrassment, my voice cracks, and I drop my eyes to where my hands have tangled themselves into a knot between my knees.

Parnatsky finally stops writing and drops the pad of paper and pencil on the desk. When I glance up again, the serious cop face is gone, replaced by a look of genuine sympathy.

"Instead, you ended up finding this note and opening a whole new can of worms," she says.

I nod, miserable. "Pretty much."

She leans back in the chair and runs her hands down her face as she stretches back, letting out an exhausted sigh. Then she drops her hands to the arms of her chair, and we both stare at the note sitting between us on the desk. A potentially crucial missing clue in Connor's own handwriting.

"What do you do now?" I ask. "With the note. Does it get put into evidence?"

"Yeah," she says. "That's about it."

"What do you think it means?"

"You want the truth?" she asks, her voice weary. "I honestly don't know."

"Oh," I say.

"Don't get me wrong, Mac," she says. "I'm really glad that you brought this to me. It was the right thing to do, obviously, no question about it. The only problem is, it doesn't change anything. I wish it did—I really do—but this note really just confirms what we already suspected. Even if you'd come to us with this note the day Connor's body was discovered, it wouldn't really have made any difference."

I lean forward in my chair, wondering what she means.

"Out of the four victims, Connor was the only one not found close to home. He was the only one not killed with poison."

I nod—everyone in town knows that Connor put up a good fight against the killer, which is why his death looked different. Parnatsky continues, "We think that Connor somehow began to suspect who the killer was, but instead of coming to us with the information, chose to take matters into his own hands and begin an investigation of his own. We think he caught the murderer off guard, which is why there was a struggle between the two."

I sink back into my chair, deflated, as I realize there's nothing fresh about my brilliant theory. "You think he set a trap for the killer?" I ask.

She nods. "We think he spied on the person for a while,

then decided to take things to the next step. Not to speak ill of the dead, but it was an extremely stupid thing to do, and as you and I both know, it had horrible consequences. If he'd come to us instead of taking matters into his own hands, he'd probably still be alive."

Instead, I think, *he came to me.*

As if reading my mind, she holds up the note. "The silver lining here is that you didn't find this when you were supposed to. That you didn't go with him to the caves that night. Otherwise we might have been left with two murder victims, instead of one."

"Or maybe I would have helped him," I say, my throat tightening. "Maybe he just needed backup, and things would have worked out differently."

She puts the note down on the desk and, to my surprise, smiles kindly at me.

"Mac, I know why you feel that way, but there's no reason to think that the two of you together would have managed any better than he did alone. Remember, we're talking about confronting a brutal murderer. Seriously, you should count your blessings, as hard as that may be."

I don't say anything. I don't feel lucky; just useless.

"I do have one more question," she says. "Why did he pick you?" She reaches down for the note and holds it up, turning it so I can see his handwriting. "Why do you suppose that is?"

"I really don't know," I say. "Maybe because he was in a hurry, and I was the closest friend he could reach out to. I live—lived—right across the street from him."

"There's nothing else you can think of?" she asks. "One of the most common things we heard about Connor during the investigation was that he had a lot of friends. He probably could have turned to a lot of people, but he chose you. No offense, Mac, but I don't get the impression that you're much of a tough guy."

"He had a lot of friends," I agree. "I mean, everyone loved him, but..." I think for a moment, then choose my words carefully, allowing myself to say out loud what I've been thinking for years. "He would have had a hard time finding someone as dependable as me. I think he knew I was loyal."

"Loyal," she repeats. She picks up the note from the desk and reads. *"Keep this to yourself.* You think you would have? Kept it to yourself?"

I don't need to think about this one. "Absolutely. Connor was my best friend. If he'd wanted me to keep it quiet while he figured things out, I would have."

She nods slowly. "Then I really do think it's a good thing you didn't find this note that day." She scans it one more time, then drops it back onto the desk and points at it. "Have you shown this to anyone? Your parents? Your friends?"

"No."

She purses her lips. "Keep it that way. Can you do that much for me? The last thing I need is for a bunch of gossip to start circulating that we've opened a new lead." I nod, and after another glance at the note, she slumps back in her chair. She looks exhausted.

"Chief Parnatsky," I say, "are you really sure that the killer was a drifter? Why would Connor come to me, if it were just a drifter?"

"We are sure," she says. "We combed through this town person by person, and there is no indication that anyone in

Camera Cove had anything to do with the murders. Not one clue leading us anywhere internal. When the farmhouse hideout was discovered, it answered a lot of questions for us. Unfortunately, it answered them too late to catch anyone. But it's been a year. The killer is gone. My best advice, Mac? Try not to think about this anymore."

She stands, picks up the bag of comics, and hands it back to me. Then she holds up the note.

"I'm going to keep this and put it into evidence," she says. "Thanks for bringing it in to me. If you think of anything else, definitely let me know."

"Okay. I will."

I stand to leave, and she comes around the desk to shake my hand.

"Do you have a summer job lined up?" she asks.

"Actually, I'm just heading to my first shift," I say. "I'm going to be the summer student at the library."

"That was Connor's job last year, wasn't it?"

"Yeah," I say. "That's what gave me the idea to apply. I know he really liked it."

She smiles. "They're lucky to have you. Thanks again for coming in, Mac. Remember what I said: try to put this out of your mind. You've been through a lot, and you deserve to move on."

"Thanks," I say. "I will."

At the reception area, I turn and glance back down the hallway. She's still in the doorway, her body sagged against the frame, watching me leave. I lift my hand, but she just turns and walks back into her office, shutting the door behind her.

SEVEN

I LEAVE THE STATION feeling deflated. I realize that
I'd been expecting shock and excitement at the revelation of
Connor's note, that it would somehow set things in motion
and the murders would finally be solved. I can see now how
unrealistic that was. Discovering Connor's note was like a
punch to the gut, but in the end, it doesn't mean anything.

Except that I missed the chance to save my best friend.

It's already starting to get hot outside. The morning mist
has burned off, and the quaint, colorful heritage buildings on
Main Street are emerging from the gloom. The sidewalks are
starting to show some signs of life too. People wander in and
out of shops and stop to consult maps.

Last summer, during the killings, the tourism industry
more or less dried up, leaving a lot of businesses in bad shape.
This year, things have kind of started to get back to normal,
but there's no denying that the typical crowds have dwindled.

There's also a noticeable difference in the tourists themselves. There are still retirees in matching track suits and sun visors, and small clusters of Asian and European tourists examining guidebooks, but now they're accompanied by a newer breed of visitor. I think of them as the murder tourists: people who travel to Camera Cove not for the seafood, the beaches, or the seafaring heritage, but to follow the path of death that ran through here last year.

There's a group of murder tourists across the street right now. They're easy to recognize, and not just because they stand out from the usual crowd—a pale and guarded-looking younger couple, dressed head to toe in heavy black clothing; a single, middle-aged man with an expensive camera and a fishing vest full of pens and notepads; and two small, weasely women, probably sisters, sucking on Virginia Slims—but because they're all standing around listening to Cubby French.

Cubby French, early thirties, short, and pear-shaped, is gesticulating wildly as he describes some juicy bit of Camera Cove gossip. He's wearing his standard uniform—a bright red T-shirt, and a matching baseball cap that holds back his dirty blond ponytail. The shirt and hat are both emblazoned with his logo: *Camera Cove Mystery Tours* in gothic letters that drip with garishly illustrated blood.

Cubby turns and points across at town hall. I can't hear what he's saying, but I imagine it's something about a botched investigation. Almost everyone in Camera Cove thinks Cubby is a dirtbag for profiting off the killings, but a lot of people do agree with him about the way the police handled things. All that time wasted on investigating locals, when they should have been sweeping the woods, looking for drifters. If they had, they might well have found the cellar beneath the abandoned farmhouse earlier, and maybe the killer wouldn't have escaped.

Cubby leads his group across the street and onto the town square, just as I'm crossing to the library. I'm trying to hurry so I don't have to hear them, and one of the chain-smoking women turns and watches me, almost suspiciously. I shiver and walk away.

On the grass outside the library, vendors are starting to set up their market stalls. I spot my neighbor Joe Anderson setting up his farm table.

For as long as I can remember, Mr. Anderson has run a produce stand in the town square, full of the many varieties of vegetables that he grows on his old farm. When his wife was still alive, he also sold pickles and jams and delicious baked goods. My mother told me that when I was little, the Andersons even sold meat at the market—chops and roasts and ground beef and pork from the cattle and pigs that used to live in the barn. Now it's just fresh produce, but that's impressive enough, considering Mr. Anderson does all the work himself. I walk over to greet him.

"Mac!" he says, "How the devil are you?"

"I'm doing well," I say, accepting his outstretched hand.

"I bet you are," he shakes his head slowly in disbelief. "A high school graduate. If that doesn't make me feel old, I don't think anything would. It seems like yesterday you were all just kids, running around the fields, asking to feed the goats."

I laugh. "Makes me feel pretty old too, I guess."

He scoffs, good natured. "Nonsense. You're standing on the cusp of your future. Nothing old about being at the peak of youth." His face drops suddenly and unexpectedly. "It's only a shame that Connor isn't here to share this moment with the rest of you." His voice catches.

I nod and drop my gaze to the ground, feeling awkward at the sight of him getting emotional.

"That's enough of that," he says, quickly pulling himself together. "Don't pay any attention to an old man. What brings you into town on this beautiful morning?"

I point at the library. "Starting my summer job today."

"Oh, that's right," he says. "Your mother mentioned something about that. We'll be seeing plenty of each other. I'll have my stand here every morning for the rest of the summer."

"You're a busy guy," I say.

"I love it. I meet lots of people, and I get to chat with folks all day long." He holds up a zucchini. "And make a few bucks while I'm at it. Business is steady, but the real money is in the junk tables." He gestures to the tables that have set up alongside his. "Tourists don't want to buy lettuce or beans, but they love a good rummage sale."

I glance across from us, and sure enough, tourists are already flocking around the tables selling used clothes, furniture, dishes, and toys.

"Don't worry about me, though," he says. "I have my regulars, the ones who know that anything grown outdoors on a real farm is going to taste a lot better than what you can get at the grocery store."

I pull my phone out of my pocket to check the time. "I'd better hustle. I need to get to work."

"You bet," he says. "Stop by the farm for a visit someday."

I run up the library steps, glancing back at Mr. Anderson to wave. I tell myself that I'll make an effort to visit him sometime over the next few weeks.

The air conditioning inside the library is a welcome relief after the sticky heat outside. A couple of people mill about near the magazines, while some others are set up at the wide, white tables at the far end. The librarian, Libby Utley, is behind the checkout counter, organizing stacks of books. She looks up as I enter.

"You're here," she observes, as she finishes stacking the books onto her rolling cart. She pushes the cart out from behind the counter and stops beside me. "We might as well get started," she says. "Drop your bag in the office, and I'll start showing you how the shelving system works."

I used to visit Connor at the library sometimes, hang with him while he shelved books and dealt with patrons, so I've seen the system in action. Once I get used to the shelving system, it's actually pretty easy. When I return with my empty cart, Libby looks at me approvingly.

"Good work," she says. "Last year's student wasn't quite as efficient, although I hate to speak ill of him after what happened. Did you know him?"

"Yes," I manage, my mouth dry. "Connor. He was a friend of mine. That's why I applied for the job."

"Well, he might not have been the best at shelving books, but he made up for it in other ways," she says. "The patrons loved him. He spent half of his time chatting them up and making friends, and to be honest, it was nice. Everyone loved him. And he...well, why don't you come see?"

I follow her as she leads me through the stacks to the children's area, a separate alcove at the back of the library, and my stomach clenches as I realize where we're going. Beyond the small furniture, low bookshelves, and colorful mats on the floor, a giant, unfinished mural dominates the back wall, a mural I haven't seen since last summer.

The painting is bright and colorful, and it's populated by almost a hundred townspeople wandering along Main Street, smiling and chatting and participating in various activities. Some kids chase one another around the fountain while two women chat excitedly with each other. An old man feeds pigeons from a bench. A dog, painted from behind, chases a squirrel toward a tree. The perspective is amazing. Figures at the back of the painting recede into a false horizon, and those at the front seem to be walking out of the painting and into the room.

Even to my untrained eyes, Connor's work is clearly an impressive piece of art. Caught off guard, I realize with embarrassment that I am on the verge of tears. Connor was so excited about the mural as he was doing it, and he never even got to finish it. Never got to take his incredible talent out into the world.

What a waste.

I have forgotten that Libby is with me until she clears her throat.

"He was talented," she says. "He used to sketch the patrons… not that they knew. He was so sneaky about it. Eventually I realized I had to give him an outlet so he would stop, and that's how he ended up doing the mural. Then he just spent most of his time working on this, instead of shelving books or dusting the shelves."

I smile, remembering how Connor had found a way to put his energy toward his art, instead of his actual duties.

"I think there's an opportunity here," says Libby. "Especially seeing as you were his friend. I'd like you to help me figure out how to raise some money to finish it. We can have an unveiling. Name it in his honor. Do you think that's a good idea?"

"Yeah," I say, my throat tight. "I think it's a great idea."

"Good," she says. "Your actual duties will have to take priority, of course, but I get the feeling you're the man for the job."

The bell on the door rings, and we turn to see a middle-aged couple, both in khaki shorts and sun visors, with fanny packs around their waists, looking around as if they've never seen a library before.

"I'll be with you in one second, folks," Libby calls across the library. Quieter, to me, she says, "Tourists. They'll be in and out of here all summer, looking for maps, asking for directions, just hanging out. Mostly using the Wi-Fi. I wish the town council would finally build a visitor center."

She trots away to help them, and I'm left staring at the mural.

Even incomplete, it's obvious how well Connor had planned it out—the biggest, most ambitious work of art he'd ever tackled. Helping to get it finished, to complete his vision, would be incredibly satisfying. In a small way, it could even be an opportunity to make up for my missed opportunity.

Then I see it. Near the center of the mural, but still unfinished, is the lightly sketched outline of five people clustered together in a group.

It's us. Connor and Carrie, Ben and Doris, and me. We're together, the way we were in his sketch from the time capsule. This was how Connor saw us. Before he died and our group fell apart, our lives had still revolved around each other, and that's exactly how he wanted to portray us in this mural—our friendship at the center of this small world.

If the tables were turned, and it was my murder that had gone unsolved, Connor wouldn't have given up on it. I know he wouldn't. The real question is whether I'm willing to be the kind of friend that he was.

I think of the note again. We all believed the killer was a drifter, but suddenly I'm not so sure. If the killer was a drifter, why would Connor have risked a confrontation? Why wouldn't he have just gone to the cops with his theory?

For that matter, why would he have asked me to come with him to the beach? For backup? That just doesn't make sense. Like Parnatsky said, I'm no tough guy. But maybe Connor thought he was on the verge of getting some kind of proof, and he wanted someone else to be able to confirm his story. Someone he could trust.

When I found Connor's note, the seed of an idea had planted itself into my mind. Now, the more I try to stomp it down, the bigger it gets. I think Connor knew the killer. I think something more complicated was going on beneath the surface of Camera Cove last summer, and Connor was the perfect person to notice it. And in order to figure out who was responsible and get justice for Connor, I need to try to see the town from his perspective.

I find Libby in the sorting area. "I think I have an idea," I say. "I think I know how we can make some money for the mural."

EIGHT

A FEW DAYS LATER, I sit in the library van, uneasy, and stare across the quiet, tree-lined street. I'm trying to convince myself to get out and walk across. That the end justifies the means. That there's no other way to find out what happened.

The house is a simple Cape Cod, with gray shingles and white trim. Thick bushes of wild roses surround it, and four brightly painted Adirondack chairs—red, blue, green, and yellow—sit facing the street from the veranda. A flag flutters crisply in the breeze at the top of a flag pole. It's the kind of house that could convince someone to leave behind their big-city life and move to the seaside.

From what I already know about George Smith and his family, that's exactly what they did—picked up and moved across the country from Milwaukee, settling in Camera Cove. Just over a year later, he was dead—the Catalog Killer's first victim.

Now I'm parked outside his house, trying to convince myself to go up and ring the doorbell. It makes me almost sick to my stomach, but I remind myself that Connor learned what was happening by paying attention. He noticed something about the victims that led him to the killer. He's not here to pay attention any longer, but I am, and if I'm going to dig into this mystery, there's only one way to do it.

I reach across to the passenger seat to grab one of the flyers I printed off this morning, then I take a deep breath and get out of the van. I cross to the sidewalk on the other side and stop, staring down the flagstone path that leads to the front door. My conscience gives my insides a tight, harsh twist, and I'm about to turn on my heel and drop the entire plan, when I see a curtain flutter in the front window. Someone has spotted me. It's too late to turn back now.

I try to look natural as I stroll up the walkway and climb the steps to the front door. I ring the doorbell and almost immediately the door opens, and an elderly lady peers out at me.

"Hello," I say, holding out the flyer. "I'm here on behalf of the local library. We're doing a funding drive and hoping to collect unwanted household belongings for a rummage sale."

"Rummage sale?" she asks, reluctantly taking the flyer.

"Yes," I say. "We'll be holding it on the day of the parade, when there will be lots of people around."

It was Mr. Anderson who gave me the idea when he pointed out the junk tables in the town square. Libby loved it. "We'll kill two birds with one stone," she said. "We'll raise some cash for the mural and get some community outreach in at the same time!"

I didn't tell her that I was actually hoping to kill a third bird with the same stone—that this was the perfect excuse to get close to the other victims and to make my way into their homes so I could start to gather clues.

The old lady looks at the flyer. In the background, I hear a child scream, and she turns to look back into the house.

"I'm sorry," she says. "It's not a good time."

She's about to close the door when someone calls out from somewhere inside. A moment later, a younger woman appears in the doorway, a toddler on her hip.

"Who is it, Mom?" the younger woman asks.

"Someone looking for donations. I was just telling him we can't help."

The younger woman adjusts the baby on her hip and reaches out for the flyer. She glances at it, then hands the baby to her mother and beckons for me to follow her.

"We've got some stuff," she says.

The older woman frowns, and I hesitate on the step. "Emily," she says, "why are you bothering with this right now?"

"We have to get rid of all this crap anyway," Emily says. "I don't want to take anything with me. Nothing." She turns and glances past me down the walk. "Is that your van?"

I nod.

"You'll seriously take anything?"

"I'll take whatever might work for our sale," I say.

"Emily," her mother protests. "We can have a yard sale ourselves. You don't have to do this."

"Mom!" snaps Emily. "Stop arguing with me! I don't want a yard sale. I don't want to look at this stuff anymore. I just want it gone."

She turns and strides down the hallway, and the older

woman steps aside to let me in. I make a move to kick off my flip-flops, but she holds her hand up.

"Don't worry about that. This house is a disaster. Go ahead, follow her," she says, with a voice that clearly implies that I'm responsible for this unfortunate situation.

I move down the hallway after Emily Smith, wondering what could possibly have made me think this was a good idea. At the end of the hallway is a messy kitchen, and two school-aged children are coloring at the table. They don't look up at me. Emily is standing at a doorway, waiting for me.

"Most of the stuff is in here," she says, opening the door and reaching in to turn on a light.

I follow her into the side door of the garage. A bunch of hockey equipment is piled up in the middle of the floor, and some tools are scattered around the room.

"Take whatever you want," she says. Her voice trails off, and I notice her gaze move to the workbench at the back of the room. I realize with horror that this must be where they found George Smith.

Emily and the kids had been out running errands when the killer had made his way into the house, unimpeded, and laced a beer with strychnine—a beer that George Smith then drank. After George had died, the killer then dragged his body into the garage and positioned him so he was slumped over his workbench.

The older kids found him when they returned home. They thought he was sleeping.

The catalog image had been pinned to the arm of George's shirt, and the half empty bottle of poisoned beer had been left on the kitchen counter for the police to find, wiped free of fingerprints.

"He was always trying to fix things," Emily says, and I realize that she's moved closer, so that she's standing right next to me. I can smell wine on her breath, and the faint stench of cigarettes on her clothes. A closet smoker, I guess. I recognize the scent from hanging around with Carrie.

"He couldn't fix this," she says. She gestures to the table, the packed boxes—all the broken parts of a life she never expected.

A loud noise jerks me from my daze, and I nearly jump out of my skin. Emily's mother is standing by the door to the kitchen, her hand on the button for the garage door, which is sliding open with a metallic shudder, flooding the space with bright daylight.

"Emily," she says, and her voice is firm and mildly stern, as though she's caught a kid repeating an act she shouldn't be doing. "Come on in. Leave the guy alone."

Emily makes a loose sweeping gesture around the room.

"Take whatever you want," she says again. "Sports equipment. Tools. Whatever. I don't want any of it, so you're doing me a favor. Just pile it by the garage door, and then you can back up your van and load it up."

I swallow and try to look normal. "Thank you very much," I say. "The library will really be helped by this."

She turns and walks up the few steps to the kitchen, and her mother follows her, closing the door with a soft *click* behind them. I back the van up to the garage door and open the back hatch. Now that I'm alone in the room, I stand and look around, suddenly unsure of what to do next.

The plan I've come up with is pretty basic: get close to the crime scenes, learn what I can about the victims, and work my way out from there. But now I'm inside a victim's house, alone in the spot where the murder took place, and I'm drawing a blank.

I try to put myself in Connor's head. At some point he obviously learned something that convinced him to start investigating. Was it a connection between the victims? A conversation that he'd overheard?

I walk over to the workbench where Smith's body was found, reach out, and run my hand along the surface. Some tools have been piled up, and a couple of empty boxes are sitting on the floor next to the bench. It's as if someone started to think about packing but didn't get very far.

Am I looking for something obvious? An incriminating photograph wedged between the pages of a book, maybe, or a map to a secret rendezvous spot? Even if there had been such a thing, the police have obviously scoured this garage from top to bottom. Forensics people have probably scooped fingernails and hair into little bags and run tests on them back at the lab. Still, there's got to be *something* that can point me in the right direction.

I set to work collecting things for the library sale, hoping that something will jump out at me. I begin with the sports equipment. I drag the hockey bag to the door, followed by a set of golf clubs and an old tennis racket. George Smith was obviously a bit of a jock, I realize, as I pull a pair of men's cross-country skis across the garage floor. The sports equipment takes up a lot of space in the van, and I haven't even started to look at the rest of the stuff in the garage.

A few boxes stacked against the wall are full of old issues of *Sports Illustrated*. I huff them into the back seat before turning to see if there's anything else to take.

On a shelf on the other side of the garage, a stack of kitchenware has been messily arranged. Knives, heavy pots, various expensive looking kitchen gadgets. It looks too nice to take, so I leave it.

I'm about to close up the van when the door to the kitchen opens again, and the older woman, Emily Smith's mother, looks down at me from the top of the steps. She's holding a glass of wine, and I can see that just past her, in the kitchen, the kids are arguing over a toy at the table. She ignores them and walks down the steps to me.

"You'll have to excuse my daughter," she says. "She hasn't been the same since George died. She should have come back home with me, but she couldn't give herself the space."

I nod as if I am supposed to understand. It's clear from her oversharing and the slightly glassy look in her eye that the woman has been drinking. Now would be a good time to try and find out information. But as it stands, my mind is blank, and I have no idea what to ask—let alone look for. If Connor was looking for a shrewd detective to help him out, he was barking up the wrong tree.

"Will she—your daughter I mean—will she be sad to leave?" I ask. "I mean, didn't they have any friends around here?"

The woman snorts. "Not Emily. She says she was too busy taking care of the kids, but I know better. I grew up in a small town myself. I know how cold people can be to newcomers. Camera Cove is a pretty little place, no question, but the welcome wagon didn't exactly get rolled out for them. She can't wait to get the hell out of this place, and to tell you the truth, neither can I."

"Why did they stay?" I ask.

She shrugs. "George did what he wanted. He was having an affair, you know."

My eyes widen.

"Oh, he was," she says, catching my surprise, and I can tell that she's relishing this opportunity to gossip. "I'm not sure who it was with, but he was messing around with someone. He was gone all the time. Seemed like every time I talked to Emily on the phone, he was out of the house, supposedly wandering the beach."

It's as if a little bell goes off inside my head. Connor was found at the beach. Could there be a connection?

She takes a long sip of her wine, then leans toward me conspiratorially.

"Emily doesn't know, and I'm not about to bring it up, under the circumstances, but I know the signs, believe me. 'Long walks on the beach' indeed. Don't get me started on Emily's father. George's problem was that he was never happy. He was always looking for something new, something better. Why the hell do you think they ended up here? No offense."

I make kind of a strangled sound, trying to let her know there's been no offense taken.

"Did you, you know, tell the cops about all this?" I ask.

She scoffs. "The cops? They didn't bother to talk to me. I was hundreds of miles away when it all happened. Besides, it's not like George's affair would have made a difference in the investigation. It had nothing to do with his murder. It would have just been something salacious for the gossip rags to include in their stories. I wasn't about to introduce more pain into my daughter's life."

I don't know what to say, so I just stand there. She takes another swig of the wine, and her eyes shift away from mine, as if she's embarrassed to have said so much. She gestures toward the shelf in the corner, changing the subject. "You're not going to take the kitchen stuff?" she asks.

I shake my head. "It seemed too nice to take."

"Go ahead and grab it, sweetie," she says. "It all belonged to George. He was the cook, not Emily. To be honest, I don't know how she'd have managed to feed her kids if I hadn't shown up. Anyway, pack that stuff up; you'll make a few bucks on it. Then do me a favor and go along on your merry way."

I'm happy to take the hint. I grab a cardboard box and quickly fill it up, then drag it out to the van. When I turn back, she's standing in the garage, wine in one hand, a cigarette in the other. She presses the button, and the door begins to drop. She watches me until it's descended below her face. Then she turns and walks back into the house, her body disappearing as she recedes.

NINE

WHEN I GET HOME, I'm kind of shaken from my encounter with Emily Smith and her mother. I knew it wouldn't be easy to get up close and personal with the victims' families, but now that I've actually done it, I feel conflicted. For a brief moment, I wonder if I should stop now and just leave well enough alone, but then I think of everything I learned from George's mother-in-law and realize that I need to keep going. If I'm going to follow through, I need to brace myself for more uncomfortable moments.

In the meantime, I need some air. I grab Hobo and clip him to his leash. "Come on, boy," I say. "Let's go for a walk."

We walk to the end of the road and down onto the path to the lookout. I can't get the Smith family out of my head. I don't even know his kids' names, and I doubt they even registered my presence, but I'm sure I'll remember their faces vividly for a very long time.

I let Hobo off his leash, and he bounds off into the bushes.

A few moments later he runs back to me, carrying a stick. I settle myself into a seat in the heather and absentmindedly toss it for him as I run through the bits and pieces of information I've gathered so far.

I was hoping for a physical clue at the Smith house—something concrete and tangible that I could hold and examine and consider—but it's obvious to me now how naive that was. This isn't some crime show; I'm not going to stumble onto some crucial piece of evidence that leads me to the killer. For one thing, the murders happened almost a year ago, and it's not realistic to think that I'll find a clue hanging about on the floor of someone's garage.

I stare down at Camera Cove, neatly situated against the sea. From here, it looks like any other well maintained little town; people are going about their everyday business, as if nothing serious has ever happened here. But every single one of them knows the same thing I do—things can change forever in the blink of an eye. We've been told over and over again that the Catalog Killer is gone, and that we're safe. But didn't we think we were safe before?

And isn't he still out there somewhere?

A chill runs down my spine at the thought, and I shiver. I stand and yell for Hobo. "Come on, boy," I say. "Let's get out of here."

When we stroll back onto the main road, I spot Mr. Anderson stooped in his giant garden, weeding. My father has told me that Mr. Anderson doesn't need to keep up the produce stand, that it's more of a hobby for him than anything, but it looks like a massive task for the old man.

He looks up and notices me, smiling broadly, then stands, pulling off his gardening gloves as he approaches the fence.

"How are you doing, Mac?" He wipes the sweat off his forehead with the back of his hand, leaving a smear of dirt.

"Do you need some help, Mr. Anderson?" I ask. I look past him at the garden patch, and I can tell that he's barely made a dent.

"Well, I certainly wouldn't say no," he says. "If you're sure you have the time."

"I definitely do," I say, tying Hobo to the fence and hiking myself up to jump over. "I could use the exercise."

I quickly get to work, pulling weeds from a row of carrots, using my fingers to loosen the soil and let it breath. As kids, the five of us often helped out in the garden, and although it's been years, it comes back to me quickly.

"You've still got the touch," Mr. Anderson tells me, as he stops to observe.

"I used to like helping out," I say.

He chuckles. "I think you were the only one. I remember Connor doing as little as he could get away with to collect his five bucks at the end of a session, and you were lucky to get Carrie here at all. Doris and Ben were good workers, though. What joy it brought Margaret and me to see kids out in the fields. We were never able to have our own, so you guys were the next best thing."

The work feels good, almost as if I'm doing penance for spying on the Smith family. The sun beats down on us, and Hobo lies in the shade of a bush beside the fence, panting. Mr. Anderson brings him some water and gives him a good scratch.

"I've often thought of getting another dog," he says. "But since Margaret died, it's hard to imagine replacing Prince. Still, it's weird. There's always been a dog on the farm…but then, there were always cows and sheep and horses too, and I just can't even think about keeping all of that up. This old veggie garden is about the most I can handle, and even this is getting hard."

"You've been here for a long time, haven't you?" I ask, a theory forming in my mind.

"You bet we have," he says. "The Andersons have lived here for over a hundred and twenty years. It's tough to farm by the sea. Would have been wiser of my great-great-grandfather to find a parcel of land inland, but he was a stubborn old goat. Insisted on farming near the water, so he could at least console his aching back with the best views around."

He stands to take a break and stares around with a satisfied look at the land surrounding him. Down in the distance, the ocean sparkles and glimmers, and the coastline nestles the town against it. Except for the tiny subdivision of five houses scattered along Anderson Lane, we're pretty remote.

"Did you ever hear stories about people smuggling stuff in and out of the caves?" I ask him. I've been thinking about this ever since George Smith's mother-in-law told me he was constantly down at the beach. What if he wasn't having an affair, but had somehow gotten caught up in the drug trade in the caves? Could that have been a more concrete tie to Connor?

Mr. Anderson looks at me and grins. "Only my whole darn life. Matter of fact, a younger brother of my grandfather was involved in running rum, back during Prohibition times. He was quite the scoundrel in his younger years. Settled down eventually, though, like we all do. Used to take me into the caves when I was a boy. Yes, those caves have seen a lot of wild things over the years, Mac." He stops, and his smile disappears as he realizes what he's just said. "That is, I didn't mean to say..."

"It's okay. I'm really just curious about what it was like back in the day. Back when there were pirates and rumrunners like your uncle. There are lots of rumors about drugs being hidden in those caves, even today. It's just an interesting coincidence."

He makes a disapproving face. "Yes, well, I don't doubt it. I wouldn't call it a coincidence though. It's a natural thing, really. Those caves are a good hiding place. They run up and down the length of the coast, and they're hard to access. You really need to know the terrain like the back of your hand, and more important than that, you need to be able to handle a boat. Someone like my uncle, who grew up moving boats in and out of coves and inlets, fishing and lord knows what else, had that kind of knowledge. These days, I suppose there are still some people around with the same kind of know-how."

"People like Junior Merlin," I volunteer.

He gives me a knowing look and the hint of a rueful smile. "The Merlins have lived on their little spit of land for almost as long as the Andersons have lived up here on this hill. I daresay they've got plenty of knowledge of the ins and outs of the coastline around these parts. Beyond that, I can't tell you much without resorting to pure speculation. Not sure if you've noticed this, but around Camera Cove, speculation turns into rumor, and rumor turns into verified fact without a whole lot of nudging."

"Yeah, for sure," I say. "I was just wondering."

He nods and pulls off his gloves, slapping them together to shake off the dirt. "Well, Mac," he says, "I think I'm going to take my weary bones back up to the house, have a sit, and watch the ball game for a while. Much obliged for the help. I'll see you in the town square."

"You bet," I tell him.

I collect Hobo and walk away. When I glance back over my shoulder, he's still looking after me, a wistful look on his face.

TEN

JOEY STANDISH, aka Victim Number Three, lived in Brookfield Estates, a trailer park about a ten-minute drive from town. As I head up the coast toward it, the quaint, colorful Victorians and weathered gray Cape Cods disappear behind me. Soon, I pass a sad, unoccupied collection of vacation cottages, fallen into disrepair. The Wandering Surf Cottages have been closed for business for as long as I can remember, sitting just far enough away from the town center to be inconvenient.

The cottages also mark the edge of a much rougher area. I pass one or two barely viable farms, several more that have been abandoned entirely, and the occasional unkempt bungalow or split level.

After a few more minutes, I drive past a small, rundown, rural school, where a bunch of kids are playing on the weedy playground. They turn to look at my car, their game forgotten by the distraction of an unfamiliar visitor. A chill runs down my spine.

Just past the school, a large faded plywood sign announces I'm at Brookfield Estates in chipped, cheerful lettering. The actual "estate" is a collection of trailers lined up in rows. I turn in and park in a little visitors' lot just past the sign, then I get out of the car and look around.

A couple of trailers are well-kept: flowers are neatly planted around freshly painted wooden steps, and some have little birdhouses and whirligigs stuck in the ground for decoration. Many of them, however, are pretty grim. There are more than a few broken windows around, patched with plywood or duct-taped plastic sheeting. Broken toys and rusted trikes are scattered on patchy bits of lawn, and lines of bottles that once held beer and hard liquor are arranged neatly along the outer edges of rickety wooden steps, as if they've been deliberatively collected like commemorative plates.

It was hard enough to build up the nerve to approach George and Emily Smith's house. Brookfield Estates is a completely different ball game—the kind of place I've never stepped foot in. A couple of shirtless men are sitting on lawn chairs outside one of the trailers, smoking cigarettes and staring openly in my direction. An elderly woman in a housedress is hanging clothes on a line, leaning out from her railing and taking her time with the laundry, one eye on me. In the trailer nearest me, a curtain pulls open an inch, then abruptly shuts again.

I open the back door of the car and pull a bunch of flyers from the seat. I'm losing my nerve. I close the door and nearly jump out of my skin as a small gang of preteens—the same ones I just saw at the playground—come strolling down the lane toward me, some of them pushing bikes.

"Who are you?" asks one of them. He's obviously the ring-leader and stands at the front of the formation as if they're a group of ragtag geese.

"I'm from…from town," I say, trying not to be spooked by a bunch of kids.

"I'm from…from town," he repeats, in a quavering girlish fal-setto. He dangles a wrist in front of him and bats his eyelashes, and his posse erupts in nasty, raucous laughter. To my horror, I feel my face turn crimson. I turn away, trying to ignore them as I close the door and pretend to dig for my keys in my pocket.

I turn back and realize that the kids haven't moved. They don't show any signs of leaving. I'm sure that I'm the most interesting thing that's happened to them all day. The woman hanging laundry has gone back inside her trailer, and the men with the beer have gotten into a heated argument and aren't paying any attention to us at all.

I'm starting to wonder whether or not I'm going to have to physically push my way through the throng of kids, when a voice yells across the parking lot at us.

"Hey!"

We all turn toward the trailer with the peeping curtains in time to see a young black guy emerge onto the steps, the screen door slamming shut behind him. He's probably around my age, tall and lean, with short cropped hair, and he's wear-ing a faded red T-shirt over cutoffs. For a long moment, the kids and I stare, waiting for him to say something else. He pulls a pair of sunglasses down off his head and puts them on, then he steps down from the trailer's porch and saunters across the parking lot toward us.

"Melvin," the guy says as he approaches, and the ringleader of my tormentors sets his jaw and tilts his chin defiantly.

"Yeah?" says the kid.

"What the hell are you all doing over here, bothering this guy?"

Some of the younger kids are already dispersing, heading back up the hill toward the schoolyard, with brief glances over their shoulders.

"Shit, Quill," says Melvin, still trying to sound in control although he's obviously not. "What do you care?"

"Melvin, don't you know a goddamn thing about manners?" asks Quill. "You don't even know what this guy is doing here." He turns to me suddenly and pulls his shades up to look at me. I'm struck by his eyes; dark and intent, they pierce right through me. "So what are you doing here, stranger?"

I hold a flyer out to him. "It's a donation drive," I say, managing not to stammer. "I'm looking for items for a fundraising sale we'll be having for the town library next month."

He glances at the flyer and hands it back to me.

"Not sure you're gonna find much around here," he says. He glances over his shoulder at the rundown trailer park, then turns back to me and raises an eyebrow, as if to suggest we both know full well that the residents of Brookfield Estates Trailer Park aren't going to cough up much for the charity drive. "Charity usually comes into this place. Doesn't go out much."

"This isn't charity," I say, scrambling for an excuse. "Not really. We all use the library."

Melvin, who I realize is still standing nearby, watching the exchange with interest, lets out a harsh hoot of laughter.

"Maybe you use it, you fucking pussy," he says. "Nobody around here is going into town to use the fucking library."

Quill whips around, and with a speed and strength that surprises me, grabs Melvin by the scruff of the neck.

"Ow, Quill!" yells Melvin. "What the hell?" He reaches up with both hands and tries to pull the older boy's hands off his neck, with no luck.

"First of all," says Quill. "What did I tell you about that kind of shit? You don't say pussy, or fruit, or faggot. If you say anything, you say gay, and you say it without a snarl in your shit-eating little mouth. You say it like you say toaster, or dog, or Mom, like it's a normal, boring, everyday thing. You hear me?"

My face burns, and I realize that this guy has somehow managed to out me to a gang of juvenile delinquents. I'd prefer to just take the pussy insult and move on.

"Jesus Christ," says Melvin. "Yes, I hear you. I'm sorry, Quill. I won't say it again."

The older kid gives Melvin a shove away. "Second of all," he says, as Melvin reaches up to rub at the back of his neck, "you know damn well that people from around here use the library. Used to use it, anyway. So keep your stupid ignorant trap shut, you got me?"

Melvin nods, sheepishly. "Yeah, Quill." He grabs his bike and hurriedly turns and walks away, trying his best to look like he doesn't give a damn.

Quill turns back to me. "Sorry about that," he says. "Lot of people around here weren't raised to have basic manners. Come on. Let's see if we can find you some handouts."

I follow him as he walks along the gravel path between the trailers. He stops in front of the two shirtless guys playing cards.

"Either of you guys got anything to give away to the library rummage sale?" he asks.

The men grunt, not looking up from their cards.

"Would mean a lot to Joey. You know how much she loved the library," Quill persists. At the mention of her name, I freeze, wondering what he means. Wondering how well he knew her.

The men pause in their game, and after a moment of consideration, they both stand up.

"Might have some old tools," says one of them, before turning and crossing the field to step up into a trailer across the way.

The other one looks at me from behind a pair of thick black plastic shades, the kind that are supposed to cover a pair of real glasses. "You got any use for some old horror movie DVDs?" he asks.

"Uh, yeah," I say. "Sure."

The second guy walks up into the trailer they're sitting in front of. After a couple of minutes, they're both back, several random items shoved into plastic shopping bags.

"Thanks a lot," I say, taking the bags.

"No problem," the guys say, but they're looking at Quill. "Anything for Joey."

Quill nods tightly at them, then follows me as I bring the bags to the van and shove them in through the rear door. I shut it and follow Quill as he starts to walk into the park.

"Why did you say it would mean a lot to Joey?" I ask, trying to sound casual.

He turns and looks at me, his eyes slightly narrowed. "You know who Joey was?"

"Yeah," I say. "I mean, everyone did, didn't they? She was all over the news for weeks. She and the rest of them, I mean. Did you know her well?"

"She was my cousin," he says, in a way that tells me he's done talking about her. He turns and ascends the rickety steps to a trailer.

Although his back is to me, and there's no way for him to see the look of surprise cross my face, he speaks over his shoulder. "It's not that complicated, townie. Our mothers are sisters. My dad is black."

My face goes hot with embarrassment at such a stupid mistake, but before I can respond, the door to the trailer opens, and an old lady sticks her head out. She listens as Quill gives her the pitch. She ends up donating an old coin collection that belonged to her aunt.

Quill seems to have some clout in the park. In about a half hour, he helps me score all kinds of old crap from people in the trailer park, including some surprisingly good loot.

The only problem is that I haven't been able to bring the conversation back around to Joey. Quill likes to talk—to me, to the residents of the park, to the dogs we pass as we move around. The only thing he doesn't seem to want to talk about is his cousin, which means I'm going to have to figure out how to bring her up.

Finally, as we bring the final load of stuff back to the van, I realize I need to start asking questions before I run out of time.

"So you've lived here your whole life?" I ask Quill, when he's leaned over to shove a cardboard box into the van.

"Lived here?" he laughs. "I don't live here. I live in Portland with my folks."

"Oh," I say, surprised.

"I'm here to spend some time with my aunt," he says. A shadow crosses his face, and he glances away.

"Your aunt," I repeat. "You mean Joey's mom?"

He turns to face me and leans back against the van, crossing his arms over his chest. His smile is gone. "So are you going to fill me in?"

"What do you mean?" I try to smile, but I'm pretty sure I end up grimacing instead.

"Why are you here?" he asks. "I mean, why are you really here?"

"I told you that," I bluff. "I'm collecting items for the library drive."

He relaxes deeper into his slouch, which doesn't seem possible, and scrutinizes me over his sunglasses. "Cool," he says. "I thought—I don't know—when I mentioned my cousin, I thought maybe you were here for that. I've gotten kind of used to people hanging around, looking for info about Joey."

Before I can help it, my eyes shift away from his. I look back right away and nod, trying my best to look casual, but it doesn't work.

"What the fuck, man?" he says, straightening up. "Are you kidding me right now? Have you been playing me this whole time?" He gives me a disgusted look, then turns to leave. "That's some bullshit, man."

"No," I protest. "Wait. Seriously."

He turns back, raising an eyebrow.

"My friend," I say, choosing my words carefully. "One of my best friends, actually. He was killed too."

His eyes widen, and he lets out a long low whistle. "No shit," he says. "No fucking shit? Connor Williams?" He leans back against the car.

I nod. "I knew him since we were little kids. We grew up on the same block. There were five of us."

"And now there are four."

I nod.

"So that's why you're here?" he asks. "To poke around?"

"Kind of," I say. "I guess. I mean, the rummage sale is happening, but it was my idea. The library is trying to make money to finish a mural that Connor started, and I thought maybe this would be a way to learn more about the victims. Somebody must have overlooked something."

He chews on his lower lip, considering this, his eyes narrowed at me. "So you're trying to tell me that you're running your own investigation?"

I nod tentatively. "I guess you could say that."

"And you really think you can solve this, when they had so many cops around here for so many months?"

I shrug. "I don't know if I can solve anything. But someone, somewhere, knows who did it, and I do know that the cops didn't manage to figure it out."

"Well, you're right about that," he says. "Goddamn cops are useless. I don't know, though. I can't see how some teenager is going to do a better job on his own than they did."

He turns his head to the side to spit. I wonder if he's lost interest entirely.

"I guess I should get out of here," I say. I turn for the car door, and he reaches out and grabs my arm.

"Wait," he says. "Just hang on a minute."

I turn to him, trying to appear calm and curious, but the feeling of his warm hand on the bare flesh of my wrist sends a rush of heat up my arm and down through the rest of my body.

"Why now?" he asks. "It's been a year. Why did you decide to start asking questions now?"

Part of me wants to tell him about the note, but I don't even know this guy, and something stops me. Instead, I give him another, equally truthful answer.

"I can't stop thinking about it," I say. "I'm beginning to think I'll never be able to stop thinking about it. If I don't do something about it, I might go out of my mind."

He stares at me, not moving. His hand is still on my arm, but I feel his fingers slowly relax, and then he steps back and nods, as if he's made up his mind about something.

"I know what you mean," he says, and his tough guy attitude has faded away. "I can't let it go either. I've spent the past year going over every possibility, and..." He frowns and throws his hands in the air in a sign of defeat. "Nothing. I keep coming up with excuses to come back to the trailer park, hoping somebody will drop some information, or my aunt will remember something. I just want to learn...I don't know, something. Anything at all. You know?"

"Yeah," I say, nodding. "I do know."

We stare at each other, and I wonder if he's thinking what I'm thinking—that I'm not the only person still trying to solve this mystery, and there's comfort in knowing I'm not alone.

"Did Joey have any relationships?" I ask him. "Like, were there any guys around that might be worth looking into?"

He seems to consider this, then shrugs. "If she was with somebody, it's news to me. Not that she would have necessarily told me. Joey was pretty private about a lot of things."

"But you think it's possible?" I ask.

"Maybe," he says. "She was a good-looking girl, and guys were always chasing after her. But if she was with someone, it wasn't anyone from the park. There's no way she could have kept that a secret. Besides, nobody came forward after she died to say they'd been with her."

"Maybe someone had a good reason for not coming forward," I say.

His eyes drop to the ground and he chews on his bottom lip, thinking it all through. "Listen," he says, instead of answering. "Maybe we can help each other out. Why don't you come back on Saturday afternoon? There's a baseball tournament up at the school field, and the trailer park will be pretty much deserted. We can fill each other in on what we know. I'm not saying it will help any, but maybe if we put our heads together..." He shrugs.

"Okay," I say. "Saturday. I can do that."

He smiles. "Cool. Okay."

"Can I ask you one more question?" I ask him.

"Shoot."

"Was Joey into drugs at all?"

He answers immediately. "No. Definitely, absolutely no way. Not a chance. Her dad was into that shit, at least he was when he was still around. She wouldn't touch a cigarette or a beer, let alone any kind of drugs."

He seems more than convinced. For now, I'll assume that he's telling the truth. "Got it," I say. "So I'll see you on Saturday?"

"Yeah. Afternoon, around this time." He winks. "We'll have the place all to ourselves."

He yawns, then reaches his arms above his head, interlacing the fingers of his hands and pulling himself upward into a long, tight stretch. A wide strip of perfect, smooth skin between his shirt and the low-slung waist of his shorts reveals itself, and I turn from the sight, fumbling for the car door.

I get into the van and put the key in the ignition, aware of a weakness in my legs, and then I turn it on and make a slow 360 degree turn in the driveway. I glance in the rearview mirror as I pull up toward the exit, and see Quill walking languidly back to the trailer.

A rough shout catches my attention, and I snap back to reality. Melvin and his gang stroll back into the park, pushing their bikes. They surround the van on all sides as they move past, so I'm stuck until they've moved around me, like cows on a rural road. Melvin stops at the driver's side window, and I force myself to make eye contact. He gives me the finger and laughs, and I'm finally able to pull away.

ELEVEN

THERE ARE A LOT of thoughts running through my head after I leave Brookfield Estates, but I can't focus on anything except one.

Quill.

If I didn't know better, I might have thought he was flirting with me. I know it's impossible, though. Someone like Quill—confident, engaging, comfortable in his own body—couldn't be further out of my league. I try to push his face out of my mind.

It doesn't work. My mind immediately drifts back to the clean, smooth lines of his body, the strap of his loose tank top drifting to the edge of his taut, bony shoulder, his beautiful eyes, and the full lips that curl up at one corner as if he's got a secret he wants to tell me.

I force myself to shift my mind away from Quill, and instead, I think about Connor, and why he was in the caves that night.

It seems likely that he was there to face the killer, but by all accounts, there have been other illegal things happening in those caves for years. What if they were somehow connected, or got tangled up with one another somehow? It gives me an idea. I pull out my phone and send a text.

I get a reply almost immediately.

Hey Mac, whatsup? asks Carrie.

I need to see you. I text back. Ant too.

There's a long pause before she writes me back again.

???

Please, it's important. I can meet you anywhere.

Another long pause, then **Fine. Park at the beach tonight at 9. We'll meet you there.**

×　×　×

The beach parking lot is mostly empty when I arrive, with just a few cars parked near the boardwalk. I drive to the far end of the lot—the empty section that looks out on the caves.

Carrie and Ant are about fifteen minutes late, which doesn't surprise me since Carrie is never on time for anything. Then Ant's truck, a beat-up old Chevy, comes sliding into the lot, and pulls into the spot next to mine, his lights shining out toward the caves.

Carrie looks down at me from the passenger seat and waves. Behind her, Ant cranes his neck, trying to make out who I am. Carrie rolls down her window, and I do the same.

"Hi, Mac," she says. "What's up?"

"Hey," I say. "Do you guys mind if I get in?"

Ant says something inaudible, and Carrie turns to respond. I only vaguely make out what she's saying. I hear something about "friends" and "kids" and "cut him some slack." She turns back to me.

"Sure," she says. "Come on."

I get out of my car, and she opens the truck door for me. I climb up, and she slides along the bench seat, making room.

I know Ant Merlin as well as anyone in town, by reputation if not personally. He's three or four years older than me and Carrie, a small, wiry guy. When he was still in high school, he was always getting in trouble; petty theft, loitering, underage drinking, public intoxication.

His brother had always called him Pissant, and the name stuck, all the way through elementary school and junior high. Eventually he'd put a stop to it with his fists, and the world—or at least the world around us—had settled on the compromise: Ant. A weird handle, but I guess it kind of suited him. Besides, I couldn't tell you his real name if you paid me.

Carrie insists that he's changed. I'll reserve judgment for now.

"Hey," I say. "I'm Mac." I hold my hand out, and he narrows his eyes, skeptically, before reaching out and shaking it. "I need to talk to you—that's why I asked Carrie if I could meet up with you guys."

"Need to talk to me?" he asks, suspicious. "Alright, buddy, what's this about?"

I can tell by the tone of his voice that he isn't going to sit around making small talk for long. Carrie is watching me curiously.

I take a deep breath, then plunge in. "I want to know if any of the Catalog Killer's victims had anything to do with your brother."

Carrie leans back and puts her hand over her face. "Mac, what the hell?"

Ant reacts more aggressively. "What. The. Fuck. Carrie? What is this shit?"

"I'm sorry," I say. "It's important."

"My brother had nothing to do with that!" he says. "I don't much like the guy, but he's not a goddamn serial killer!"

"I'm not saying he is," I say, holding up my hands to show I mean no harm. "I'm just working through a...kind of a theory."

"A theory?" asks Carrie, in disbelief.

"Connor was found in the caves," I say. "Lots of people say that there's drug smuggling happening through those caves. I'm wondering if the two things are somehow connected."

"This is unbelievable," says Ant. "You don't think the cops were all over our house after those murders? They didn't leave us alone for weeks. It was bullshit."

"I know that," I agree, "and I honestly don't think your brother had anything to do with the murders. What I'm wondering is whether they were connected in some other way."

"Like what?" asks Ant.

"I don't really know," I have to admit. "It was just a hunch."

He laughs. "A hunch. Like this is *Scooby-Doo* or something. Listen, I'm not going to say this again; my brother had no connection to any of those victims. If he had, I would have heard about it."

"Mac," says Carrie. "What's all this about, really?"

They both look at me, Carrie with genuine concern, Ant with a kind of irritated curiosity. I wish I could just show them the photo I took of the note and explain to them that I missed out on a clear opportunity to help Connor, but I can't. Maybe if it was just Carrie, I would, but not here, with Ant; it feels like exposing too much of myself.

"I feel responsible," I say finally. "I feel like I should have paid attention and noticed something. Maybe I could have helped him."

"Responsible?" says Carrie, incredulously. "Mac, how could you be responsible for something like this? How could you be any more responsible than any of the rest of us?"

I hesitate for a moment, my phone with the photo of the note burning a hole in my pocket, but in the end, something holds me back from sharing it. Carrie knows me, and knew Connor, as well as anyone. If I blame myself, she might blame me too. "I know it's stupid," I say instead.

"I think I know how you feel, man," Ant says suddenly. Carrie and I both look at him, surprised. "Seriously. When my mom died, I was only about eight years old. She was in a car accident, kind of a fluke. Got rear-ended into a tree. They said if the car had gone an inch to the side, she might have been okay, but that was how it went down."

Carrie reaches out and puts her hand on his leg, and he covers it with one of his own, squeezing.

"I spent years thinking I should have known it was going to happen," he goes on. "Like I could have maybe stopped it if I'd gone with her to the store that day. Or if I'd been quicker getting ready for school that day. Or if I'd eaten my supper without complaining the night before. I mean, I know now that I had nothing to do with it, obviously. But for a long time, that's all I could think about—how I screwed up and my mom was dead."

"Oh, Ant," says Carrie. She leans over and nestles back against his chest, and he kisses the top of her head. For the first time, I can see that they really do like each other, a lot.

"Yeah," I say. "It's kind of like that."

"So I get it, man," says Ant. "But you've got to know that there's nothing you could have done about it. You've also got to know that my brother, miserable son of a bitch that he is, had nothing to do with it."

I nod. "I believe it. I just had to ask."

"That's alright, man," says Ant, as if we've just cleared up a small misunderstanding and that's the end of that.

Carrie sits up straight again and looks me in the eye. "Mac, I know you want to learn who killed Connor. I know that. But you aren't going to, okay? The cops couldn't figure it out, and a whole year's worth of people coming up with wild theories didn't make a difference, so you should do yourself a favor and move on with your life."

"I'll try," I tell her.

Back in my car, after they've driven away, I think about Ant's story. I'm kind of surprised how comforted it makes me feel, to know that someone else feels the same way about things they can't change.

There's one big difference between Ant's story and mine, though. Ant knows what happened to his mother. There's no mystery there, nothing to solve.

When it comes to me and Connor, there's unresolved business, and I intend to get to the bottom of it.

TWELVE

WHEN I NEAR Brookfield Estates on Saturday, I start to worry that I'm going to run into Melvin and his gang again, but as I drive by the playground, I can see that it's empty. I pull in and park just past the sign.

As if he's been watching for me, Quill comes strolling nonchalantly out from who knows where, his thumbs hitched into the pockets of his denim cutoffs, and the bottom of his long, faded purple tank draped over his wrists. He leans casually against my car, looking down at me through the open window.

"Hey," I say.

"Hey, yourself," he says.

The trailer park seems like a ghost town, with just a few scattered signs of life; some TVs chattering through open windows, an old man working on a truck. As if on cue, I hear the hollow thunk of a ball hitting an aluminum bat in the distance, and a muffled holler as a crowd screams.

"Game should go on for a while," says Quill. "Gives us a good chance to check things out." He pauses and smirks at me. "Alone."

Without warning, he pivots on his heel and starts to walk away. I expect him to head toward his aunt's trailer, but instead, he goes in the opposite direction. I follow him, and we wander through the empty trailer park.

"Man I hate this place," he says. "Joey couldn't wait to get the hell out of here."

"She was going to leave?" I ask.

"Fucking right she was," he says, sounding almost angry. "You think she'd stick around here? Joey was one of the smartest people you'd ever meet. She was always reading, always thinking. She had all kinds of ideas and loved learning how to do just about anything. She was figuring out her exit strategy."

"What was she going to do?" I ask him. We've left the trailers behind, and we're pushing our way onto a tangled field at the back of the park.

"Not sure," he says. "She would have gotten some kind of scholarship or something. She talked about maybe doing an apprenticeship and then working for herself. Whatever she ended up doing, she would've been successful."

He leads me onto a narrow path that's been trodden through the high weeds, and we cross the field to where a low muddy embankment, littered with garbage, descends to a small trickling stream. I wonder if this is the brook and field that gives the trailer park its name. I follow him across it and into a grove of trees.

"We used to spend so much time here," he says. "Me and Joey. We pretended it was an enchanted kingdom. Some of the other kids played here too, and Joey would give us all roles. She wanted to write books. She was creative. Always making stuff up out of her head—stories, forts, clothes—anything she thought of, she could make it. She wanted to live a big life, to see the world, make her mark."

His voice is softer than I've heard it yet, missing the brashness that has characterized his declarations up to this point.

We stop at a giant tree, and he reaches out and strokes the heavy rutted bark.

"Anyway," he says. "This is it. This is where she ended up."

The tree is split in the middle and curved into a crook.

"Just sitting in this tree, like a doll or something," he says. "Staring up into the sky like she had nowhere better in the world to be. Totally messed up."

"Who found her?" I ask, almost afraid of the answer.

"Some kids," he says, matter-of-fact. He hoists himself up into the center of the tree and climbs up to nestle himself into the crook, positioning himself so that he looks ready to take a nap. He slowly lifts one arm and places it behind his head, tilts his head back, parts his lips, and closes his eyes.

I inadvertently take a couple of steps back, but my eyes don't leave the tree. He just stays there, motionless, and the whole forest seems to grow quiet and still. A feeling of unreality settles on the grove like a light mist. Quill's features seem to have softened. His face, framed by a narrow, fragile branch, is suddenly delicate, feminine. For the first time, I can see the resemblance between him and his cousin, and I feel as if I'm staring back in time at Joey Standish as she was upon her death.

Quill's mouth opens very slightly. "This is how she was when they found her," he says, his voice barely more than a whisper.

Then, with a series of quick movements, he breaks the spell, opening his eyes, pushing himself back into a seated position, and vaulting himself out of the tree to stand in front of me. He reaches out a hand and rubs at a spot on the tree's heavy outstretched limb, where the bark has been peeled away. "This is where the catalog picture was stapled. Didn't even look like Joey. Like I said, messed up. Let's get the hell out of here."

He turns and begins to walk back the way we came. I pull my phone out of my pocket and take a couple quick shots of the tree, then hurry to follow him away from the woods, across the creek, and back through the weedy, garbage-strewn field.

The trailer that Joey lived in with her mother is especially grim. Lacy yellow curtains that I'm pretty sure used to be white are pulled tight to block the tiny windows. More than anything, the trailer looks defeated.

Quill moves aggressively up the rickety wooden steps and pulls open the screen door. "Come on," he says. When I hesitate, he makes a gesture of impatience. "There's nobody here. Her mom's at the tavern down the highway, just like every other Saturday afternoon."

If the outside of the trailer is depressing, the inside is a hundred times worse. A small kitchen opens into a living room, and both are laden with empty beer cans and ashtrays full of butts. Fast food wrappers and empty pizza boxes are strewn all over the floor.

"It wasn't always like this," Quill says, catching the way I look around the room.

He seems different since we walked inside the trailer—tense—and I instinctively throw up my hands against the defensiveness in his voice. "No," I say. "I know, I mean. I'm sure."

"You don't know anything," he says, angrily. "It was better when Joey was still here. She kept her mom on the straight and narrow. More or less. They had a decent thing going on. Polly—that's my aunt—she'd keep the place pretty clean, and Joey did most of the cooking. She was a great cook, actually. I told you she was creative, didn't I?"

I nod, although it's not really a question.

"She could cook anything she wanted. Lasagna, tamales, roast chicken, you name it. She made a lot of her own clothes. She even learned some mechanics stuff from some of the guys here in the park. I'm telling you, she could figure out how to do anything. She didn't want to stay here," he tells me again. "She wouldn't have."

He turns abruptly and strides down the narrow hallway. After a second, I follow him. He pushes open a door, and when I catch up, I can tell right away that we're in Joey's bedroom. I get the impression that it hasn't changed at all since she died. Girls' clothes are still strewn around the room, along with books and magazines and baskets full of cloth and paper and various craft materials.

Quill sits on the bed, pressing himself up into the corner of the wall, with his left leg thrown up into a hard angle and his right leg sprawled flat. His crotch is angled straight at me, and if he weren't wearing baggy shorts, I'd probably be stumbling backward through the bedroom door and skittering back to my car like a scared cat.

He pats the bed beside him, but I ignore the invitation and grab an old orange chair—plastic and metal like the kind you find in a school auditorium—from the desk, tossing some clothes onto the floor to take a seat.

"Jesus, you're jumpy. I'm not going to bite, unless you want me to." He grins, and I try—and fail—not to blush.

His flirtatiousness drops away, and he looks at me seriously.

"So why now?" he asks. "Why are you suddenly digging around in this, a year later?"

I wasn't sure whether I'd show Quill the note or not, but sitting across from him now, in Joey's bedroom, it seems like the only option.

"I want to show you something," I say.

"Oh, yeah?" he asks, raising an eyebrow suggestively.

I ignore his look and dig my phone out of my pocket. I scroll through the pictures until I find Connor's note. I hand Quill the phone, and he leans forward to grab it from me. His eyes widen as he reads the note.

"From Connor?" he asks, handing it back to me and dropping back down onto the bed.

I nod. "He left me this note, but I only found it a few days ago."

"That's fucked-up," he says. "So you think he knew he was meeting the killer that night?"

"Yeah," I say. "I do. Cops think so too. Told me as much."

He lets out a long whistle. "Wow."

"What about you?" I ask him. "Why are you still trying to get involved?"

His eyes drop away from mine, down toward his feet.

"Joey and I were really close," he says. "From the time we were just babies. I always felt kind of guilty about how things played out. I mean, I live in a nice house in the sub-urbs, and my folks actually care about me, about whether or not I do well in school, about who I hang out with, all that shit. Joey had it different. Her dad's a junkie and an asshole, and her mom's been a mess for years. I used to come spend a week here at the park with her every summer, and then Joey would end up spending like a month with us. When she died, it nearly killed me. I was really messed up about it. Still am. I mean, how are you supposed to process some-thing like this?"

I nod. I know exactly what he means.

"Anyway, I spent a lot of months being angry, acting out, ignoring school, not caring about anything at all, really. My parents made me go to a psychologist, and it actually kind of helped a little bit. By the time I started to calm down a little, pull my shit together, it seemed like everyone else had started to move on. I don't mean they forgot about it, or whatever, but they all—my parents, Joey's mom, everyone—they just kind of accepted that it wasn't going to be solved and started trying to get past it. Now they all want me to get past it too."

I think about my parents, how worried they've been about me; about Carrie and Doris, telling me to move on with my life; about Chief Parnatsky, saying that the investigation is over and there's no point in trying to find something that isn't going to be found.

"The thing is," says Quill, and it's like he's reading a script straight out of my mind. "I don't want to get past it. I think there's an answer out there, and I want to do everything I can to figure it out."

He stops, and we stare at each other, not speaking. In that moment, something passes between us. Over the past year, the frustration of not knowing what really happened has settled on me like a fog, but now it turns out there's someone trying to find a way through it with me.

"It sounds like we both want exactly the same thing," I say.

Quill smiles. "Two heads are better than one, right? Okay. Cool. Tell me what you've figured out so far."

"Not a lot," I admit. "I mean, there's the note, but it doesn't really tell me much. I did visit George Smith's house."

He lifts his chin, regarding me with new interest. "No shit? Did you pull the whole 'I'm raising cash for the library' thing?"

I blush, embarrassed. "Maybe."

He laughs. "You are one sneaky piece of work. I love it. So what did you find out?"

"Well, the whole thing felt really sleazy. His wife didn't say much—she was kind of distracted and a bit weird. But his mother-in-law told me that she thought he'd been having an affair."

Quill's eyes widen. "Whoa."

"Yeah," I say, "but here's the thing. Her only evidence is that George was apparently spending a lot of time at the beach. She seems to think that he was meeting some woman there, but I wonder if it might've been something else entirely."

"Like what?" Quill asks, his attention totally focused on me.

"Well, Connor's body was found in the sea caves at the end of the beach, which is weird to begin with. A lot of people think those caves are used for drug smuggling. So I wonder if there's a connection."

He contemplates this, sitting up and leaning forward to hug his knees. "Do you remember when you asked if any of the guys who were into Joey might have had something to do with this?"

I nod, interested to hear where he's going with this.

"Well, the thing is," he says, "I'm pretty sure that she was seeing someone, and he wasn't from the park."

My eyes widen. "Seriously? Why didn't you mention it?"

He shrugs. "I wasn't sure I could trust you. I'm not in the habit of spreading Joey's private business around."

"Fair enough," I say. "So what do you know about him?"

He shakes his head, lips pursed. "Nothing. That's the thing. She never came out and said anything, but I could always tell when Joey started hooking up with someone. Her texts would get kind of cryptic, and she was slow to hit me back. Usually she'd come out with it after a couple of weeks, but that didn't happen this time. I wasn't going to start playing her games, so I didn't press her."

"You didn't tell this to the police?"

He drops back against the headboard and rolls his eyes. "Do I really have to explain to you why I didn't want to talk to the cops?" he says. "Besides, I didn't have any proof, and the guy didn't come forward, so it's not like there was much I could say. I figured something would show up in her texts or whatever, and they'd have someone to look into, but as far as I know, that didn't happen."

I mull this over. "So at least three out of the four victims had a secret that they didn't share with anyone—not even their best friends. Don't you think they might have been connected?"

"Yeah," he says, "maybe. But Joey definitely wasn't screwing around with George Smith. He was way too old for her and not her type. She wasn't into drugs, either; I know that for sure."

"Would she date someone who was into drugs?" I ask.

He chews on his lip, thinking about it. "I really don't think so. That kind of thing just wasn't Joey's style."

"We're missing something," I admit.

"Well, that just means we're going to have to dig deeper," says Quill. He smiles slyly. "Maybe you need a partner with you on your next round of visits—someone to help you with all those heavy library donations."

I think about it. It's dishonest enough—entering peoples' houses under false pretenses—without bringing along someone who doesn't even work at the library. On the other hand, I've thought back on my visit to the Smith house a hundred times, wishing I'd had the guts and the clear head to ask more questions and find out more. Something tells me Quill might be better at it than me.

"Yeah," I say. "That might work."

"Awesome," he says, jumping up from the bed. He leans toward me and throws me a wide high five. When our hands connect, he grips, and our fingers slide together, connecting.

The mood in the room changes. Quill stands over me, looking down into my face. Our hands are frozen together, and I feel almost trapped, not sure what's going to happen next. I want him to pull me up out of the chair, against him, but I'm also afraid of the exact same thing. The panic must show on my face, because he slides his hand away from mine, gently, and then takes a step back and sits on the bed.

"Can I ask you something?" he says.

"Yeah," I say, trying my best to sound laid back.

"Was there something between you and Connor? I mean, more than just being friends?"

"No!" I say, too quickly. I try to cover it with a laugh, but it comes out sounding strained. "Not at all. We were just really good friends. We grew up together, like you and Joey."

"That's cool," he says, nodding.

But something tells me he isn't convinced.

THIRTEEN

EVERYONE EXPECTED that Christopher Brindle would be mayor someday. He was a handsome young lawyer, with a pretty, friendly wife and a baby, and when he was elected to town council, it just seemed like a matter of time.

Then his wife, Maria, was murdered—Victim Number Two—and within six months, he was remarried to a neighbor, who just happened to be his dead wife's best friend. None of that had gone down very well with the public. Despite the fact that cops were unable to find anything linking Brindle to the murders, it wasn't long before the scrutiny forced him to step down from the town council.

Chris Brindle and his new wife, Celeste, moved, which unfortunately means we won't get to check out the crime scene while we talk to them. Their new place, in a ragged strip of town houses, is a far cry from the nice Cape Cod house that was all over the news when Maria Brindle's body was found.

"I thought this guy was rich," says Quill, as I park on the street.

"He had to quit the town council after the murders," I say. "I don't know what he does now."

Quill rings the doorbell and we stand, waiting. In the entryway of the town house next door, a curtain shifts, and I glimpse eyes peering nosily out at us. The curtain snaps shut when the door opens.

The woman in front of us is tiny—barely five feet tall—with big eyes and tightly cropped black hair. She's wearing an apron over jeans and a black sweater, and as she stares up at us, smiling broadly, she wipes her hands on a cloth and throws it over her shoulder.

"Hello, there," she says. "How can I help you?"

I smile and hand her a flyer. "We're doing a donation drive for the local library," I say.

"Come on in," she chirps. "I'm sure I can find something in here for you."

We follow her into the town house and stand in the foyer. The house is a bit small and kind of rough around the edges, with scuffed paint and a large stain on the carpet in the corner. Something smells bad, burnt, and there's a bit of smoke in the air. She smiles apologetically.

"I'm not much of a cook," she says. "I'm trying to learn. My husband's former wife was a fabulous cook." She blushes, and her face drops as she realizes what she's said. "I talk too much…" she says, trailing off. "What kind of stuff are you looking for?"

"We're not picky," I say. "We'll take pretty much anything that you're willing to get rid of, as long as it's in good shape.

People have given us bags of clothes, kitchen stuff, sports equipment, books."

"I've got some old pots and pans in the basement," she says. "Do you mind hanging out here for a minute while I go down and check?"

She opens a door on the other side of the foyer and disappears down some steps. As soon as she's gone, Quill kicks off his shoes and tiptoes quickly further into the house.

"What are you doing?" I whisper furiously behind him. He turns back and grins at me.

"Hurry up!" he whispers back.

I can hear Celeste banging around in the basement. I hesitate for a second, then I step out of my shoes and follow him.

Quill has moved into the kitchen. It's dated, like the rest of the house, but it's cozy, with colorful dish towels hanging on the oven door and a couple of potted plants on the windowsill. A casserole sits on the stove, its top blackened and charred.

"Look," says Quill.

He's staring at the fridge. In the center of the door, surrounded by a mess of coupons and photos and bills, is a beautiful black and white photograph of a young woman with curly black hair. She's holding a baby and smiling broadly at the camera.

I recognize the woman, and the photograph, immediately. It's Maria Brindle in the same picture that was used in news reports about her murder.

There's a noise, and we turn to find Celeste in the doorway of the kitchen, holding a cardboard box. Her smile fades when she finds us there. I feel a tight pang of guilt, like a knife between my ribs.

"I'm really sorry," says Quill. "I yelled down, but you must not have heard us. We've been at this all day, and we're super thirsty. Is it okay if we grab a glass of water?"

Her face brightens again, as she immediately buys his explanation.

"Of course," she says. She puts the box on the counter and moves around us, filling glasses from the tap and handing them to us.

"Thanks a million," says Quill. "I have to ask this, I'm sorry. Is that a picture of Maria Brindle on the refrigerator?"

I turn to stare at him, my eyes wide, willing him to shut up, but he ignores me. Celeste looks flustered, turning to glance at the photo. Her mouth drops open and she begins to speak, then stops and starts again.

"Yes," she says. "Maria was my husband's wife, and a very good friend of mine."

"I'm so sorry," says Quill, and the waver in his voice catches me off guard. "I shouldn't have asked. It's just...I was cousins with one of the other victims. Joey Standish. I saw the photo of Maria and I..." he trails off, and Celeste's eyes widen with sympathy. She steps toward him and puts her hand on his arm.

"I know," she says. "That monster took so much from us."

Quill covers his face with his hand, and I wonder if he's about to burst into tears.

"Oh my goodness," says Celeste. "Please, come into the living room and sit down for a minute."

She leads the way, stepping out of the room ahead of Quill. He drops his hand from his face and turns to glance quickly at me. To my shock, he flashes a quick grin, then his face drops back into its miserable disguise, and he follows her into the living room.

Celeste gestures for us to take a seat on a couch, and she sits across from us in a wingback armchair. Quill pretends to gather himself, and I just sit quietly. If he's going to play this kind of game, he's on his own.

"I'm sorry," he says finally. His eyes are dry, but his voice is full of tears, and I can tell by the sympathetic look on her face that Celeste is convinced.

"It's okay," she says, soothingly.

"People just don't understand," he says.

She nods repeatedly, and I can see that she's choking back tears. "I know what you mean," she says. "It's been really difficult for Chris, and for me too."

"People were nice, at the beginning," says Quill. "But I know that some people even kind of blamed Joey for her own death, like she put herself in that position."

Celeste sits forward in her chair now, her eyes gleaming.

"People were horrible to us," she says, her voice thick and emotional. "They said all kinds of terrible things. We had to move, just to get away from the old neighborhood."

"Really?" asks Quill, leaning forward, his elbows on his knees. "That's awful."

Now that Celeste's talking, it's like she can't stop. "Our friends abandoned us. Even our families are acting distant. People think that Chris and I are terrible people. They assume that we were having an affair before she died."

My stomach twists. I can't believe that we've tricked her

into unloading on us like this. I glance at Quill, wondering if he feels as guilty as I do, but he's sitting forward, staring intently at Celeste as she speaks.

"Everyone had it backward," she says. "I loved Maria. Chris loved Maria. But she was unhappy for a while before she died. She used to tell me that she wanted to leave Chris, but that he was trying to hold the marriage together. Then she died before anything was resolved, and Chris and I found comfort in one another."

She stops suddenly and stares across at us, as if she's only just realizing that we're in the room.

"I'm sorry," she says weakly. "I don't know what came over me. I shouldn't be telling you these things."

Quill looks at me, his eyes widening meaningfully, as if he's trying to send me a message, and I realize that he wants me to step in and help him out. I don't know what to say. He's so much better at this than I am. But the room has fallen into an uncomfortable silence.

"Do you know why?" I ask, stumbling my way toward an actual question. "I mean, why she wanted to leave him?"

She looks awkward. "I don't know," she says. "She wouldn't say. She was vague. Distant." She stands. "Really," she says, "I've said too much. Please forgive me. This isn't appropriate."

"It's okay," says Quill. "I know what it's like to have all this stuff bottled up. The murders made us all a little bit crazy."

She smiles at him, grateful that he's given her an excuse. "Yes, I think you're right."

We all turn toward the sound of a door opening.

"Celeste?" a man's voice calls from the entryway.

"That's my husband," she whispers. "Please don't say anything about this."

A moment later, Christopher Brindle enters the room. He's holding a briefcase and is wearing a suit. The top button of his shirt is undone, and the tie is loosened. He stops and stares at us, then toward his wife.

"Hi, honey," she says, "These nice young guys are here to collect some donations for the library."

"Yes," says Quill. He stands up from the couch, and I follow his lead. "We're throwing our first annual rummage sale. Should be quite the event."

Celeste walks over to hug him, and Christopher's face softens as he leans down to kiss her on the cheek.

"Supper smells great, honey," he says, teasingly.

She blushes and giggles. "I'm trying!" she says. "I swear to God, I'll get it right eventually!"

"I know that, Celeste," he says. "I'm only picking on you." He leans down and kisses her again, and I get the odd feeling that he's doing it for our benefit.

"You're early," she says, pulling away. "I wasn't expecting you for a couple more hours."

"We should get going," I say, shooting a glance at Quill. He nods, and we move around the couple and into the hallway.

"Don't forget your stuff," says Celeste. She takes the box out of the kitchen and hands it to me.

"This is great," I say. "Thank you so much." I grab the box, ready to get out of there, when a loud crackling wail fills the room. We all turn toward the sound, and I notice the baby monitor on the counter for the first time.

"Ashleigh's awake," says Celeste. "I'll go get her."

She disappears upstairs, and Chris Brindle's smile disappears as he stares at us. "Do me a favor, guys," he says. "Don't come back here, okay?"

"Uh, yeah," says Quill. "For sure."

"I don't know if you realize who we are," he continues. "But we don't appreciate uninvited guests coming around here. Got it?"

My mouth is dry, but I somehow manage to croak out a response. "We're sorry. We didn't mean to intrude."

Chris steps out of the way and lets us pass, and we move back to the front door. Quill steps into his shoes, and then I hand him the box as I wriggle my feet back into my sneakers. The whole time, Chris stands at the entrance to the foyer, staring at us. His eyes are narrowed and suspicious, a look that seems as if it's settled there permanently.

My hand is on the doorknob when Celeste appears, holding a young toddler in her arms. The little girl looks at us, wide-eyed, then turns toward her father and stretches out her arms. Our presence instantly forgotten, he turns to her, beaming, and grabs her from her stepmother.

"Say 'bye-bye,'" says Celeste, and the little family turns to look at us as I open the door and step aside for Quill to move around me with the box.

"Thanks again," I say, before I step outside. Celeste smiles at me, waving Ashleigh's hand for her. Christopher Brindle watches us, stone-faced, as I back out the door and close it, finally, behind me.

FOURTEEN

MY HANDS ARE SHAKING as I shove the keys into the ignition, but Quill is laughing.

"Holy shit!" he says. "That was awesome!"

"Awesome?" I ask, incredulous, as I drive us away from the town house. "It was awful! I can't believe you did that!"

"Did what?" he asks, surprised.

"You totally threw the ball to me when I wasn't ready for it," I say. "You were doing such a good job asking her questions. I don't know why you dragged me into it. I almost ruined everything!"

He scoffs. "You weren't that bad. You just need some more practice. Besides, until I came along, weren't you planning to do all this on your own?"

"Fine," I agree, reluctantly. "But next time we do something like that, at least make sure I'm ready for it."

"We should go somewhere," he says. "Somewhere we can talk everything over."

I think about it. "There's a coffee shop near the beach," I tell him. "We could go there."

"Perfect."

When we're finally sitting in quiet corner booth, Quill with a latte and me with an iced tea, we look at each other. I let out a deep breath, and then, surprising myself, I start laughing.

Quill looks at me, surprised, and then he starts laughing too. After a minute, when we've calmed down, he looks at me. "So you caught that, right?"

I nod. "Maria had a secret too. She wanted to leave her husband."

"I don't blame her," says Quill. "Her husband seems like an asshole. But how does that tie in with Joey and Connor and George Smith? Do you think maybe he was the murderer?"

I shake my head. "The cops totally ruled him out."

Quill looks at me with wide eyes, as if he's just thought of something. "Mac, what's the one thing that all four victims had in common?" he asks.

I think about this. "They were all hiding something from the people in their lives."

He nods. "So what if the killer used that to his advantage? Like, wouldn't it be easier to plan such elaborate murders if you knew your victim was preoccupied with some secret, behind-the-scenes stuff?"

I think about this. It makes sense. "Especially if the killer got to know the victims' routines. If George Smith was running around on his wife, he was probably spending his energy worrying about how to not get caught. The fact that someone was following him wouldn't have been on his radar. And

Connor's secret was that he had figured out the identity of the killer."

"Or," says Quill, "maybe it wasn't."

I give him a quizzical look and he explains.

"Maybe Connor had a completely different secret. Maybe the Catalog Killer was able to capitalize on that and somehow convince him to visit the caves that night."

I think about this, trying to fit the pieces together. "If that's true, then why did he want me to come to the caves with him?"

Quill shrugs. "Who knows? But the note didn't say anything about hunting a murderer; it was totally vague. It could have been anything, and whatever it was, could it really be any weirder than wanting you to help him identify and catch a serial killer?"

I have to admit that he's right. I haven't been able to figure out why Connor chose me to help him. It makes total sense that he could have had a different, actual secret.

The only problem is that I have literally no idea what it would be.

"So the killer watched each of the victims, discovered something they were hiding, and took advantage of this information to set up his murders."

I nod, slowly. "Maybe Connor went to the caves that night, thinking he was going for a completely different reason—something related to whatever he was hiding—and was ambushed."

"That makes sense," says Quill. "It also explains how the killer was ready with a catalog image, poison, everything. He showed up prepared."

We go silent, staring into our drinks, and I know we're both imagining the same macabre scene.

Quill shakes his head. "Changing the subject. Before all this happened, did you have a plan for what you were going to do next? With your life, I mean?"

I shrug. "I guess so. I didn't have it all mapped out or anything, but I knew I'd go to college. I mean, I had no idea what I'd take or anything like that, but I loved the idea of leaving town, getting a dorm room and a roommate, making new friends. Joining clubs."

He laughs. "Joining clubs? Like the chess club? The badminton club?"

I smile. "You know what I mean. College stuff. Doing something interesting, taking classes with brilliant professors, sitting on the quad and talking about serious books. Going to open mic nights, meeting people…"

"Kissing boys?" he asks.

I blush and drop my gaze to my drink. "Maybe."

He reaches out and puts his hand on mine, rubs his thumb gently over my knuckles.

"What about now?" he asks.

I meet his gaze again. "I don't think about any of it anymore, except when I have to. When my parents nag me, or when I need to pay a room deposit, or something stupid like that. I don't think about what courses I want to take, or what friends I'll make, or…or any of it. It's just a thing I have to do now, because my life is going to keep on going, whether it makes sense or not, and I guess the best I can hope for is that it works out okay somehow."

"I know what you mean," Quill says. "My future has seemed so empty and irrelevant since Joey died, because I know she doesn't get those chances now. All the things I wanted from my life...I just stopped wanting them. And nothing else has stepped up to fill in the space. But lately..."

His eyes drop, out of shyness or embarrassment or both, and his thumb stops moving over the top of my hand for a moment. Then he picks up my hand from the table and turns it over, cupping it between his. I watch this, mesmerized for a moment, and then I lift my eyes back to his and find that he's staring right at me, a small smile on his face.

"Things have felt different, since I met you," he says.

My heart leaps, and I smile back at him. Unfortunately, our waitress chooses this moment to interrupt, and Quill lets go of my hand, but even later, as I drive him back to the trailer park, I can still feel the imprint of his touch against my skin. I keep running his words over and over in my mind, wishing I could hear them again for the first time, again and again and again.

As I pull over onto the shoulder near the Brookfield Estates road sign to let Quill out, he turns to me and frowns. "So this totally sucks, but I spoke to my parents this morning, and they want me to come back home for a while. I don't really have much choice in the matter, so I'm leaving this evening."

"Oh," I say. "Shit."

He shrugs. "To be honest, I'm pretty happy to get the hell out of the park, but I hate not being here to help my aunt."

"When can you come back?" I ask.

"I don't know," he says. "Maybe next weekend for a couple of days? I'll see if I can borrow my mom's car."

I think about this. "We could go to the Abernathy house, where the killer was hiding out. That's not a trip I want to make on my own."

He smiles. "I'll protect you, don't worry. What will you do in the meantime?"

"I still have to visit Connor's parents," I say. "And I should do it alone."

"You sure you want to tackle that on your own?" he asks. "I feel like I should be with you. If you wait, we could go together."

"Trust me," I say. "It's the last thing I want to do, but I need to do it, and it'll be less complicated this way."

"Suit yourself," he says. "But text me the minute you're done."

"I will," I promise.

He nods, satisfied, and reaches for the door handle, but then, instead of getting out of the van, he slides himself across the seat to me and runs a hand around my waist, pulling me into him. I react without thinking, reaching up with my right hand to grab the back of his head and pull him toward me, and then we're kissing.

He pulls back, and we both stare at each other. Since I met Quill, I've been telling myself that something like this couldn't happen, but now that it has, it feels like everything since that moment has been leading up to this.

"Let's pick up this conversation next time," he says, turning and jumping out of the van. He runs down the pitted gravel driveway into the trailer park, without looking back.

As I drive away from the park, my face is still flushed and warm, so I open the windows to let in some air. But the hot summer breeze doesn't do much to cool the memory of Quill's hand around my waist, his lips on mine. Something perfect has happened. All I want to do is turn around, chase Quill down, and make sure he means what I think he meant by his parting words. For the first time since Connor died, a new obsession takes up my mind, and during the entire drive back to town, I don't think about the Catalog Killer once.

FIFTEEN

IN A WAY, Victim Number Four's house is the easiest for me to visit, since it's literally right across the street. The reality, though, is not nearly that simple, and it takes me several days to work up the courage to visit. As I walk up the steps to the front door, I'm well aware that I haven't been inside Connor's house since the reception after his funeral. I didn't want to go to the reception, but my parents insisted, and I stood around in the corner with Ben and Carrie and Doris, the four of us mumbling, shell-shocked.

Although I see Connor's father from time to time, coming and going from the house to his truck, I haven't seen his mother outside of their house since Connor died. Every couple of weeks, my mom takes a casserole across the street, returning gray-faced.

"That poor woman," she always says. "She'll never get over this." After these visits, she usually goes upstairs for a nap.

The curtains are drawn tight, and the flowers in the pots

around the front door are wilted and sad. I hesitate for a moment, wondering if I'm making a terrible mistake, then I push the bell.

I wait for a long time. Having rung the doorbell once, I'm not willing to do it again, but just when I'm about to turn on my heels and get out of there, I hear the bolt turn in the lock. It opens a crack, and an eye peers out at me.

"Mrs. Williams," I say. "It's me. Mac."

The door opens wider, revealing Connor's mom. She looks like she's aged several years since I last saw her up close. Her face is pale and drawn tight, her eyes are hollow and empty, and her entire body sags in defeat, as if she's shrunk several inches. Still, she manages a slight smile.

"Mac," she says, and her voice seems to come at me a half step after she opens her mouth, like the sound skipping on a buffering video. "Come in. Please."

She opens the door a bit wider, then turns to pad away down the hall toward the kitchen. I come inside and push my shoes off, then follow her. The living room is dark, but a thin shaft of light breaks through the drapes in the center of the picture window. The wooden coffee table gleams in the light, and I can see that the room is spotless, the pillows on the sofa arranged perfectly, the books that fill the shelves on either side of the mantle spine-straight.

The kitchen is equally immaculate, every surface gleaming, every window as clear as crystal. The house doesn't feel the way I remember it. The kitchen in Connor's house used to look more like my own; newspapers and magazines piled at the end of the breakfast bar, dirty dishes stacked next to the sink. I have the uncomfortable thought that it's like a house in a catalog, with no real evidence that anyone actually lives here.

Connor's mom stands in the middle of the kitchen, staring at the wall as if she's trying to remember what she's doing here. I wait in the doorway, and eventually she turns slowly toward me, a movement that seems to take a lot of effort. She stares at me then, her face flat but her eyes intense. I don't know what to say to her, and I wish with everything inside of me that I hadn't come.

"Can I offer you a soda?" she asks me, abruptly.

"Sure," I say. "Thanks."

I take a seat at the breakfast bar at the counter and watch as she finds a can of Pepsi in the fridge and pours it into a glass for me.

"I've wanted to visit for a while now," I say, and I immediately feel guilty about the lie. I haven't wanted to visit this house at all. I'm only here because there's no other option.

She puts the soda in front of me and smiles. She isn't exactly waiting for me to continue, although I'm sure I could keep talking for as long as I want.

Finally, she says, "You were good friends. That's often the way with neighbors. Do you know how Connor got his name?"

I shake my head. "He never told me."

She laughs, a hollow scraping sound, as if she's trying out the idea of laughing for the first time. She must decide it doesn't work, because she stops abruptly, her face going back to the grim mask she's been wearing since I arrived.

"I got his name from a graveyard," she says. "A graveyard!

What a stupid thing to do. I never even told his father; just said the name as if I'd come up with it out of nowhere. I'd gone walking one day, and when I came to the old graveyard near the Catholic church down on Glebe Street, I went in, and there was this grave, all by itself. An old stone grave, covered with lichen. And the last name jumped out at me. Connor. What kind of person does that?" Her face is frantic, as if she really needs an answer from me right now.

"I think it's probably pretty common," I say. "People find baby names in all kinds of places."

"I stood there, eight months pregnant, looking down at the grave," she says. Her eyes are distant, and I can tell that she's remembering the scene. "I didn't know who the hell was there under the ground, but I thought to myself, if this baby is a boy, I'll name him Connor, and that was that. Stupid, stupid, stupid. Sometimes I think I cursed him."

"No," I say suddenly, intensely aware of how different she is now from the nice lady I grew up with. Something is wrong with her. I wonder if she's on some kind of drugs.

She goes silent, but her face is still horrible, pinched and drawn into a mask of terror. Desperate for something to break this mood, I grab for the bag of comics and push it across the counter to her. She snaps out of her trance and stares at them, questioning.

"These were Connor's," I say. "He—he lent them to me, and I never got them back to him. I thought it was right to return them."

She smiles faintly, and I am relieved to see that the expression brings back a semi-normal look to her eyes.

"Oh, Mac," she says. "You didn't need to worry yourself about that. You could have kept them."

"I know," I say. "But I didn't feel right about it. They were his, after all."

She stands. "Come with me."

I follow her up the stairs and to the door of Connor's room. It's exactly the way I remember it—neatly organized, everything put away properly. She walks into the room and stands at the desk, staring out the window.

"Close the door, will you?" she asks. "I try to keep it sealed off. I know that's crazy; you don't need to tell me. Connor's father thinks we should junk it all, throw everything away, but it's not his decision to make."

It doesn't seem crazy to me at all. I can understand what she means. Where the rest of the house smells of lemon cleaner, dryer sheets, and dish soap, this room smells of Connor; the scent of pencil shavings and paint, body wash and sweat. It's faint, but it's unmistakable, as if he were in here just a few minutes ago.

"I sit here sometimes and watch you," she says, not looking at me, still staring out the window. "I hope you don't mind."

I open my mouth to speak, but my voice is dry, and I have nothing to say.

"I come in here once every day," she says. "Always at a different time. I try to imagine myself in his mind, try to understand where his thoughts were taking him. I know it's crazy, but I keep thinking that if I had the chance to go back, I could change how things turned out. I could have stopped him from going out there. Anyway, sometimes you're in your room, and I sit at the desk and look across at you." She turns away from the window to look at me. "I'm sure the two of you did that many times, didn't you?"

I nod, and a memory floats into my consciousness: me and Connor as kids, standing in the windows of our darkened bedrooms, whispering into our moms' cellphones, pretending we were spies. I don't mention that I've seen her watching me.

"I can't help thinking that if he'd only been able to leave Camera Cove, things would have turned out differently. If he'd gone away to private school, perhaps."

"He could have been a world-famous artist," I say.

"Yes," she says. "Yes, I suppose he could have. It's all he wanted to do, despite his father's best efforts to convince him otherwise. We paid for private lessons, you know. Astrid Billingsley is the best artist in this area, and she usually doesn't take students, but she said Connor had great promise. She said he could have had a career as an artist." A change comes over her, a visible weakening that starts in her face and then works its way through her body like a wave. She places a hand on the desk and leans against it.

"I think I need to lie down," she says. "You stay here as long as you like. Connor would have liked to have a visitor." Her voice is weak, and before I even have a chance to respond, she's moving slowly across the room, as if in a daze. She closes the door softly behind her.

I stand completely still, listening to the sound of her feet as she shuffles down the hallway. After a moment, another door opens, then closes. I am alone in Connor's room.

His desk is neatly organized with his art supplies spread out all over it. His bed is made with the old plaid quilt that he had the entire time I knew him. His wall is plastered with the same posters he always had: the first Iron Man movie and a small one-pager for a Botticelli exhibit that his parents took him to see in Boston. I wonder if there's still a small stash of dried-up weed in his hiding place, the shallow cavity beneath his dresser's bottom drawer.

I think of Joey Standish's room in the trailer park. Her room has also been kept exactly the same; and I wonder, what is the point of this? Doesn't it just prolong the agony of losing a child?

I scan the room, looking for a clue of some sort. The bulletin board is stuck with the typical stuff: applications to Pratt and the Rhode Island School of Design that he never got to fill out; grad photos; a ticket stub from the KISS concert he somehow convinced us all to go see in Portland. *They're the ultimate performance artists!* I remember him saying, pestering us until we finally agreed, just to shut him up. The concert ended up being awesome.

The weight of what I'm trying to accomplish suddenly drops onto my shoulders, making me weary. I don't even know what I'm looking for, let alone how to find it. I'd thought it would be better to visit Connor's house by myself, but I wish that Quill were here, asking the right questions, noticing the right things.

I pull the chair away from the desk and sit down. I stare out his bedroom window through the rain, at my house and at my own bedroom window.

I wonder if Connor ever watched me when I didn't realize it.

I imagine him sitting in this very spot, looking up from his homework or his latest drawing or sculpture, and noticing me at my desk. What did he think of me in those moments, really? Did he think of me at all, or did he only watch me because I happened to be directly in his line of sight?

I sink back into my chair and think about the times I sat in this room, listening to Connor tell me about the latest artists he was obsessed with—Damien Hirst, Frida Kahlo, Hieronymus Bosch—and his plans to eventually become a legendary artist himself. He liked to read books about people who lived wild, dramatic lives: Jack Kerouac, dropping everything and hitting the road. Bonnie and Clyde, on the run from society.

"That's what I want, Mac," he'd tell me, his eyes gleaming and his hands gesturing wildly. "I want to go out into the world and live a huge, crazy life and then turn it into art. And to be an artist, you need to live outside the margins."

"You are an artist," I told him. "You're the most talented person I know."

"I'm learning the basics," he said. "I need to get out of here and start living a life I can put into my art."

I thought he sold himself short. All around me is evidence of Connor's art. Beside his desk is a wide, deep shelf, covered with old jars and food containers full of art supplies—brushes and pencils and various tubes of paints and piles of pastels. The lower shelves are stacked with paper.

Sitting in the center of the desk is a thick, black sketchbook. I reach for it and press my hand down on the cover, as if feeling for a pulse. I pick up the book and am about to open it, when I hear a creak on the stairs.

"Joyce?"

I manage to get the book back onto the desk and spin around, holding the bag of comics in front of me like a shield, before the door to Connor's room is pushed open.

It's Connor's father. A look of bewilderment appears on his face.

"What's going on?" he asks, his voice angry. "Where's Joyce?"

"She went to bed," I say.

He stays there, silent, waiting for an explanation. Dumbly, I shove the bag of comics out in front of me.

"I had these," I stammer. "They were Connor's. I—I've wanted to bring them back since...for a while. Mrs. Williams wanted me to see his room, but she said she needed to go to sleep. She—she looked kind of exhausted, and maybe upset," I add.

His face softens slightly, and he steps into the room side-ways, holding an arm out toward the hallway in a gesture that it's time to leave. I put the comic books on the desk, then walk past him out of the room. He closes the door softly behind us.

In the kitchen downstairs, Mr. Williams grips the edge of the counter with both hands. Like his wife, he seems to have gotten smaller, and his shoulders slump as he tries to figure out what to say. Connor's father was always decisive—a straight-talker. He's the kind of man who likes to give firm handshakes and pass out free advice about colleges and careers; but now he's at a loss for words.

"She…" he begins, then stops and stares at the floor as if trying to find the right thing to say. "Joyce is not the same. Obviously none of us are, but she hasn't left the house in almost a year, other than to sit in the backyard and stare at the trees."

He stops and looks out the window at their backyard.

"I should go," I say.

He snaps out of his daydream and moves around the counter, holding his hand out for me to shake. His grip is firm and solid.

"Thanks for coming, Mac," says Mr. Williams. "It was thoughtful of you to return Connor's things."

"No problem," I say.

He chews on his inner lip, as if he's trying to figure out how to say something. "I don't want you to get the wrong idea, Mac, but I need you to do me a favor. I'm sure that someday Joyce will want nothing more than to see you, to see all of Connor's friends. But for the time being, I think it's best that you give her some distance and stay away from here. She's in rough shape, and she'll be in bed for days, after a visit like this."

"I'm sorry," I stammer.

He waves my apology away, with forced affability. He fishes in the breast pocket of his jumpsuit and pulls out a business card, handing it to me. I stare at it, grateful for an opportunity to look away from his face. WILLIAMS & WILLIAMS GENERAL CONTRACTING.

"Nothing to apologize for, Mac. You were just being a good friend, and I appreciate that. If you ever want to talk about anything, or if any of Connor's other belongings pop up, call my cell phone. It's on the card. Any time at all. Just stay away from Joyce."

"Yes," I say, moving to the porch, anxious to escape. "I will." I slip into my sneakers and bend to tie them. I can feel him moving up behind me—the pressure of the space between us as he prompts me toward the door.

"Good-bye, Mac," he says.

"Thanks. See you later, Mr. Williams."

As I push through the screen door, I can feel him behind me, watching me leave. I can't get out of there fast enough.

SIXTEEN

AFTER I LEAVE Connor's house, I grab my bike and head into town, to the beach. I need to think.

I lock up in the parking lot and walk along the boardwalk until I come to an unoccupied bench, weathered gray from the sun and salty air. I sit and stare down over the dunes toward the water. The beach is crowded. Clusters of tourists and local families hang out near the lifeguard stand; teenagers mingle further along near the caves, far enough away from the parking lot that they can drink beer and smoke weed. A group of people in bright blue shirts drifts along the edges of the dunes. They're carrying large blue recycling bags and are stooping to pick up trash.

Everything about the scene is calm and normal, but in the distance, the mouth of the caves yawns open like a reminder.

I pull my phone from my pocket and call Quill. He answers on the first ring.

"Hey!" he says. I hear traffic behind him, a burst of laughter, and conversation.

"Hey, there. How's it going?" I ask.

"Great! Sorry about the noise. I'm downtown—just met up with a few friends."

"Oh, that's cool," I say, with a pang of jealousy. I wish I was hanging out in the city with Quill and his friends, instead of reeling from visiting Connor's house.

"It'd be cooler if you were here," he says. "Oh hey, that reminds me. My folks want to meet you. They say you should come over for dinner."

"Your folks?" I ask, surprised. The jealousy is replaced by something completely different—a blend of anxiety and excitement and happiness. "You told them about me?"

"Yeah," he says. "Of course. I mean, I didn't tell them that we're lying our way into people's houses, trying to hunt down a serial killer. I just told them I met a cool guy."

My mouth stretches into what I'm sure is a ridiculous grin, and I lean back in the bench, speechless. It literally never occurred to me that I should tell my parents about Quill, and in a million years I wouldn't have expected him to talk about me like this.

"Hello?" he says. His voice changes. "Hey, I'm sorry. I wasn't trying to assume anything. I just thought after—you know—after we kissed, that maybe you were into me."

"Yes!" I say. "I am!" He laughs, and I feel myself blush. "I just never really talk to my parents about that kind of stuff."

"What kind of stuff?" he asks, teasing. "You got a lineup of boyfriends you want to tell me about? The truth is, my folks like to stay on top of what's happening with me, especially since last year. They really didn't want me to hang out at the park for a week, so they were psyched to hear that I met you. They think it's healthy. It's cool. My parents are cool. You'll see. So what's up, anyway?"

"Well, I just visited Connor's parents," I say, glancing up and down the boardwalk to make sure that nobody is in hearing range.

"No shit? How'd it go? You learn anything?"

"Not really," I say. A woman approaches with her dog, and I lean forward with my elbows on my knees and drop my voice. "They're super messed up. His mom is on pills or something, and I think she's living in some kind of weird fantasy world. Then his dad came home and found me snooping around Connor's room. He was really strange and awkward about it, not that I can blame him. Still, he just seems off. They both do. It's sad, and kind of creepy. I feel pretty shitty about the whole thing."

"Don't," says Quill. "You're trying to solve their son's murder; they'll thank you if you're successful. You didn't find anything in his room?"

"I didn't have much time to look," I say. "I wish you'd been there. You probably could have sweet-talked them into letting us look through Connor's stuff."

"I wish I were there too," he says. "All I can think about is what we can do to find out more."

"Well, get back here soon," I say.

"I'll try. I know you want to go to the house where the killer was staying," he says. "I'm hoping my mom will let me go back sometime in the next week, now that I have a boy to visit. I'll let you know what happens."

In the background, I hear someone say Quill's name.

"Hang on a sec, Mac," he says. He turns away and I hear muffled conversation, then he comes back. "Hey, we're heading to catch a movie. I'll text you later on, okay?"

"Yeah," I say. "Sounds good. Can I ask you something?"

"Shoot."

"You're not going to tell your friends about us looking into the murders, are you?"

"Not a chance," he says, and I can hear a smile in his voice. "But I've already told them about you."

I'm still smiling a few minutes later when I hear someone call my name.

My head jerks up, and I'm surprised out of my daydream. The group of beach cleaners is closer now, and I see that one of them is approaching me, an arm raised in greeting. It's Doris, striding purposefully over the sand toward me, her hair pulled back into a perfect ponytail that's sticking out the back of a baseball cap. She's wearing sensible, ankle-length khakis and a bright blue T-shirt that reads *Camera Cove Beautification Committee.* She's also dragging a recycling bag, half full of cans and bottles, through the sand beside her. I shove my phone into my pocket.

"What are you doing here?" she asks, dropping her bag in the sand and climbing up onto the boardwalk.

"Just hanging out," I say.

"You're not just looking for reasons to be sad, are you?" she asks. She tilts her head toward the caves.

I shake my head. She collapses onto the bench next to me.

"Good," she says. "Don't spend the summer moping about."

I point at her recycling bag. "Looks like you're keeping yourself busy."

"It's a good resume builder," she says. "Someone's got to clean up after the tourists and dirtbags."

"Find anything good?"

"Just garbage. Bunch of lowlifes. Another good reminder of why I can't wait to get out of this place."

"Doris," I say tentatively. "Do you think the cops did a good job? On the Catalog Killer?"

Her chin drops, and she eyes me suspiciously over the top of her sunglasses. "Are you ripping off the scab, Mac?"

I know I'm taking a chance, talking to Doris, but I feel like she might have a clearer perspective on things than I do. She wasn't as close to Connor as I was, or Quill was to Joey, and she's one of the smartest people I know. She also lived through the murders, just like I did.

"They didn't catch anyone," I say. "It's a small town. It went on for months. Somebody must have seen something that they didn't think to tell the cops."

"Maybe," she says, "but I don't see what that has to do with you."

I consider telling her about the note, but I worry that she'll just make some sarcastic comment about comic books.

"It doesn't," I say. "You're right. I shouldn't even be thinking about it."

"There's no point, Mac," she says. "You've held yourself together pretty well so far. Don't start getting all wound up now, or you'll just end up like Ben or Connor's mom."

"Yeah," I say. "You're probably right."

"I'm totally right," she says. "People are just acting weird right now because it's been a year."

I smile, attempting to look as if I agree, although I don't.

She glances down the beach and stands. "I should go. I have to wrap up here and then head to softball practice."

"You're playing softball?" I ask, surprised. I've never known Doris to watch a sport, let alone play one.

"No," she says. "Coaching first graders. I started last year so I could get some athletics on my college applications without having to actually play. It was kind of fun, believe it or not, so I decided to do it again this year. The kids are cute."

I shake my head, smiling. "You definitely earned every penny of your scholarship," I say.

"Yes," she says, matter-of-fact. "Anyway, I'd better run. Catch you later, Mac. Try not to sit here getting all existential. Get laid or something, will you?"

She stands to leave.

"I went to see Connor's parents today," I blurt out.

Doris looks at me for a moment without saying anything, then sits back down beside me.

"You're ripping off the scab," she says. She purses her lips and shakes her head. "Now are you going to tell me what's going on?"

The temptation to talk to someone else who knew Connor is just too great to ignore. I fish my phone out of my pocket and scroll through until I find the picture I took of the note. I hand her the phone and she squints at the photo, then looks over at me, an eyebrow raised.

"When the hell did this turn up?"

I tell her about the comic books, bringing the note to the cops, and about how Parnatsky didn't want to listen to me.

"And so you decided to just run your own investigation?"

I shrug. "Connor obviously wanted me to help him," I say. "If nobody else is able to figure it out, I kind of figure I owe it to him to take a crack at it myself. What harm can it do?"

She hands my phone back. "Don't fool yourself," she says. "You could do a lot of harm. Starting with his parents. Do you really want to open up this whole can of worms for them all over again? Please don't tell me you showed them this."

"I didn't," I say. "I brought back his comics, and that's it. His mom actually seemed kind of happy to see me, I think. She took me up to his room, and then she got tired and went to lie down."

"So you had a chance to look around his room?" she asks. Despite her initial skepticism, Doris is starting to sound curious.

"Not for long," I say. "His dad came home before I could find anything. There's probably nothing there, but I can't know for sure."

She thinks about that. "Where else have you been, Mac?"

"I've visited all four of the victims' homes."

Her eyes widen. "How the hell did you manage that?"

"I started a donation drive," I say, "for the library. We're going to have a rummage sale on the day of the parade."

"Was this your idea?" she asks, incredulously.

I shrug. "It was the only way I could figure out how to get into those houses."

"Holy smokes, Mac," she says. "I seriously wouldn't have given you the credit. You're a regular Sherlock Holmes. So what did you find out?"

"Not a whole lot," I admit. "A bunch of dead ends, to be honest."

"That's a shame," she says.

"What do you mean? I thought you said this is a bad idea."

"Sure it is," she says. "But if you're going to do it, you might as well do it properly. You need some help."

Now it's my turn to be skeptical. "Help?"

"You need someone who isn't going to get all emotional about things," she says. "Someone like me."

I could tell Doris that I already have help, but for some reason I hold back. I don't want her to know about Quill; at least, not yet. Whatever it is that Quill and I have, for now it's just between the two of us, and I kind of like it that way.

"I don't know what else there is to do," I say instead.

"Well, have you been to the Abernathy house?"

"Not yet," I say. I'm about to tell her that I've been planning on it, but she cuts me off with a deep sigh.

"That settles it," she says. "You definitely need my help." She sighs and closes her eyes, claps her hands on her lap as if preparing for something big, then stands up and looks down at me. "Okay. Tomorrow morning. Pick me up at eight?"

I stare at her, bewildered, trying to figure out how to say no. But then it occurs to me: Doris is smart, and no-bullshit, and most importantly, she knew Connor. Maybe she can shed some light on things in a way that Quill and I can't. Why wouldn't I want her help? I'm supposed to go with Quill, but he just said himself that it could be another week until he's able to get back here. Who knows? Maybe it will be kind of cool to hang out with Doris again.

"Okay," I say. "Eight it is. Thanks, Doris."

"I just want you to know that I'm not promising anything. If this doesn't lead anywhere, I'm out."

She hops neatly off the boardwalk, grabs her recycling bag, and disappears back into the dunes, and I'm left wondering what just happened.

SEVENTEEN

THE HOUSE IS DEEP in the forest that sits between the highway and the township, a thick stretch of overgrowth, pine, spruce, and mixed hardwood. Most of it is public land, but it's backed against old farms, long since abandoned, deserted by families who got sick of trying to pull a living out of the rocky terrain.

Doris and I follow Abernathy Road—an underused country byway riddled with clusters of deep potholes—past a dozen of these old farmhouses, each of them deteriorating in its own way. Two or three of the places we pass are still inhabited, although it's hard to imagine the kind of lives people live inside them. On several more of the old lots, sad, shabby bungalows have been built instead. No working farms, but we do see loads of vegetable gardens and some chicken coops. One of the yards even has a cow, chewing mournfully on some patchy grass.

"God," says Doris, "what a miserable existence. It's bad

enough living in town. Imagine being stuck out here in the sticks, living through this kind of monotony."

"I think a lot of people like living in the country," I say. We pass a house that's obviously been abandoned entirely, with broken windows and a front porch that has a shrub growing up through it, busting through the steps and pressing against the house. "I guess a lot of people move away, too."

"That's the best place to be," she says. I glance across to the passenger seat. I don't hate Camera Cove the way Doris does, but I don't feel all that different from her either. Even before the murders, I hadn't given a lot of thought to sticking around after high school, let alone moving back later on, but now it seems totally unthinkable.

Even today, as we head deep into no-man's land, Doris looks organized and prepared for anything. She's wearing hiking boots, and though it's hot as hell out, she's got jeans on. She catches me glancing at them. "We're going to be pushing through bushes and thorns," she says. "Might as well be protected."

I park alongside a dried-up old ditch and we get out. There's nothing but fields and trees around us, the hum of summer insects, and the thick, sweet smell of rot from a swampy culvert stamped down with old chip bags and beer cans.

We cross the road and step onto the rutted track that leads into the old farm. "Are we sure this is it?" I ask, staring doubtfully toward the thicket of alders at the back of the tangled, overgrown field.

"This is it," she says definitively. "My sister and her boyfriend took us for a drive here after the place was discovered last summer." She points up to the alders. "There were cops streaming in and out of that thicket."

There's nobody here now. Just us.

"Are we sure this is a good idea?" I ask, suddenly nervous. Reading news stories about a serial killer's hidden lair is one thing. Exploring it in person is something else entirely.

But Doris is already trudging ahead of me with purpose. "We're here, Mac," she says. "Grow a pair."

I shudder and follow her through the field to the edge of the woods, asking myself why I didn't just wait for Quill. But the truth is, Doris is tackling this with a determination that I'm forced to admire. Besides, Quill and I talked again last night and made plans; tomorrow I'm having dinner with him and his parents, a prospect that is both exciting and almost as terrifying as this visit to the Abernathy house.

The wood is bordered by a thick, dense tangle of sharp bushes, but eventually we come to an opening which reveals a well-trodden path. A piece of police tape, faded and tattered from a long winter, waves raggedly from a tree branch.

As we move out of the sun and into the dappled shade of the forest, my skin gets goosebumps and a hush falls over us. The dull rumble of the highway in the distance gradually disappears, and the hot summer wind that chased us across the field into the woods breaks up into tendrils that twist away into the trees.

This is a dirty forest. A blanket of leaves, matted together like paper, covers the forest floor, and there are piles of old garbage scattered about: broken glass and rusted appliances, the skeleton of an old bicycle, the rusted chassis of a pickup truck. I turn my gaze up, following the poplar trees as they point toward the sky, competing for sun. A branch snaps under my foot, and a flurry of starlings sweep out of a tree in a furious rush, escaping to someplace safer. I follow their path, and when my eyes drop back down, Doris stands facing me, her arms crossed across her chest, annoyed.

"Are you coming?" she asks, and without waiting for me to answer, she turns and takes off further into the woods.

I shake off my anxiety and hurry after her.

The house is a mirage, a ghost, an apparition rising out of the thin and rapidly growing alder trees. It's a two-story farmhouse, ragged with peeling dirty yellow paint and a slightly sagging peaked roof that's missing half of its shingles. A tangle of thick vines are netted in and around the rungs and up the support posts of a veranda that runs along the front. Two tall, pointed dormers stick out from the roof. The windows are dark, but as we step forward, a patch of errant sunlight finds a break in the trees and catches on the glass, creating the illusion of two eyes opening from a sleep and watching us as we approach.

It would be disturbing enough, even if you didn't know a serial killer had camped out here during a spree.

"I'll give you this much," says Doris. "This place is really creepy."

Still, she leads the way, and I follow as we walk up the narrow pathway toward the house and up the creaking steps, across the porch, and through the threshold of the beaten wooden door.

The house is in better shape inside than it appears from the exterior. The bare wood floors are slightly dusty, but a newish plastic broom settled against the wall amidst a pile of dirt and cobwebs, implies that someone has swept it recently. Similarly, all the random pieces of furniture—a couple of chairs, an old table, a linoleum-topped kitchen buffet—have been wiped down, and several random objects have been placed neatly on top of any available surfaces.

Doris begins to move briskly through the house, checking out the rooms one after the other, scanning each one thoroughly, looking for clues. I follow her, impressed at how professional she seems, like a forensic detective. At the foot of the staircase, she stops, and we look at a small wooden door with a glass knob, built into the side of the stairs.

"This is it," she says, reaching forward and pulling the door open.

She pulls a flashlight out of her bag, and I turn on my phone's light. We both lean forward, pointing our beams down into the gaping dark hole. A rough wooden staircase descends into the cellar.

Doris takes a deep breath. "Here goes nothing," she says, and takes a step through the door.

I grab her arm.

"Wait," I say.

"What?" she asks, shaking off my hand. "Are you worried he's still down there? Mac, if you're serious about exploring this, you have to take the emotion out of it and think of it as a homework assignment."

Despite my anxiety, I laugh.

"Homework?" I say.

She looks irritated, but then begins to laugh herself.

"Hey," she says. "You have to work with your strengths, right?"

The tension broken, we step into the basement staircase and move down into the cellar.

The cellar floor is made of packed dirt, and a warren of rooms branches out from a long hallway. It smells like damp and mildew. I shine my light around the space and take in the framed-in walls, paneled with rough hewn pine boards, gray with age. The door closest to us is wide open, and I steel myself before stepping up to the threshold and shining my light inside. I half expect to see something gruesome, but only a pile of old bricks and the broken remains of some ancient furniture fill the space.

Doris has shone her light to the end of the hallway, where a door stands half ajar. She hesitates for the first time since we arrived here, then swallows and marches toward it as if to prove this entire mission is completely mundane.

"Wait—" I say, but it's too late. She's pushed the door open, and the flashlight reveals a large room. I follow her down the hallway and we come to a stop, taking in the space.

"Shit," I say. Doris nods. Against one wall is a workbench, old and wooden. A paper calendar, curled up on the edges, is tacked to the wall above it—the only evidence that seems to have been left behind. On the other side of the room, five stone steps lead up from the ground to double doors, set into the ceiling on an angle—old cellar doors, built to bring firewood and wheelbarrows in and out of the house. The room rings with a hollow emptiness, as if something left behind a bad feeling.

"This is it, huh?" Doris says thoughtfully, as she walks around the room poking her light into corners. "This is where the son of a bitch slept? I can't believe somebody actually slept here."

But it's true; it's one of the few things we actually know about the person who killed Connor and the other unlucky victims. Somebody stayed here—a hiding spot so unlikely and grim that nobody would ever notice him coming and going.

I do know that the police found a cell phone charger, a roll of plastic, a bed, some empty food cans, and some thin latex gloves, along with a half-empty box of rat poison. Someone had taken great care not to be identified. They'd found a site that could be used as a hideaway, with nothing concrete that would lead to a criminal.

In the corner of the room, a small window, thick with years of grime, lets in a swampy, murky light.

I move over to it and realize that someone has swiped a hand over the glass from the outside, smearing a hole into the filth. I wonder how long ago it happened, whether a cop did it, or if not, if they noticed it.

"Look at this," I say.

There's no answer. When I turn around, Doris isn't standing there any longer. My skin crawls, and a wave of panic rolls upward from my knees.

"Doris?" I call out. Again, she doesn't answer.

The room closes in on me, and I begin to feel nauseous. I move out of the room, push toward the stairs, and run up into the house.

"Doris?"

My voice falls flat, and I imagine the sound waves being sucked into the years of dust. A flurry of images rushes in front of me. Families living here, babies being born, people growing old, and then, like a monster in the night, the murderer climbing into this den and holing up downstairs.

"Doris!" This time, I'm yelling. I need to get out of the house, and I scramble out to the porch and onto the back step.

"Doris!"

I stop and wait, trying to hear past the rushing blood in my head.

"Mac!"

She sounds urgent, and it's coming from the other side of the house. I race around the side, terrified and blindly trying to get to her.

On the other side of the house, a thick patch of knotweed looms tall and sinister.

"Mac!"

"Where are you?" I holler.

"Over here!"

I follow the sound of her voice, thrashing through the weeds until I finally find her, kneeling on a small bank of dirt. She's alone, and I gasp with relief. She looks up at me, and her face is wide and incredulous, but not scared. She looks exhilarated, but when she catches sight of me, her face falls.

"What the hell is the matter?" she asks.

"Jesus Christ, Doris," I say. "You disappeared and I didn't know where you went, and then I was in the basement by myself..." I trail off, and she stands up.

"Shit, Mac," she says. "I'm sorry. I just wanted to get out of there. It smelled weird."

"Yeah," I say.

"I'm sorry," she says again. "I thought you heard me leave."

"It's okay," I say. "I just got worried."

I realize that she's staring at something on the ground. "Look," she says.

I step toward her. The thing she's looking at is covered in mud, and the glass is cracked, but I'd recognize it anywhere. A green face, the Hulk, stares up at me from the face of the cheap Timex.

"It's Connor's watch," I say, my voice catching.

We use a stick to carefully lift the watch out of the dirt and put it into a Ziploc bag that Doris, prepared as always, pulls out of her backpack.

So Connor really was here—watching the house, staking out the killer. It's what I've suspected all along, but I don't feel satisfied. Instead I feel a sudden and unexpected anger at Connor. He could have gone to the cops and stopped all of this, gotten the Catalog Killer arrested. He could have put an end to the terrible mystery that still haunts us, given all of us a chance to start moving on.

He could have lived.

"I think I need to get out of here," I say, once Doris has carefully put the evidence into her purse.

"We've found enough for one day," she agrees.

As we walk back through the woods, I keep glancing back at the house. I don't like it being at my back, and although the dark, gaping windows on the upper floor reveal nothing more than the slowly shifting shadows, I have the horrible, unsettled feeling of being watched.

I'm relieved when we emerge into the field and the blazing

sun, and I pick up my step as we push through the hay to the car. I press the unlock button before I even get there, and Doris climbs into the passenger seat. I move around and am about to climb in behind the wheel when I stop.

"Hurry up!" Doris yells from the car. "It's like a sauna in here!"

But I can't move. My feet are planted to the ground, and I stare at the driver's side window, at the eyeball that has been drawn carefully in the dust.

EIGHTEEN

"IT MUST HAVE BEEN done this morning," says Doris. "In town. You know how people are always writing things on car windows, like *clean me* and stuff like that. Some jerk was walking by and drew it in the dirt."

"But I would have seen it," I protest. A chill still echoes up and down my spine.

"Maybe, maybe not," she says. "Look." She steps to the side, pulling me by the arm until the light from the sun is directed into a glare against the glass. Sure enough, the eye disappears. "See?" she says. "You just didn't notice it because you were distracted, and we were talking the whole way out here. It's just some random thing."

"It still freaks me out," I say. "What if someone knows what we're doing, and they're trying to get us to stop?"

"You've been watching too many horror movies, Mac," she says.

I can't relax. I spin around, staring at the fields and trees around us.

"Mac!" she says, clamping onto my arm with a reassuring hand. "There's nobody here! Look around." I follow her fingertip as she draws an arc around the surrounding fields, but all I see is a million opportunities to hide.

Before I realize what she's doing, she's brushed the eyeball off the car with the back of her hand.

"What are you doing?" I ask. "I didn't even get to take a picture yet!"

She rolls her eyes. "Just forget about it. It's creepy, I'll give you that, but it doesn't mean anything. Let's get the hell out of here."

As we drive away, I glance at the rearview mirror repeatedly, waiting for a figure to rise from the hay and stare after us. It isn't until we turn onto the main road and the farm is far behind us that I finally relax.

"What are we going to do about the watch?" Doris asks.

"I don't know," I admit. "It's probably worth taking to the police."

Doris nods. "I think we should go there right away. I don't want to end up in trouble for hanging on to evidence. That's just what I need right before I escape to Cornell."

This time, the receptionist recognizes me right away, and we're soon back in Parnatsky's office.

"Where did you find this?" asks Parnatsky. She's leaning forward in her chair, her hands clamped to the edge of her desk, staring at Connor's watch as if she's afraid to touch it, as if she's afraid it will bite her.

"It was in the mud outside the Abernathy house," says Doris.

The chief narrows her eyes. "What were you kids doing out there?"

"Looking around," says Doris. "It's not a crime site any-more. We're welcome to go there, aren't we?"

"It's still private property," says Parnatsky.

Doris raises her eyes to the ceiling. "Whoever owns that land has been out of the picture for years. You know that."

"You're missing the point," says Parnatsky. "Or more likely, you're avoiding the point." She looks directly at me. "You're searching for something, aren't you? You've been looking for something ever since you found that note."

I nod, keeping her gaze. "What am I supposed to do? Just pretend that nothing happened?"

"I'm sorry," interjects Doris, "but I'm a little confused. Shouldn't you be thanking us for bringing you a valuable clue in the investigation you screwed up?"

I shoot her a dirty look, but Doris's eyes are focused on Parnatsky.

Parnatsky leans back into her chair and stares up at the ceiling. She sighs. "Guys, I get why this is so important to you. I really, really do. Connor was one of your best friends, and you want to find out what happened to him, but I have to tell you, none of this makes any difference."

"You're only saying that because you didn't find it," says Doris. I recognize her temper bubbling up, the way it did when we were kids, and I silently will her to stop. I don't think we're going to get into trouble, but I don't want to piss the woman off more than we already have.

Parnatsky grits her teeth together and sucks air slowly into her lungs before lightly clapping her hands onto the desk and standing up. She stares down at us, and I realize for the first time how tall she really is. Every time I've been around her, I've been on the other side of a desk or table, or she's been behind the wheel of a car.

"I'm going to say this one more time," she says, through clenched teeth. "We have done as much as we can. The feds did as much as they could. I appreciate that you both want to do something, and I am glad that you felt that your best option was to bring these things to me as you found them, but like I said to you already, Mac, none of this tells us anything about what happened to Connor, or to the rest of the victims, that we didn't already know."

"Oh, come on!" yells Doris, and I close my eyes, realizing that she's past the point of being reasoned with. "You're just saying all this bullshit because you know that you blew it!"

"Doris," I hiss, "shut up!"

But Doris isn't anywhere close to shutting up. Shutting up just isn't her style.

"Eventually things will have to get back to normal, right? Even if they don't, I'll be gone, so I'm not really sure why I care, but chances are people will forget and move on. So if that's your excellent policing strategy—hoping that people will forget what you screwed up—by all means, go ahead and sit on your ass. But when other people who actually care about this case go out and do the heavy lifting for you, the least you could do is pretend to be interested in what they find!"

Doris is on her feet now, glaring at Parnatsky from across the desk. I can tell that the cop wants to reach out and grab her by the neck, but instead she drops into the chair, and Doris is left standing there.

"Are you done?" Parnatsky asks, after a moment.

Doris's face stays tight, but she seems to realize that she's gone over the top, because she sits back down into the chair. The air is full of tension, and although I feel like I should say something to break up the uncomfortable silence, I draw a blank.

"Listen," says Parnatsky, finally. "I know everyone thinks we blew this investigation, but the reality is, we are very open to every single clue. It's just that we already knew Connor had figured out the killer's identity. This evidence, just like Mac's note, only proves something we already knew."

"So you can't do anything," says Doris. It's a statement, not a question.

"There isn't much more to do," says Parnatsky. "I'll be straight with you both. Officially, the investigation is still open, but at this point we don't have any reason to think that the killer is still in Camera Cove, or that he left behind any kind of clue that we didn't already find."

"There was nothing in the house?" I ask.

"There was lots in the house," she says. "But he cleaned his tracks well enough to keep us from finding anything useful. No prints, no hairs, no fibers, nothing that led us anywhere but to dead ends."

Doris's chair scrapes abruptly back, and she stands, grabbing her bag from the floor beside her.

"Okay," she says. "I've heard enough. I get the picture."

She turns and leaves, the heavy wooden door swinging back with a low creak before it hits the wall.

I look at Parnatsky, who is rubbing at her temples. I want

to apologize, but I don't know what for. We're all feeling the same thing. Helpless.

"I'd better follow her," I say. She nods without looking up, and I move to the door.

"Mac," says Parnatsky. I stop in my tracks and turn back to her. "Don't think I don't care."

"I don't think that," I say.

"We've done everything we could," she says. "If there were something to look into, I'd do it."

"I know," I say.

"You need to stop; let the past be the past. Digging around isn't going to make anything better."

"It's not going to get better either way," I say.

Doris is outside, sitting on the stone railing of the stairs. She looks remarkably calm, considering her blowup inside.

"They don't know what they're doing," she says.

"She tried," I say.

"I don't know why I offered to help you," she says. "It was a mistake. I can't let myself get caught up in this. I'm sorry, Mac. I need to focus on the fall, on getting out of here."

"It's okay," I tell her.

"You should leave it alone," she says. "Seriously. I knew it was a bad idea to help you, but I thought..." she trails off.

"You thought what?" I ask.

"I thought I could convince you that this whole thing is a stupid idea," she says. "People are talking, Mac."

"Talking?"

"They're saying you're unhinged over Connor's death. That you were—"

"What?" I ask, getting irritated.

"People are saying you were in love with him, and you're starting to go a bit nuts."

"In love with him?" I ask, my mind spinning. "Who is saying that?"

"Everyone," she says. "Everyone thinks you were in love with Connor. To be honest, they thought you were in love with him before he even died. The way you hung off his every word, always staring at him like a heart-eyes emoji."

For a moment, I'm speechless. Is this really what people think of me? "I didn't—it isn't true," I say, finally.

"I know that, Mac," she says, and her eyes are kind but pitying. "It's just hard to be a gay kid in a small town. People say stuff. And…" she trails off.

"And what?" I ask.

"I didn't want to tell you this, but people have started to notice things."

"What kind of things?" I ask.

"I know you think you've kept it a big secret, but people are starting to suspect that you're poking around into the murders."

"How would anyone know that?" I ask, shocked.

"Come on, Mac," she says. "All it takes is one person seeing you go in to Patricia Parnatsky, and another one to see you leaving George Smith's house, and someone else to see you driving around near the trailer park. You know what this town is like. News travels. And now that you're spending all this time obsessing over the murders, people are starting to talk again."

I'm almost shaking. I take a step back from her, steadying

myself against the stone railing of the stairs. "Who…who is saying shit like that?"

Doris reaches out and grabs my arm. I look at her, and her eyes are piercing and serious.

"Mac, just forget about them. It doesn't matter. I didn't want to tell you any of this. I know we aren't super close, not like you were with Connor and Carrie, but you're still my friend, and I hate to think of you ruining your future over this. Please, just move on. Get through the summer, get yourself to college, and forget that this stupid town ever existed."

She lets go of my arm, then abruptly turns and walks down the steps. As she leaves, I realize that there isn't much reason not to take her advice.

Maybe I should leave it alone. I've hit nothing but dead ends, and I'm forced to ask myself…

What is it that I'm *really* looking for?

NINETEEN

QUILL LIVES IN a really nice neighborhood just a few minutes' drive from the Portland city center. I find his street, quiet and leafy, lined with elegant, narrow town houses. I slow down until I spot his address, then circle the block four times before I park, gathering my nerve.

I've never been on a date before, let alone met a guy's parents. I check my hair in the rearview mirror, take a deep breath, and get out of the car.

He answers the door almost as soon as I've rung the bell, leaning out to give me a quick kiss on the lips.

"Hey!" he says. "Come on in!"

I look him up and down and smile. He's wearing a pale blue button-down and chinos, a far cry from the tank tops and shorts I'm used to. "You clean up nice."

He laughs. "My mom told me I had to dress up for dinner, since it's a 'special occasion.'" He makes air quotes over the final two words.

"Oh shit," I say. "No pressure or anything." I'm in shorts and a polo shirt. I don't look messy or anything, but I'm far from dressed up.

"You look great," he says. He leans in and whispers. "They're just thrilled that I'm thinking about a boy instead of obsessing over Joey's death. They don't realize that with you, I get to do both!"

I laugh and follow him through the heavy wooden door into a wide, bright hallway. Expensive looking artwork lines the crisp, white walls, and fresh flowers sit in a vase atop a classy antique table.

"Wow," I say. "Nice place."

"Thanks," he says. "Come on, meet my folks."

Quill's parents are on the back deck, which looks down on a small backyard that's full of flowers and even has a tiny fountain.

"You must be Mac," says his mom. "Welcome! I'm Val." She shakes my hand and smiles. She's attractive, older than I expected, and I can see a faint resemblance to Joey.

Quill's dad is flipping burgers on the grill. He closes the lid and turns around to me, and I'm faced with an older, taller version of Quill. "How's it going, Mac?" he asks, reaching out to give me a firm, manly handshake. "I hear you're keeping Quill out of trouble."

"It's mutual," I say.

"Don't believe him," says Quill. "Mac's never been in trouble a day in his life."

We eat dinner on the deck, burgers and some salads. Quill's parents are really nice. They ask a lot of questions about living in

Camera Cove—not about the murders, which is refreshing, but about growing up in the same small town that my parents grew up in. They also grill me, lightly, about my plans after the summer, and they seem pleased to hear that I'm going to Amherst.

"We're going to hang out in my room for a while," says Quill, after we've eaten dessert.

"Keep the door open," his mother warns. I feel myself blush, but Quill just laughs.

His room is in the basement. "Your parents are nice," I say, taking a seat in an old armchair as he flops onto his bed.

"Yeah, they're pretty cool," he says. He leans forward, eagerly. "So are you going to tell me about the Abernathy house or what?"

I didn't really think that we'd be jumping into this so quickly. I was kind of hoping that we'd spend some time just hanging out, but I can tell from the look on his face that he's dying to hear what happened, so I fill him in on my trip to the old house with Doris, leaving out the part where Doris told me that I'm crazy for chasing after an answer.

"So the watch brings us back to square one," says Quill, after I've filled him in. "Connor was following the killer after all."

"It has to mean that," I say. "Why else would he have been at the house, unless he was really following the actual Catalog Killer?"

Quill nods, thinking it over. "It's the only explanation. That's good though, right?"

"How?" I ask.

"Detective work is all about proving and disproving theories," he says. "We came up with one theory, and then new evidence disproved it. Now we've narrowed things down."

He jumps off his bed and rummages around underneath for a minute before pulling out a beat-up old backpack. He pulls a couple of books out of the bag and hands them to me. One is called *Unsolved Serial Killers of the Twentieth Century* and the other is called *Silver-Tongued Devil: History's Most Notorious Human Monsters.*

"Got these online," he says. "Research."

I flip through one of the books, stopping in the middle at the thick collection of photographs. Pictures of Ted Bundy, Charles Manson, and Jeffrey Dahmer stare blankly out from the pages. The images are unsettling, reminding me that a real person was responsible for the horrors of last summer. A human, not some faceless boogeyman, killed all those people. A sick feeling works its way up from my stomach. I shut the book and push it back across the bed.

Quill, however, isn't unnerved. On the contrary, he's almost gleeful as he talks about what he's learned from his research.

"The thing about serial killers is that they all had their own thing. It was like a game or a compulsion for most of these assholes. Almost all of them are guys, and almost all of them had a pattern that they followed. Have you ever heard of the Alphabet Killer?"

I shake my head.

"Three little girls were murdered, back in the 70s," he says. "Each of the girls had first and last names that started with the same letter, and each of them was found in a town that had a name that started with the same letter. Michelle Maenza was found in Macedon, Wanda Walkowicz was found in Webster. You get the idea."

"Who did it?" I ask.

"They never found the killer," he says. "Originally, the cops thought it must be somebody from the area who was able to research his victims. But they were never able to find a suspect, and so the official word was that it was probably a drifter. Sound familiar?"

I nod. It sounds too familiar.

"There are lots of theories online," he says. "You'd be shocked at how many conspiracy theorists there are out there. Cubby French isn't the only person obsessed with this case."

He flips through the other book, *Silver-Tongued Devil*, until he finds the page he's looking for and reads aloud.

"Perhaps what makes many serial killers terrifying is their ability to melt into their communities, to smile at their neighbors, and to go about their days as if there is nothing unusual in their minds at all. For every antisocial freak like Jeffrey Dahmer, there's a birthday clown, a friendly neighborhood shopkeeper, or a doctor with a reputation for selflessly helping the poor."

He looks up at me. "Creepy," I say.

He nods. "You said it. A true psychopath could do it without anyone suspecting a thing."

"Right," I say. Quill looks at me with an expression that almost borders on excitement, as if the fun is just getting started. In reality, I feel the opposite: overwhelmed and exhausted.

"Are you even listening to me?" he asks.

"It's hard not to," I say. "You haven't stopped talking for ten minutes."

I regret it as soon as I've said it. I'd meant it as kind of a joke, but it doesn't land that way at all.

"Excuse me?" he says, his voice several steps beyond frosty. "In case you didn't notice, I'm trying to help you out here."

"I know that," I say. "We're helping each other out. It's just, do we have to talk about this every minute we're together? I mean, you're able to go out with your friends and have fun downtown and act like nothing is wrong, but when you're with me it's one hundred percent Catalog Killer, one hundred percent of the time."

"Come on, Mac," says Quill, "you know I'm not going to hang out with my friends and talk to them about this. You and I have this in common. This is why we're hanging out in the first place."

"Oh, really?" I ask. "I guess I thought there was more to it than that."

"There is," he says. "Of course there is. But don't you want to get to the bottom of this, so we can move on to normal lives again?"

"Yeah," I say, "I do, but I can't help feeling that you're kind of obsessed."

His jaw drops and his head snaps back.

"Obsessed?" he asks. "What the actual fuck? You're the one who came sniffing around the park in the first place!" He clasps his hands in front of his chest and flutters his eyelashes. "Excuse me, I'm wondering if you'd be willing to donate to my library beautification fund, and while you're at it, would you maybe go poke about in your dead cousin's closet and see if there are any clues lying around?"

"You're being an asshole," I say. "Maybe I've just decided that this whole thing is fucked-up. We should let them rest in peace. This isn't right."

"You can let whatever you want rest," he says, and he's obviously furious now. "I'm going to keep on looking until I can't look anymore, with or without you."

"Maybe that's for the best," I say. I stand and walk to the door. "Tell your parents thanks for the barbecue."

Quill doesn't move from the bed; just stares at me, shaking his head. "You know, Mac, I had a feeling when I met you that there was something more going on with you, but then I convinced myself that it wasn't true. I thought maybe you really did like me, and maybe something cool could happen between us. But I should have known better. I mean, it's obvious."

"What's obvious?" I ask, worried that I already know what he's going to say.

"You're in love with Connor," he says. "You're totally fucked-up in love with him, and I think you're the last person who realizes it. Now you're changing the script, putting up roadblocks, and I can't help but think that it's got more to do with Connor than it has to do with me."

"You don't know anything about my friendship with Connor," I say, and then I turn and leave.

His words keep repeating, over and over again in my mind, as I drive back to Camera Cove. Doris said almost the exact same thing, and according to her, everyone in town has the same suspicion. Are they right? Is my real reason for trying to solve Connor's murder that deep down I have feelings for him that I've never wanted to admit?

It's true what I said to Quill; he doesn't know anything about my friendship with Connor. Maybe it's also true that I don't know much about it either.

TWENTY

OVER THE NEXT WEEK, I do my best to put thoughts of the Catalog Killer to rest. My theory hasn't changed—I still think Connor was on the trail of the Catalog Killer—but I've finally convinced myself that it doesn't matter. Connor is dead, nothing is going to bring him back, and there's nothing at all to indicate that the murderer will strike in Camera Cove again.

But more than anything, I've finally realized that I wasn't drawn into Connor's search because I wanted to learn the truth, but because I couldn't let go of Connor.

The truth is, Doris and Quill were right; I did have feelings for Connor. I wouldn't say I was in love with him, but I definitely felt something more deeply than I was ever willing to admit to myself.

Maybe I wanted Connor to feel the same way, as crazy as that might have been, and his note to me was one last shred of hope that I might have meant more to him than I'd allowed myself to wish for. I know now that I was fooling myself, and like Doris said, I let it take over my mind. The case is over. I'll never know the truth, and I'm not doing anyone any good by keeping it open.

It's harder to ignore Quill.

I think about texting him a thousand times, but I can't bring myself to do it. Neither can he, it turns out. For a couple of days, I expect him to send me a message, apologizing, but when that doesn't happen, I begin to realize that whatever was starting to happen between us is probably over.

I tell myself that it's for my own good—that it's better for us to avoid each other. He has his own reasons for trying to figure out who killed his cousin, and they aren't the same as mine. If he wants to keep chasing Joey's killer, I won't stop him. But I can't be near it either.

Still, when I lie in bed at night, thinking about the summer so far, I can't keep my thoughts from drifting toward him. His quick, deep voice, the smooth curve of his neck, his soft lips…

Dropping Quill and the mystery leaves a lot of empty space in my days, so I fill them up with work, helping Libby to prepare for our sale on parade day.

Last year, the Camera Cove anniversary parade didn't happen for the first time in almost sixty years. Nobody felt like celebrating. More to the point, people were terrified, and large, loud groups didn't seem like an antidote to the fear.

This year, desperate to get things back to normal and increase tourism numbers, the chamber of commerce and the town council have made a big push to get people excited about the town's anniversary celebrations.

Libby and I show up early to set up our table outside the library. As I drag the mountain of donations we've collected up from the basement storage room, it's clear that it's actually been a pretty successful drive. Between the signs I've posted all around town and Libby mentioning the sale to everyone who checks out a book, people have been dropping stuff off at the front desk in a steady stream.

By the time people have started to trickle into town and take up space along the sidewalks, we've got several large tables set up. George Smith's kitchen stuff squeezes into a space next to some hand-knitted sweaters, and the books, dishes, and various bric-a-brac that I've spent the summer collecting soon cover the tables and spill down onto the ground.

"This is so wonderful, Mac," says Libby, as she cheerfully wanders about, sticking bits of masking tape onto items and scrawling prices onto them with a Sharpie. "I never would have guessed we'd have so much stuff to sell."

I smile as I arrange trays of baked goods that have been donated to the sale by some of our patrons. I wonder how Libby would react if I told her that the whole thing started as an excuse to snoop around victims' houses.

Since my visit to the old house with Doris, and our conversation with Trish Parnatsky, I've felt more and more disconnected from my original plans. Driving past Connor's house this morning, on my way to set up for the parade, the familiar twinge of sadness was more muted than in recent weeks. The thrill of discovery—of feeling like I could solve this horrible case—has begun to recede. There are more important things to think about.

Like leaving. There's a lot of summer left, but I'm finally imagining myself moving away to college. To a new life with new friends, new interests, and a series of distractions that will lead me away from Camera Cove and into a happier, less complicated future. *Maybe*, I even allow myself to think, *I'll find a boyfriend.*

I try to imagine him, what he would look like, how he would sound, the things we would do together, but when I try to focus on the vague, faceless figure in my mind, it's always Quill's face that emerges, grinning widely, his eyes sparkling and intense. When I look back on him, will I think of him as my first boyfriend? Were we really a couple? Did he want us to be? I spin it over and over in my head, and ultimately I have to concede that it doesn't matter; whatever he was to me, he isn't that now.

It's for the best, I tell myself. The only thing we had in common was the murders.

It doesn't take long to get our display arranged, but before we've even finished, some early birds have started to arrive, poking about and making shrewd offers and inquiries. I've often heard the expression "one man's junk is another man's treasure," but until you've run a small-town rummage sale, you don't realize how true it is.

Soon the crowd thickens, and people begin to line up along the streets, unfolding lawn chairs and preparing for the main event. The sales table is buzzing along, and I find that I'm really enjoying myself. Everyone is in a good mood; the main street of Camera Cove hasn't been this lively and full of togetherness since before the murders.

This is the Camera Cove I grew up in. This is what the killer stole from us. And for the first time since Connor died, I begin to think that maybe we'll get it back. Not right now, but someday.

"Hey, these were my dad's!"

I am jerked out of my daydream to see a kid stopped in front of my table, holding a pair of hockey skates in front of me accusingly. A woman reaches around from behind and puts her hand on the kid's shoulder.

"That's okay, Georgie. We donated them to the sale."

My mouth goes dry when I see that it's Emily Smith. The child, I recognize now, is George Smith's son, and he's staring intently at the skates that used to belong to his father. The skates that I took under false pretenses.

Emily gently takes the skates from Georgie and puts them back on the table, then she turns to smile at me.

"Hi there," I say, forcing a smile. "It's good to see you."

"We're leaving on Monday," she tells me. "Finally sold the house. Shipped everything ahead with my mother. I wanted the kids to have one more chance to see the parade. George took them to it the year we moved here."

I nod. "That's nice," I say. "It's good to get back to normal, after last year."

I cringe inwardly as I realize my blunder. Her smile drops.

"Yes, I suppose it's good for the town," she says briskly, "but I'm happy to leave. Can't get the hell out of here fast enough, to tell you the truth. I feel bad for any of you who have to stay in this godforsaken place."

She grabs Georgie by the arm and, without another word, pulls him away from the table and back toward the crowd that's waiting for the parade to begin. In the distance, I hear the first trills of the marching band from the direction of the baseball field behind the school, where the floats and parade participants always line up to get organized.

The band gets louder and then, suddenly, they appear from behind the school, leading the way. The crowd cheers, and people stand and watch, full of happy anticipation as the parade makes its way along in front of us. Behind the marching band, two little girls in warrior princess costumes march along beside beribboned and cheerful looking ponies.

The floats cover all the bases. Most of them have been pulled together on the fly by various businesses and organizations. The hospital has a stereo playing Motown music, and various doctors, nurses, and other healthcare employees perform an elaborate, choreographed lip sync. Kids dive for candy that's thrown from the floats, and as the parade marches past, I swell with more and more town pride—the likes of which I haven't felt since I was a kid.

Then a murmur runs through the crowd ahead of me, and smiles turn to frowns. A man yells something indistinguishable, but obviously angry. I crane my neck, trying to make out what it is that has turned the crowd's mood so quickly. Then I see it.

Cubby French has positioned himself in the middle of the action. He's wearing a grim reaper costume: a long black robe with a hood and a sickle. On a sign that hangs around his neck, I read *Camera Cove Murder Tours: Only the Best Put the Rumors to the Test.*

"What on earth is he thinking?" says Libby, angrily. "What an idiot."

Cubby seems to be enjoying his effect on the crowd, smugly marching along with a wide, shit-eating grin. He stops smiling, however, when, with a scream, someone runs out of the crowd on the other side of the street and full-on tackles him.

For a moment, they roll around on the ground, but Cubby is easily outmatched by the other guy, who manages to maneuver things so that Cubby lands on his back, his arms pinned to his sides and his legs kicking uselessly in the air. His assailant, screaming almost incoherently, turns sideways, and I get a glance at his face.

It's Ben.

For a moment, the parade halts. The band stops playing, and the crowd goes completely silent as they watch the scene unfolding in front of them.

"You're a freak!" Ben yells into Cubby's face. "A perverted freak! What kind of person would do something like this? People died!"

The crowd near them parts, and Patricia Parnatsky pushes her way past people and up to the scene. Her presence seems to wake up the crowd, and a couple of large, beefy men step forward to help her as she pulls Ben off Cubby.

Cubby scrambles to his feet, his robe in disarray. "That punk attacked me!" he yells, pointing at Ben, who is standing breathlessly to the side, held back by one of the men.

"He only did what everyone else here wanted to!" yells a voice from the crowd, which results in a cheer from onlookers.

Parnatsky walks up to Cubby, and they have a quick and heated conversation. After a moment, he shakes his head and turns to glare at Ben before storming away. As he exits, the crowd claps. Parnatsky walks over to Ben, who has shrugged off the men who were holding him back and is now standing sheepishly to the side. She looks stern, but I see her put a hand on his shoulder as she speaks to him, and after a second he nods. Then he turns and disappears in the opposite direction of Cubby.

Cubby's sickle sits in the middle of the street. Someone runs forward and grabs it out of the way, which seems to break the spell. The parade starts up again.

Nobody is buying anything at the moment—everyone is busy watching the parade.

"Libby," I ask, "are you okay to watch things for a few minutes? I was going to run across the street and try to find a hot dog or something."

"Absolutely," she says, waving me away. "Take your time. We're not going to need to keep this up much longer. Almost everything is gone!"

The parade has picked up steam again, and people are cheering and shouting it on. I find a break between a float and the local Girl Scout troop and skitter across the street, pushing along in front of the crowd in the direction where Ben disappeared. It would be impossible to spot him in this crowd, but I have a feeling he didn't stick around to watch the rest of the parade.

I cut away from the crowds and the noise of the parade, and when I'm on an empty side street, I start to jog.

TWENTY-ONE

I'M HALF A BLOCK from the beach when I spot Ben. He's walking slowly along the sidewalk, hunched, his hood up and his hands in his pockets. If he hears me approach, he doesn't register it, but when I slow my pace to step along beside him, he turns to glance at me without surprise.

"Are you okay?" I ask him.

He shrugs and turns to look out at the water.

"What was that all about?"

Now he looks at me, disgusted. "What do you think it was about? The guy is a monster. He needed to be knocked down a few pegs."

"Yeah," I say, "you're right. But why now?"

"Nobody else was doing anything about it," he says, as if this is the most matter-of-fact explanation in the world, as if his freak-out were just a normal occurrence.

I don't push it. We've reached a set of stairs leading down to the beach, and when he steps onto them, I follow.

On the boardwalk, we stop to sit on a bench.

"Are you okay?" he asks me suddenly.

"Me?" I ask, surprised at the question. "Yeah, of course. I'm fine."

He reaches up to scratch the side of his head, embarrassed. "I'm sorry I freaked out that night, at the bonfire."

Misery and helplessness are written all over Ben's face. I might have idolized Connor, but Ben idolized him too, just in a different way. I'd wanted Connor's attention and approval, but Ben had wanted to *be* him, to fill a room the way he did, to make girls turn their heads, to have Connor's natural talent. Maybe it makes sense that out of all of Connor's friends, Ben and I are the ones having the hardest time getting over his death. We've just chosen dramatically different ways of showing it.

"It's okay, Ben," I say. "I understand where you're coming from. You don't have to apologize to me."

"Yeah, but I do," he says. His face is visibly upset. "I just—I don't know what's wrong with me. I've been acting like I'm the only one who even cares that Connor is gone. You and him were easily as close as he and I were."

I shrug. "It's been hard. I get it."

"You were a good friend to him," says Ben. "Better than he deserved."

Now I'm genuinely confused.

"What do you mean?"

"Never mind," he says. "It doesn't matter."

I press him. "Seriously, man. You can't just say something like that and then expect me to forget about it."

"Fine," he says. "Connor knew how you felt about him."

"What are you talking about?"

"Come on, Mac. You idolized him, and he knew that. He knew it went beyond that too. That you—you felt things for him."

I don't protest.

"He loved you, Mac," says Ben. "I know he did. But that didn't stop him from making fun of you sometimes. I mean, the way you talked to him about those comic books. I think he only kept it up because he didn't want to hurt your feelings. But that didn't stop him from tearing you down a bit behind your back. He called you his lovesick little buddy."

I feel like I've been slapped. I can't speak.

"Don't take it too personally," says Ben. "It's not like you were his only target. I'm sure he had shit to say about me too, and you have to remember how much he used to tease Doris. We aren't supposed to say this stuff, because he got murdered, but you do realize that he could be kind of an asshole, right?"

I know he's right. Connor was always rolling his eyes about Ben, calling him stupid or borderline illiterate. I feel a wave of shame, thinking about how easily I ignored it, how quick I was to laugh at those jokes. It's no better than the way I'd laughed when we were younger, when Connor would make fun of Doris so badly that she'd run home crying. Of course Connor had made fun of me. How could I have thought otherwise?

"He might've been kind of an asshole, but he was still our friend," I protest.

"Our friend, huh? Is *that* why you're out there fishing around for answers?" he asks. "It was a serial killer, Mac! Don't you get that yet? Some asshole came and ruined everything for all of us and then disappeared. There are no answers! Everyone in town knows what you're doing, and they're all laughing at you."

My face flushes red-hot with shame. I want to tell him that he's right, that I've already started to put Connor and the Catalog Killer behind me, but something has set him off, and he doesn't give me the chance.

"You and Cubby French are the only two people in town who are forcing this thing to stay alive," he goes on. "For what? To make yourself feel more involved in Connor's life? I hate to sling the truth at you like this, Mac, but Connor had flaws just like the rest of us, and the sooner you realize that, the sooner you'll be able to move on."

I'm pissed and confused, and instead of telling him that I've already started to move on, I try to throw some of his own venom back on him. "Oh, like you're doing such a great job of moving on," I say. "You've been making a fool out of yourself in public every chance you get."

"The difference is that I want to get over it!" Ben is yelling at me. He's so mad, he's almost spitting.

"Yeah, right," I say. "Do you know what I think? I think you were so pissed off when you learned that Connor and Carrie had hooked up, you've never gotten over it. And now you're stooping so low, you're willing to talk a bunch of shit about your dead best friend."

Ben looks as if I've just punched him in the face. He pulls

away from me, and for a minute, I worry that he's actually going to haul back and hit me. Instead, he narrows his eyes at me, and when he speaks, his voice is low and full of venom.

"Maybe this little adventure of yours makes you feel important. Like you're Connor's knight in shining armor, riding in to avenge him. But I'll tell you something. If he were still alive, he'd be the first one to talk about how pathetic you are."

"I'm not staying to listen to this," I say, standing up and turning to leave. As I do so, something catches my eye. A face at the top of the stairs pulls quickly out of view, as if it's been caught watching us. I turn to Ben to see if he noticed it, but he's already up from the bench and stalking away from me.

I make a split-second decision and rush for the stairs. The steps are steep, but I take them two at a time. By the time I get to the top, I'm completely out of breath.

Other than a few tourists strolling along the sightseeing walkway at the top of the stairs, the street seems empty. I look in both directions, and I'm about to give up when I catch a flash in the mirror of a car that's parked close to the boardwalk. Someone is hurrying into the narrow alleyway between the back of a fish-and-chips shop and a house.

The figure is average height and of slim build, and they're wearing a navy blue sweatshirt with the hood pulled up, over plain, gray shorts. Because of the odd way they're moving—slightly stooped and shuffling forward as if trying to move fast and avoid detection—I can't tell if it's a man or a woman.

Without even thinking, I run across the street and almost collide with a cyclist in full racing gear. The woman on the bike yells, and I wave apologetically but don't stop. I hurry through the alley, adrenaline rushing through my bloodstream and canceling out any panic I might be feeling. A couple cats run out of my way, scrambling to escape from the stinky metal trash cans they've been scavenging.

Suddenly, I'm back on Main Street. The parade has ended, but people are milling about in its chaotic, exciting aftermath. Parents are stopped in small clusters, talking animatedly. No doubt most of them are discussing Cubby and Ben's disruption of the parade. Laughing children dart about, playing tag, grabbing balloons from clowns, and chowing down on the candy they managed to snag from the floats.

I cast my gaze frantically about the crowd, trying to pick out the dark hoodie from the throngs. Then I see the figure strolling away, hands deep in shorts pockets, still hunched to avoid detection. Staying close to the edge of the activities, I move along the sidewalk, trying to keep them in sight.

I'm so distracted that I don't see the woman walking with three miniature poodles until she's right in front of me. I try to step over the leashes, but I find myself tangled up in a mass of yapping fuzz balls. The woman is apologetic, and I try to look friendly, but my prey is getting close to the edge of the crowd, and I know that once they disappear out of sight, they'll be gone entirely.

I manage to get untangled, then I scan the crowd. For a moment, I think I've lost sight again, then I notice the hoodie standing at the edge of the crowd, back still to me. The figure has stopped and is looking back and forth. I push my way through the clustered throngs until I'm just a few people away.

The figure stiffens, as if realizing it's been seen, and then its head begins to turn.

"Mac!" A hand grabs me by the shoulder, and I almost jump out of my skin. I spin around on my heel and am immediately enveloped in a hug from Anna Silver.

"Oh," I say. "Hey, Anna, how's it going?"

"Isn't this fun!?" she asks. "I love parade day. It honestly feels like things are getting back to normal, don't you think?"

I smile and nod, wondering if she can hear my heart pounding, even over the crowd. I'm still reeling from the chase and my fight with Ben.

"Yeah," I manage to say. "It's really cool, isn't it?"

I glance quickly over my shoulder, but the figure is gone. I curse internally.

"You never did text me!" Anna says, playfully swatting at my arm.

"Oh, you're right," I say, vaguely remembering our conversation in the caves. "Sorry about that."

I'm distracted, thinking about the stalker, and my argument with Ben is also spinning around in my mind. As I remember the caves the two thoughts collide, sparking another memory. My attention snaps back to Anna.

"Anna," I say. "You're pretty good friends with Taryn Watts, right?"

She nods. "Yeah, we've been besties since we were little."

"Do you remember back in junior year when she and Connor dated for a little while?"

Something flickers in her eyes—a momentary uncertainty—but she keeps smiling.

"Yeah," she says. "Of course. Connor was all she talked about for months. When they started going out, I was so excited for her."

"They had a pretty messy breakup, didn't they?" I ask.

The look returns, but this time, it doesn't fly away so quickly, and her face grows serious. "You could say that," she says. "Why do you ask?"

"I'm just wondering," I say. "I heard she was really upset about it for a long time."

She doesn't say anything for a few seconds, then, hesitantly, "I don't like to speak ill of the dead, Mac, but you were one of his best friends, so I'll tell you. Connor was awful to Taryn. Like, straight up mean. He didn't hit her or anything like that. If he had, we—I mean me and her other friends—would have done something. It was different, harder to pin down. It was all mind games, like setting up dates and not showing up, and then pretending they'd never made plans. Stupid shit like that."

"He gaslighted her?" I ask, shocked.

"Yeah," she says. "Among other mindfucks, pardon my French. It was awful. We couldn't convince her to dump him, and it wasn't like there was anything we could say to our parents or teachers. It would have sounded like teenage drama. It was serious, though. Believe me."

I'm totally confused. "But she was so upset at the funeral."

She makes a wry face at that. "She was upset because she never got the chance to confront him over how he treated her. She hated him, Mac, and then someone killed him. It was a mess, and she's still not totally over it."

"Do you know if he treated anyone else like that?" I ask.

"I've heard rumors," she says. "But I think people mostly let it drop after he died."

I must look like I've seen a ghost, because she reaches out and puts a hand on my arm.

"I'm sorry, Mac," she says. "It's all water under the bridge now. I know he was a really good friend to you, so don't let it get to you. Camera Cove is just starting to get back to normal. It'd be a shame if these sad thoughts sent you in the opposite direction."

I nod, distracted. "You're right. I shouldn't even think about it."

"Exactly!" she says, and now her bubbly personality has returned. "Anyway, you have to promise to get coffee with me before the summer's over. If we're going to be at the same school, I feel like we should get to know each other a bit better!"

"Yeah," I say, barely hearing myself speak. "That sounds great, Anna."

I make my way back to the library, my mind racing. I've always known that Connor had a bit of a mean streak, but Ben's tirade has put it in a new perspective for me. I think of what he said about Connor making fun of Doris. She was always his easiest target—serious, skeptical, a stick in the mud.

Usually when he called her out, it was because she was standing in the way of us having fun, but there were other times—times I'd forgotten or maybe even pushed to the back of my mind—when it went beyond that. Doris's family didn't have a lot of money, and I remember him making jabs about her clothes, her bagged lunches, the series of beat-up, second-hand cars her parents drove.

Now, within the last hour, I've learned that Connor was a shitty boyfriend to Taryn Watts, to say the least, and maybe even to other girls. And if Ben is telling the truth, Connor was saying terrible things about me, mocking me behind my back. Maybe he suspected all along that I had feelings for him that went beyond friendship. Maybe I was easy to joke about.

Behind all of this is a darker realization. If Ben and Doris and even someone as nice as Anna Silver saw the nasty side of Connor's character so clearly, might it stand to reason that other people did too?

What if someone took an offense to heart and couldn't let it go?

What if someone went looking for revenge?

It doesn't fit—not perfectly, at least. Could someone have been so upset about Connor's mean streak that they'd plan a series of murders, just to get back at him? It doesn't make sense. It's just too complicated.

I stop dead in my tracks as I reach the library.

What if I've been looking at this wrong the entire time? What if someone didn't plan a killing spree to get back at Connor, but took advantage of one, instead?

What if there were two murderers all along? The Catalog Killer—the person who was responsible for the first three deaths—and another person, who was responsible for Connor's?

It's like a series of clues snaps into place, just like that. Could someone have had a serious grudge against Connor? Serious enough that they lured him to the caves, killed him, and planted a catalog picture to make it look like the Catalog Killer's original plan of killing a whole "family"?

The more I think about it, the more it makes sense. The more I think about it, the more a cold chill begins to creep down my spine. Were there two killers the whole time?

Was one of them following me today?

TWENTY-TWO

BACK IN THE LIBRARY the next day, I grab the shelving cart, desperate to hide away in the stacks and think. The old metal trolley squeaks and limps along as I push it through the stacks, stopping in order to replace books on the shelves.

I can't very well go back to the cops with my new theory. If I tried to convince Parnatsky for the third time that she should listen to me, I'd be laughed out of the building, or worse. I picture her calling my parents, telling them I need an intervention.

What I really want is to talk to Quill, but I'm afraid and kind of ashamed. Have I messed things up too much already?

A commotion in the children's area interrupts my thoughts.

"This won't do!" a voice says loudly. "It simply won't do!"

I hear Libby's muted voice trying to explain something to someone, and I leave the cart to see what is going on.

Libby is standing in front of the mural and speaking to an elderly woman. The woman has long gray hair tied back with a bright scarf, and her dress is equally bright and wispy. Her arms are covered with bangles, large gemstones stud her fingers, and a collection of beads and feathers dangles around her neck.

The woman is gesturing wildly at the mural, walking back and forth in front of it and pointing at the unfinished portion of the large painting.

"No, no, no," she says. "It simply won't do."

Libby sees me coming and looks relieved. "Astrid," she says. "I'd like you to meet Mac Bell. He's our summer student this year."

The woman glances at me distractedly.

"Mac was one of Connor's best friends," says Libby. "If it weren't for Mac's excellent idea of looking for donations for yesterday's sale, we probably wouldn't have the money to pay anyone at all."

Now the woman turns to look at me with actual interest.

"Well, I'm sure this young man will agree with me that it is truly unacceptable that this fine piece of public art, the tragic *legacy* of Connor Williams's snuffed out talent, has not been served, to say the least."

Libby turns to me to explain. "Astrid was Connor's art teacher," she says. "Because she was so involved with Connor's work, we've asked her to consult on the best way to complete the mural."

I realize that this is the art teacher Connor's mother mentioned.

"'Involved' is an understatement," says Astrid, with a grand flourish at the mural. "I was his mentor. We spent many hours together at my studio, working through his sketches, deciding on the best approach to take, sharing opinions on perspective and subtext. It was a huge project, and he took it on with great panache!"

With a dramatic groan, she throws herself into one of the small children's armchairs and puts the back of her hand against her forehead. The effect is almost surreal—the tall, angular woman draped uncomfortably across the tiny yellow armchair.

"It's just too much," she says. "I'm at a loss. Part of me wants to leave the piece unfinished, as a reflection of his own unfinished life. The rest of me, of course, believes it should be completed, but only by someone intimately involved with Connor's vision and direction as an artist."

Libby shoots me a brief, conspiratorial eye roll, then turns back to Astrid with an ingratiating smile. "If we do decide to go ahead with the mural, who do you think we should hire to do the work?" she asks.

Astrid quickly clambers out of the chair with a shocked look.

"Doesn't it go without saying?" she demands. "There's nobody else on earth, let alone here in Camera Cove, with a better grasp of what Connor was trying to achieve here. If you don't hire me to finish the mural, I will protest! I will take my fight to the streets! I won't rest until his vision is vindicated!"

"Wonderful," says Libby, calmly. "I'm so happy to hear that you're interested. I was hoping you'd agree to finish the mural for us. I'm sure it's what Connor would have wanted."

Astrid looks somewhat disappointed, as if she were hoping for more of a fight, but she drops her shoulders and gives in.

"Very well," she says. "I'll begin next week."

She turns back to the mural and bows deeply toward it, then with a flourish and a swirl of fabrics, she swoops out of the building.

"That went better than I expected," says Libby.

"Seriously?" I ask. "She seems a bit nuts."

"Oh, that was nothing," she says. "A few years back, she made a sculpture for the hospital grounds, and when they placed it improperly, she chained herself to the flagpole."

The excitement over, I return to my shelving duties. I'm just getting back to work when I hear a tapping on the other side of the shelves.

"Pssst," someone whispers, and I stop and bend over to peer through a crack. A pair of eyes that I'd recognize anywhere look back at me. Quill. He disappears, and I pull back from the shelf, wondering where he's gone, but a moment later he appears at the end of the stack, pretending to look through a book.

"What are you doing here?" I ask.

He drops the book on a table and winks at me. "I heard the library was for checking things out," he says. I hide my blush by grabbing the book and placing it on my shelving cart.

"I'm glad you're here," I say. "I didn't know if I'd see you again, after…"

He nods. "I know," he says. "It was messed up. We both just kind of went off on each other." I'm happy to see that he looks as relieved as I am that we're finally having a conversation.

"I've been dying to talk to you," I say. "I'm really sorry. I shouldn't have—"

He cuts me off. "Don't apologize, Mac," he says. "If anyone should be sorry, it's me. I shouldn't have thrown all that stuff about Connor in your face. This whole thing has dragged up a lot of emotions. Believe me, I get it. Truce?"

"Truce," I say. I'm a bit worried that it sounds less like getting back together, and more like two guys after a bar brawl, but then he reaches out and takes my hand, just for a moment, and when I look at him, he's smiling at me in a way that lets me know I have nothing to worry about.

"So listen," he says. "That's not the only reason I'm here. I found something."

"Found something?" I ask.

"Yeah," he says. "A clue. I know you said you wanted to back away, and I considered not telling you, but I decided that this was too urgent to dick around. I need your help." He reaches back into a pocket and pulls something out, dangling it in front of me. A single key on a red plastic tag.

He holds it out to me, and I take it. The key is hanging on the tag by a short length of steel chain, and the tag itself is embossed with faded silver letters that read *Wandering Surf Guest Cottages* over the top of a sun setting into waves. On the reverse side of the tag, 17 has been punched into the plastic.

"These cottages are closed," I say. "Have been for years. Where'd you get this?"

"Do you remember when I told you that Joey and I used to play in the woods behind the park? Where her body was found? I remembered out of the blue the other day that she used to have this hiding place, where she'd keep stuff. Pieces of jewelry that she'd take from her mom, lipgloss that she'd swipe from the drugstore. Stuff like that. It was an old tin box, underneath a rock. So I remembered that box, and the next chance I got, I headed back to the park. Sure enough, the box was still there."

"And the key was in it," I finish.

"Bingo, Nancy Drew," he says. He smiles coyly and holds the key ring up, dangling it enticingly. "Wanna go check it out?"

Quill hangs out in the kids' section, reading graphic novels while I finish my shift, and a half hour later, we're out of town on the winding, dilapidated old highway that runs along the coast. As we pass tiny fishing harbors and idyllic coves, sailboats drift through the water like butterflies, and I do my best to fill Quill in on my new theory.

"So you think Connor *thought* he was onto the killer, but he was actually onto someone who just *wanted him* to think he was onto the killer?" asks Quill.

"Don't you think it makes sense?" I ask. "It even explains why the killer didn't use poison, or try to position the body."

"I guess so," he admits. "I mean, it's messed up, but what part of this isn't? The only thing I still don't get is how Connor's watch ended up at the farmhouse."

"I've been thinking about that," I say. "Let's say Connor's killer took his watch and held onto it in case it became useful. Once the Catalog Killer's hideout at the Abernathy house was found, Connor's killer dropped it at the scene to make it look like Connor had been following the actual killer the whole time."

Quill chews on his lip and nods his head slowly, thinking it through.

"It works," he says.

"It did work!" I say, excitedly. "When Doris and I found it, we brought it to Parnatsky, who immediately assumed it was just more evidence that Connor had figured out the killer's identity!"

"Mac," says Quill, and his voice doesn't match my enthusiasm. "If you're right about this, and if someone is following you because they think you're on to something, you might be in danger."

"Well, we'll just have to figure things out quickly then," I say.

He looks at me with a mix of skepticism and admiration.

"I hope we can," he says. "For your sake, if nothing else. And I'll tell you this: we'd better hope that it's not the Catalog Killer who's on to you."

"I know," I say, with a shudder.

"I don't think you totally get what I'm saying, Mac," says Quill. "If this theory is true, it means that the killer still has one victim left to go. Last I checked, he needed to knock off a teenage white boy."

I swallow hard as I mull over this new perspective.

"I didn't think about that," I say. "But maybe it's not an issue? I mean, he's been gone for a year. Maybe Connor's killer did the dirty work for him, and when he realized that the job had been done for him, he moved on."

"Maybe," says Quill, doubtfully, "but if there's one thing I've learned from those books, it's that serial killers operate on uncontrollable impulses. He might have gotten scared off for a while when he realized someone else had taken up his job, but something tells me he won't be satisfied until he finishes his project."

This new insight is still ringing in my head as we come around a turn to approach a long stretch of sand dunes. Roofs peek out over the backs of the dunes.

Quill points at a building near the road. A sign outside reads *Wandering Surf Cottages: Main Office*, and a board tacked beneath it says *Closed Indefinitely*. Directly across the road is a low, one-story house with a veranda across the front. There's a woman sitting there, her hair up in curlers, staring at us suspiciously as I slow down.

"Drive past it," he says. "I know where to go."

We continue on past the beach, and the road turns away, dragging us into a stand of spruce trees, out of sight of the cottages and the old lady with the hawk eyes.

"Pull over here," says Quill, and I slow the car down, sidling up along the gravel shoulder.

I haven't even turned off the key when he's out of the car.

TWENTY-THREE

BY THE TIME I've made my way around the back of the car, Quill is already sprinting back across the main road and onto the hill, where he waits for me. I follow him up, and together we stare down at the beach. It's wide and deserted, but not nearly as nice as the beaches closer to town. Instead of white sand and dunes, this one is rocky and bordered by red clay hills. Farther back along the coast, we get a clear view of the Wandering Surf Cottages lining the beach, defeated and deserted.

We descend a narrow path and stealthily make our way back toward the cottages, staying low and scurrying past when we get near the main office. A sign stuck prominently in the ground where the cottages are built, reads TRESPASSERS WILL BE SHOT.

"I don't know about this," I say.

"That shit is ridiculous," Quill says. "Who is going to shoot us? That old lady?"

The cottages are depressing. They were obviously once built to take advantage of the post-war tourist boom—small brightly colored housekeeping units with nice little verandas and cement block barbecue pits out front—but they're now just ramshackle shells. The paint, once cheerful pastels like canary yellow, cotton candy pink, and baby blue, is dulled and dirty and peeling in thick flakes from the walls. Unpainted plywood boards have been nailed over all of the windows. The verandas are saggy, and the barbecue pits are full of years worth of debris.

"Why would Joey have even been here?" I ask.

He shrugs. "Your guess is as good as mine." He steps up onto the veranda of the first cottage and tries the key in the front door. No luck.

He tries it in the next four cottages, and with each one, I get more apprehensive, worried that someone is watching us, calling the cops, and reporting us.

"Relax," says Quill, noticing my discomfort. "Nobody gives a shit about these places." He puts the key into a new lock, and with a rusty shudder, the bolt slides open. I freeze at the bottom of the steps as Quill turns the knob and pushes the door inward. With a flourish, he holds it open with one arm and steps to the side, using his free arm to usher me up the steps.

Anxious, and wishing he'd gone in ahead of me, I step into the little cabin.

The room is dark, dimly lit by the open door. Then Quill steps in behind me, and the door slams shut. I jump a little at the sound. Now the darkness is only broken up by thin shafts of dusty light that sneak in from cracks around the edges of the boarded up windows.

Quill laughs. "Scared of the dark?"

I ignore him and pull a flashlight from the side pouch of my backpack. The room emerges from the shadows: a small kitchenette in one corner, a couch and two chairs, and a partition with a curtain in front of it at the back.

"Check it out," says Quill, stepping toward the small kitchen counter. I shine my light at the open shelf and see what he's noticed: two candles stuck in empty beer bottles. He pulls a lighter from his pocket and lights them, placing them on the table in the middle of the room.

"That's cozy," he says.

"These are newish," I say, pointing at the bottles. "They look like recent labels."

"Do you think Joey was here?" he asks, and his usually sarcastic bravado is gone, replaced by a hushed sadness.

"She must have been," I say. "Right? She had the key."

I move into the kitchen and begin opening drawers. Most of them are empty except for a few random pieces of junk: old takeout forks, a deck of cards, a child's coloring book that looks as old as I am. Quill takes one of the candles and moves over to the wall behind the couch, where there's a small bookshelf.

"Anything good?" I ask, abandoning the kitchen and joining him to kneel on the floor next to the shelf.

"Not unless you like board games," he says, poking at a stack of old games.

We search the rest of the small cottage, but nothing

emerges. A bedroom—complete with a double bed and two bunk beds but no mattresses—yields absolutely nothing.

Finally we go back out to the main room.

"I guess that's it," I say. "Maybe we should get out of here before someone comes searching."

But instead, Quill flops onto the couch. "What's the rush? Come sit?"

If I were a better person, maybe I'd be able to keep my mind on the matter at hand. Instead, all thought of Connor and Joey disappears completely, and I find myself moving toward the couch.

I sit down awkwardly next to Quill, holding the flashlight in my hands. He reaches over and takes it from me, switching it off and placing it on the floor. The only light in the room now is the soft flicker of a couple of candles, and a few random streaks of light.

"That's nicer, isn't it?" he asks.

I nod and part my lips to speak, but the words get stuck in my throat.

Quill reaches his hand around and puts it on my shoulder, pulling me gently around to face him.

I lean toward him, closing my eyes. I can feel his warm breath against my lips.

"Quit being scared of everything, Mac," he whispers.

I feel dizzy, my mind melting away completely, when suddenly a thought snaps into my head like a lightning bolt, and I jump up from the couch.

"What the hell?" he asks, frustrated. "Are we going to keep playing chicken?"

I barely hear him; instead, I'm fumbling for the flashlight on the floor. I snap it on and rush to the back of the room.

"What is it?" he asks, his anger replaced by alarm or curiosity.

I pull a game from the top of the stack on the bookshelf.

"Ever play Clue?" I ask him.

"Who hasn't?"

I take the box to the table, handing him the flashlight. He shines it down on the box as I open it and pull away the game board. Inside are the typical pieces of an old, well-used board game: colorful plastic player figures, dull metal weapons, the tan plastic coil of rope, cards, and a small envelope.

And a piece of paper, ripped from the pad of tally sheets.

"Look," I say, my hands trembling as I reach into the box.

I flip the paper over. It's been scrawled and scratched on, the little squares filled in and *Professor Plum* and *Conservatory* circled.

"Joey" is written across the top.

Quill stares at the paper, frozen in place, for a long time. I watch him from the side of my eye, waiting for him to react, but he just stands there, hovering.

"Are you okay?" I ask, finally.

He reaches out slowly and picks up the paper. Every trace of the brashness I've come to associate with him disappears.

"I can't believe it," he whispers. "She was here, Mac. She was right here in this stupid cabin, playing board games with somebody, for fuck's sake."

The words are barely out of his mouth when our heads both snap back toward the game board. Quill reaches down and unfolds it, and, sure enough, there's another tally sheet sitting inside. Like Joey's, it's been worked over with pencil, but there's no name written anywhere on the paper.

"Goddamn it," says Quill. "Who the hell was here with her, and why would they have been playing board games?"

"You said she was seeing someone in secret," I say. I pick up the flashlight and shine it around the room again. "Maybe there's something here that we missed. Some kind of clue."

We work our way around the room again, pulling away couch cushions, peering into the darkest corners of the kitchen cupboards. Quill even takes the back of the toilet off and sticks his hand down into the depths of the murky water, coming up empty.

Eventually, we have to admit that the place is empty.

"This is such bullshit," says Quill, disgusted and defeated.

"Don't be upset," I say. "We have a clue."

"Whatever," he says, turning away from me and moving back to the door, angry. He wrenches it open, letting a shard of bright daylight into the dingy room. "You coming?" he asks.

I don't answer; I'm staring at the ceiling in the corner of the room. The daylight he's let in from outside is shining a bright, crisp-edged beam along the floor, up the wall, and onto a specific, triangular patch on the ceiling. In this light, it's obvious that one of the ceiling tiles is askew and sitting slightly off the grid from its neighbors.

"Do you see that?" I ask.

He nods. I grab one of the small wooden dining room chairs and carry it over so it's beneath the hole. When I climb onto the chair, I'm able to push the tile up, pretty easily.

"Shove it out of the way," he says.

I do as he says, and he drags a second chair over. I shine my phone light up into the opening.

"There's something up there," he says, pointing at the corner of the hole. He jumps, using his free hand to dig inside. Slowly, he prods a lumpy object toward the corner, until finally he is able to grab it and yank it out of the hole entirely.

The thing flops onto the floor, kicking up a thin cloud of dust. It's a plastic garbage bag, tied tight with duct tape, about the size of a small dog. It's lumpy and limp but thick with bulk.

"What the hell is it?" asks Quill.

"I don't know," I say. "Maybe we should get out of here and call the cops."

He gives me a quick, irritated look. "What is it with you and the cops?" He walks over, and before I have a chance to protest, he kicks the bag, which slides across the floor.

"What are you doing?" I ask.

"It's not a body," he says thoughtfully, as if that was his first guess. "It's kind of light."

He kneels beside the bag and starts to rip at the tape. "It's bound up too tight," he says. "Get me a knife from the kitchen."

Too curious to protest, I follow his instructions and bring him a serrated steak knife with a cheap plastic handle. He stabs it into the bag and cuts open a gash a few inches long. The action is aggressive, almost violent, and I step back instinctively as he drops the knife and puts his hands into the gap, pulling the rip open with a confident yank.

The garbage bag bursts open, and Quill stands, shaking the bag empty. A pile of Ziploc bags pours onto the floor. Some of them are stuffed full of pills—small white ones, multi-colored tablets, orange hexagons. Some of the bags are stuffed tight with lumpy green plant material. A few, carefully taped in neat loops, contain white powder.

Quill lets out a long, low whistle. "Holy shit," he says. "Look at all these fucking drugs."

"It's drugs?" I ask, although I already know that he's right.

"Please tell me you're kidding," he says, stooping to pick up one of the green bags. He opens it and sniffs. "That is definitely weed right there. It's old, though."

"Where do you think it came from?" I ask.

"Beats me," he says. "I can tell you it wasn't Joey's. She wouldn't go near this shit, guaranteed."

"Maybe it belongs to whoever she was with," I say. "It just seems like too much of a coincidence that she would be secretly meeting up with someone in the exact same cottage that somebody else was using to hide drugs."

"You're probably right," he says. "But I can't imagine Joey hooking up with someone who'd be into this kind of crap. I mean, Joey wouldn't even look at some dude if he was into smoking a bit of weed, let alone all of this shit." We both look at the floor, and it finally occurs to me that this is a lot of narcotics.

"So what do we do now?" I ask. "Take them to the cops?"

His laugh is incredulous. "You've got to be kidding. Can you imagine what the cops would think if I showed up with a bag of drugs? No, we leave them here and pretend we never saw them."

I chew on my lip, thinking. "I might have a better idea," I say.

TWENTY-FOUR

LIKE LAST TIME, I meet Carrie and Ant in the beach parking lot. Unlike last time, I'm not alone.

When we arrive, Carrie is sitting on the hood of Ant's truck, smoking, and Ant is pacing on the gravel. I pull up a few spaces away, and when we get out of the car and walk toward her, I look at Carrie to see if she'll react to Quill's presence. Whatever she feels, she does a good job of hiding it; just exhales a cloud of smoke and then gives us a little wave.

Ant, on the other hand, isn't as calm.

"Who is this?" he asks me, looking at Quill. Without waiting for an answer, he snaps, "This better not be about the Catalog Killer again. I told you, we didn't have anything to do with that."

"Quill," I say, ignoring Ant for the moment. "This is my friend Carrie, and this is her boyfriend, Ant. Guys, this is Quill." I almost finish the sentence with "my boyfriend," but I lose my nerve at the last second.

"Hey, Quill," says Carrie. She slides off the car and drops

her cigarette butt on the ground, crushing it under her heel before walking over to shake his hand. Then she leans in to give me a hug.

"He's cute," she whispers, very softly, before she pulls away.

"Are you going to tell us what's going on?" asks Ant.

"Ant!" says Carrie, annoyed. "Mac is one of my oldest friends. Stop being an asshole!"

"That's fine, Carrie," says Ant. "I'm happy to hang out with the guys, maybe grab a burger or catch a movie sometime, but this is the second time we've been summoned to a dark parking lot, and the last time he practically accused my family of being a bunch of serial killers."

"I didn't accuse you of anything," I say.

"Well, it sure sounded like it at the time," Ant shoots back.

"Hey!"

Carrie and Ant and I turn toward Quill, who's opened the back door of the car and pulled the backpack out. He tosses it across the parking lot, and it lands near Ant's feet.

"You might want to check that out," says Quill.

"What is it?" asks Ant, warily, making no move to pick it up.

"Open it up," I say.

He looks like he's going to argue with me, then thinks twice and grabs the backpack with an annoyed snort. He unzips it and pulls it open, and I see his face go still.

"What the fuck?"

"What is it?" asks Carrie.

He ignores her. "Where did you get this?" he asks, his voice tight. "Do you know how much shit I've been in over this?"

"Ant," says Carrie. "What is it?"

He hands her the bag, and she looks inside. She gasps.

"Jesus Christ, Mac," she says. "What are you doing with all this?"

"We found it," I say.

"Found it?" asks Ant. "My ass you found it, you little thief."

"Ant!" snaps Carrie. "Shut up and let him talk."

"We don't owe you an explanation," says Quill. "It's enough to know that we found it. I don't give a shit if you believe us or not, but that's the truth."

I do give a shit if he believes us. "We found it in the ceiling of one of the Wandering Surf Cottages," I say.

"You expect me to believe that?" asks Ant.

"It's the truth," I say.

Carrie looks at me, suspicious. "You're still poking around, trying to find out what happened to Connor, aren't you?"

I hesitate, then nod. "I have to."

"What else aren't you telling us?" she asks.

"We found something in that cabin that proves Joey Standish was there too."

Carrie's mouth drops open, and Ant points a finger at me. "Kid," he says, "I told you a hundred times. You're barking up the wrong tree if you think that my brother had anything to do with those murders."

"I'm not saying he did," I say. "But somebody took those drugs, somebody who was connected to Joey Standish, and your brother is the only person around who I can think of that would have this kind of stock hanging around."

"Oh, they're his, alright," says Ant. "They went missing last year, and who the hell do you think he blamed for it?"

My heart skips. "They've been gone for a year?"

He nods. "Every goddamn day for months, I had to listen to him bitch about those stupid missing drugs."

"He never found out who took them?" I ask.

"No," says Ant. "No matter how many arms we twisted, nobody knew anything about it, and it's not like we could call the cops and ask them to look into it."

"I need to talk to him," I say.

Ant bursts into a snorting laugh, and Carrie shakes her head at me, her face gravely serious.

"Not a good idea, Mac," she says.

"He might know something!" I say.

"He doesn't know shit," says Ant. "I told you that. He doesn't have a clue."

"Maybe when he finds out where they were, he'll have a clue," says Quill. "Won't he be happy to get them back?"

Ant glares at me, but I can tell that he's thinking.

"Yeah," he says, reluctantly. "He'll be happy to get this shit back. God knows he'll have no trouble selling it."

"Then take us to see him," I say. "Please. We just want to ask him about it."

"Mac," says Carrie, warning. "Just let it go. Connor is dead; you can't bring him back."

"You know it's not that simple, Carrie," I say.

Ant zips the bag closed and then lets it dangle by a strap, bouncing it lightly as if he's weighing it. "Fine," he says finally. "You want to see Junior? I'll bring you to Junior."

Quill and I climb into Ant's truck, squeezing into the narrow space behind the front bench seat. Ant shoves the backpack into the narrow space between us, then pulls out of the parking lot.

None of us speak as we drive away from town. There's enough tension in the truck to even keep Quill quiet. Ant pulls onto the old coast highway but turns north, the opposite direction of the cottages. A few miles out of town, Ant turns off onto a rugged gravel road that continues to twist along the shore, bringing us even closer to the water.

"Holy shit," Quill whispers. "I feel like we're just a few inches from slipping over the edge."

"Don't worry about it," says Ant, without turning around. "I've been driving on this road since I was fourteen."

"Does it ever wash out?" asks Quill.

"Yup," says Ant, simply.

Quill gives me a wide-eyed stare, then I feel his hand reach over and squeeze my knee. Outside the windows, fog is thickening.

Suddenly, with a jerk of the wheel, Ant pulls a hard right, as if we're about to drive straight into the ocean. I stifle a yelp, and then we're creeping through the fog, bumping along on a series of makeshift bridges that connect several small, rocky islands.

"What the actual fuck?" asks Quill, in a voice that's equal parts exhilarated and terrified.

"You know where we are?" Ant asks, and I know he's talking to me.

"We're on the spit," I say. I don't need to guess; I've heard stories about this place for years.

"Yup," says Ant.

Carrie turns around toward Quill. "The Merlins have lived out here for over a hundred years."

"No way," says Quill, impressed.

We drive over one last bridge, then Ant brings the truck to a stop. He and Carrie get out, then he leans his head in and looks back at us. "Come on," he says. "This is what you wanted." Quill and I exchange looks, then we squeeze our way out of the back of the truck.

Even though it's the height of summer, there's a chill in the fog. Next to me, Carrie wraps her arms around herself and shivers. We're on a small, rocky island, surrounded by drifting coils of fog and the noise of the ocean. Through the fog, I get a vague glimpse of waves snatching at a rocky shoreline.

A small house stands nearby. It gives off the impression that it grew out of the maritime soil: weathered gray shingles that look like they've spent half their lives in the ocean; a chimney built from smooth granite rocks; piles of dry seaweed banked around the perimeter. There's a skim of salt over everything.

Hard, aggressive music punches from the open downstairs windows, which let light out onto the unkempt lawn. Behind the house is a dock, built into the rocks. A beat-up old fishing boat is tied to its end, where the water is deepest. Closer to shore, a weatherworn speedboat is tied to a piling with its bow pointed out to water, ready to make a quick getaway.

"Is this your brother's house?" I ask Ant.

"My house too," he corrects. "It was willed to both of us by our old man. Junior is the oldest, though, so he pretty much decides what goes on out here, which is basically the same thing that went on when our father was still alive. Do you understand what I'm saying?"

"I'm not stupid," I say, annoyed at the patronizing way he's speaking to me. "We just brought you a bag full of illicit substances."

"Okay, fine," he says. "You're not stupid, but I'm willing to bet you don't realize how dangerous my brother is."

"Okay," I say. He turns to Quill and waits.

"Got it," says Quill.

"Just be careful when you're talking to him," Ant says. "Tell him the truth, and try not to piss him off."

He reaches into the back of the truck and pulls out the backpack, handing it to me.

"Uh, don't you want to give it to him?" I ask.

Ant laughs. "You shitting me? You're the one who begged to come and see him, special delivery and all."

Reluctantly, I take the bag and sling it over my shoulder.

Ant leads the way to the front door. Carrie turns to me, narrowing her eyes. "I swear, I can't figure you out, Mac."

She turns and follows Ant as he barges through the screen door, then Quill and I follow them into the house.

TWENTY-FIVE

THE FRONT DOOR leads directly into the kitchen. It's smoky, and people are sitting all around the table. Two women are playing cards. One of them has long red hair and wears a tracksuit. She's probably in her late thirties, but the other one, with short black hair, tight denim shorts, and a bikini top, isn't much older than me. Across from them, a heavily tattooed guy with a leather vest over a bare chest is rolling a joint. On the other side of the room, sitting in a rocking chair next to a wood stove with his hand out to scratch the top of a lazy Great Dane's head, is Junior Merlin.

I've seen Junior Merlin before. Once in a while, he comes into town to eat at the tavern or to just wander around like he owns the place. He's as huge as his brother is tiny: muscular arms and shoulders, a broad chest that presses against his tight T-shirt, a shaved head and a thick beard, and a blood-red glass eye. It used to scare the crap out of me when I was a kid and Merlin was still in high school. There are a lot of rumors about how he lost his eye; everything from a bar fight to a dare that he put a cigarette out in it. But whatever the case, he's chosen a terrifying replacement.

As we walk in behind Ant and Carrie, the room goes silent. The girls look up from their cards; the joint roller pauses in his task; the dog's face perks up to attention; and Junior Merlin lifts his chin and stares straight at us with his gruesome eye.

"Bringing friends around, Ant?" he asks in a thin, reedy voice. The question sounds almost conversational, as if he's asked what Ant had for dinner, but I can feel the tension in the room. It's instantly obvious that this isn't the kind of place where people just bring guests, whether it's Ant's house too or not.

"You're gonna want to see this, Junior," says Ant, ignoring the question. He turns to me. "Go ahead. Show him."

Every eye in the room is on me as I walk over and set the backpack in Junior's lap. Junior takes one last long look at me, then picks up the backpack and holds it out in front of him, shaking it slightly as if trying to gauge its weight.

"What is it?" he asks. His voice crackles, as if it's coming through on a bad connection.

"Open it," says Ant.

Junior drops the bag onto the floor, then bends over and unzips it. The people at the table still haven't moved. It's almost as if they're statues, trying to stay as unobtrusive as possible while they figure out what's going on. Junior reaches down and grabs the top with each hand, yanking it open.

For a long, drawn out moment, nobody moves. Junior stares into the bag, and the rest of us in the room seem to collectively hold our breath. He reaches down and sticks his hand into the bag, rummaging around briefly, staring at the different bags—pills and powders and buds—that he's pulled out from the depths.

"What is it, Junior?" the redhead asks. Junior doesn't answer her. Instead, he sits back in his chair and pulls a mitt full of baggies out of the gym bag. He holds them tight in his fist and stares at me. I stare back, mesmerized, at his hands. His knuckles seem to whiten, then turn red, and I can see the plastic bag full of bright red pills begin to compress under the pressure.

"Where the fuck did you get these?" he asks, quietly.

I open my mouth to speak, but no sound comes out.

Ant steps forward, as if to explain on my behalf, but Junior holds up a hand, his palm out, telling him to be quiet.

"I want to hear about it from him," he says, and his hand sweeps around toward me, his finger jabbing so assertively that I almost feel it in my chest from several feet away.

I swallow, and from somewhere inside, I gain a rush of confidence. This guy is a drug dealer. He might be dangerous and stupid, but he's not going to kill me in front of all these people. My friends are standing right here, in the same room. He'd have to kill them both too.

I glance back at Quill. I can tell by looking at him that he's nervous, but ready to pounce if he needs to. Behind him, Carrie is standing against the wall, arms crossed in front of her chest, face squinted up in an expression I've known my whole life. She's pissed, and I know that she isn't pissed at Junior. She's pissed at me, for putting myself in this situation.

"Kid," says Junior, and now he's rising from his chair, slowly. "I am not going to give you another chance to tell me where you got my fucking DRUGS!"

He yells the last word, and it jolts me out of my daze.

"I found them," I say. "I found them in one of those abandoned cottages on the other side of town."

"In a cottage," he repeats, as if he doesn't believe me.

"Yeah," I say. "In one of those Wandering Surf Guest Cottages on MacAskill Road. I was there with my—" I swallow again, then turn to gesture toward Quill with my chin. "With my boyfriend."

The guy in the leather vest snorts, and Junior Merlin allows him a snide half smile before getting back to the matter at hand.

"So you and your boyfriend just happened to be poking around in an abandoned cottage, and you just happened to find a giant stash of drugs that just happened to have been stolen from me last year."

I nod. "Except we didn't just happen to be there." I pause, wondering how much I should give away. "We were there looking for clues. Into the Catalog Killer murders."

There's a long and ominous silence that seems to stretch out forever.

"I sure as hell hope you aren't suggesting that I have anything to do with the fucking Catalog Killer," Junior says finally, his face blank.

"No," I say, holding up my hands in surrender. "Absolutely not. But I think that whoever stole these drugs from you was there, in the cottage, with one of the victims. We found evidence that Joey Standish had been there with somebody, secretly, and while we were looking around, we found the drugs."

"Where?" asks Junior.

I explain the whole thing in detail—how the bag had been stuffed into the ceiling.

"And you automatically assumed that these drugs had something to do with me?" asks Junior, with phony outrage.

"You're Junior Merlin," I say. "You're the only person in the county who would have this kind of stash." I'm going out on a limb, hoping that he'll hear it as flattery, not judgment, and I'm right.

He nods, as if this answer satisfies him. "Fair enough."

"I'm hoping you'll answer a question," I say. "Since I returned this stuff to you."

There's a murmur of laughter around the room at my audacity, but Junior just nods at me.

"I'm feeling benevolent, my man," he says. "Go ahead."

"Did any of the four victims ever visit you here?" I ask.

"You're assuming I know what the victims looked like," he says.

"It was all over the news for months," I say. "You're telling me you never caught a glimpse online, or on TV?"

He smiles indulgently, like he's humoring a small child. "Yeah, I saw the pictures, just like everyone else. There was a goddamn serial killer on the loose. I was glued to that shit. Had some extra security around too, if you catch my drift."

The tattooed guy at the table lets out a whistle. "Damn right."

"To answer your question," says Merlin, "no. Never saw any of them. Not that I would have. Couple of high school kids, a mini-van mom, and a middle-aged dude? Not the kind of people who usually hang out around here."

"Not even Joey?" Quill butts in. Everyone turns to look at him as he steps forward to stand next to me. "The girl," he explains. "The one from the trailer park. She wasn't here with a boyfriend or something?"

Junior shakes his head emphatically. "None of them. Not once. I don't know a goddamn thing about the Catalog Killer."

I wait for him to say something else, but he just stares down at his bag of loot, and quietly, things start to go back to normal in the room. The dark-haired girl gets up and goes to the fridge, grabs herself a beer, and opens and hands one to Junior as well. He takes a long swig and looks at me.

"I don't have anything else to tell you," he says. "Ant. Get these lovebirds out of here."

"What?" he asks.

"You heard me, I'm done here. I don't want to think about how I got ripped off today. We're going to get messed up. Aren't we, girls?"

The two women at the table laugh in unison.

Ant doesn't say anything. He just grabs his coat and walks back out the door.

"Come on," Carrie says to me. "Time to go."

Quill and I turn to follow her through the door, but Junior calls after me.

"There is one thing I'll tell you," he says. "I do think there was some connection between the murders and the drugs going missing from around here."

"Why do you say that?" I ask.

"It just didn't feel right," he says. "Everything happened around the same time. That first guy gets killed, then someone rips me off. Maybe they were trying to frame me, who knows? I do know that the cops came around, asking me a lot of questions about the killings. Guess they figured all kinds of criminals do all kinds of crimes. After the second murder, after people started saying it was a serial killer, I started getting paranoid—started worrying that some of my product was going to start showing up with the bodies. That never happened, but still...too much of a coincidence for my liking."

"But you don't have any idea who might have taken this stuff from you?" I ask, pointing at the bag.

"I sure as hell wish I did," says Junior. "For a while, I thought maybe my dumbass brother might have had something to do with it, since they were stolen out of his truck. But I always had the feeling it was something deeper than that."

"Thanks," I say. Junior turns his attention back to the dog, and we leave.

I expect Ant to still be as furious as he was when we arrived, but he's actually smiling as we get back into the truck. As we drive off the spit, he turns the radio on and puts a hand on Carrie's knee.

"No offense," says Quill, "but your brother is one scary son of a bitch."

"Try living with him," says Ant. He turns around and grins at me. "I have to tell you, you did me a real favor back there. My brother never stopped blaming me for that theft, and now at least he'll know what happened. It's a good thing you got in touch with Carrie."

"No problem," I say. "Do you mind me asking why he blamed you?"

"Because they were stolen right out of the back of my truck."

"Where were you when that happened?" I ask.

"He was with me," says Carrie, with a displeased look at Ant. "At my house."

"On our street?" I ask, surprised.

"It was just a fluke," says Ant. "Usually he runs stuff on and off the island with the boats. He's got a bunch of guys who hide shit for him, up and down the coast. That night, he needed to get rid of a bunch of shit because he got a call that the cops might pay a visit. The boats were gone, so he made me take them away in the truck."

"Which I didn't know about at the time," says Carrie, pointedly.

"He even suspected her," says Ant, bitterly.

"He suspected everybody, Ant," says Carrie.

Something else is bothering me. "Do you remember when this all happened?"

"It was after the first murder," says Ant. "Like he said, there was a lot of heat around, and Junior was so paranoid. Usually, he wouldn't ever let anything leave the island except by water. I was supposed to hide them, but I never got the chance."

Suddenly, without warning, Ant slams his hand on the dash, startling the rest of us.

"It's okay, babe," says Carrie, reaching over to rub his shoulder.

"I just hate it," he says, bitterly. "I hate that he makes me do shit like that. I hate that he made me put you in that position. I can't wait till we can get the hell out of this place."

When we return to the beach parking lot, Carrie gets out of the truck and pulls the seat forward so we can get out.

"Thanks a lot, Ant," I say.

"Yeah," says Quill. "This was a real fun evening. We should do it again sometime."

Ant laughs. "Anytime, guys."

Carrie hugs Quill. "It was good to meet you," she says. "Keep this guy out of trouble, please?"

"We'll keep each other out of trouble," says Quill. "Don't worry."

When she hugs me, we hang on for a long time. "I'm sorry you had to see that, Mac," she says softly. "I'm not with Ant because I like being around that kind of shit. I'm with him because I know he's so much better than it."

"I get it," I say, pulling back to look at her. "I really do."

She smiles. "Quill seems really great, Mac," she says. "You should think about focusing on him for a while; stop thinking about those damn murders."

"I will," I say.

Quill puts his arm around my shoulders as Ant and Carrie drive away, and her words echo in my ears. I know it's good advice, but there's no way I can follow it—not now.

"Well, I guess that was another bust," says Quill.

"Are you kidding me?" I say. "Things are finally starting to fall into place."

TWENTY-SIX

IT'S LATE, and the only place still open in town is The Salty Bean, a coffee shop near the boardwalk. It's practically empty, other than an old couple sitting at a table in the window. We buy drinks at the counter and take them to a booth in the corner.

"Are you going to keep me in suspense all night?" asks Quill.

"Okay, so here's the thing," I say. "Connor loved the idea of living large. Doing wild things. He was always talking about breaking away from Camera Cove, experiencing exciting things, living an authentic life. Does that sound familiar?"

Quill looks at me, his eyes wide. "It sounds like Joey," he says.

I nod, excited. "Do you remember the day we met, when I came to the park for donations?"

He nods.

"You said that Joey used to love going to the library. It was how you got people to give donations."

Understanding dawns on his face. "Connor was working at the library."

"Exactly," I say. I slam my hand on the table, excited. "Exactly!"

The elderly couple turns around to look at us. When I glance across at them to smile apologetically, I think I catch a glimpse of something through the window. A figure in the alley across the street that seems to melt into the shadows as I watch. I stare for a few moments until I've convinced myself that my eyes are playing tricks on me.

"Hello," says Quill. "Are you going to keep going?"

I lower my voice and lean toward him.

"So imagine this," I say. "Connor and Joey strike up a conversation at the library. They become friends. Maybe Connor flirts a bit, and Joey likes it, thinks he's cute. They start to fall for each other, and what's so nice about it is that even though they've grown up just a few miles away from each other, they don't know each other at all. They come from different worlds. She's from the park, he's from town; they go to different high schools. They've never met before, and they like that."

"I can see it," says Quill. "Opposites attract, right?" He gives me a wink, but I'm too caught up in my story to react.

"Maybe," I say, "or maybe they just like being themselves for a change. So somehow, one of them comes into the possession of a key to an abandoned cottage. Maybe Connor's dad did some carpentry work out there, boarding up cottages, and forgot to return one of the keys; maybe Joey found it on the side of the road; who knows. Now they have the perfect spot to see each other, talk to each other, without being noticed by anyone. As time goes by, they start to get serious."

Quill frowns. "Don't you think he would have told you if he was getting serious with some girl?"

I shake my head. "No. We didn't really have that kind of friendship. And besides, didn't Joey keep it from you?"

He nods.

"The other thing you need to know about Connor is that he was involved with a lot of girls. He might have been trying to keep things on the down low. Maybe it was in his best interest to keep stuff like this quiet, because he wouldn't want the other girls he was messing around with to know. He had kind of a…history, I guess you could say."

"Sounds like a real prince," says Quill.

I shrug. "He just really liked girls, and they really liked him."

"I wonder if Joey knew that's the way he was," says Quill, cynically.

I shrug again and continue laying out my theory. "Anyway, they get so serious that they start to share their ideas about the future. They both want to get out of Camera Cove. They've always planned on graduating high school first, but the more they start to talk about it, the more they realize that they want to leave sooner than later. There's just one problem."

"No money," says Quill.

"Exactly. But then, lo and behold, one evening Connor looks out of his bedroom window and sees Carrie and her boyfriend, Ant Merlin, park across the street, in front of Carrie's house. Her parents aren't home, and he sees them go inside. It's dark. The street is empty. Connor knows that Ant deals a bit of weed, and he decides on a whim to sneak across the street and look inside the truck."

"There's a backpack," says Quill. "He takes it."

"When he gets home, he realizes that there's a lot more than just some weed in the bag. He panics a bit, but realizes that this could be their ticket out of town. He hides the backpack at the cottage, and he and Joey start to think about how to unload the stuff, make some money, and leave town together. But then..." I trail off.

Quill finishes my sentence. "Joey is killed."

"Joey is killed," I repeat. "At first, he's horrified and shocked and grief-stricken. Then he starts to wonder what to do. He thinks he should maybe tell the cops, but if he goes to the cops, he'll have to explain the bag of drugs."

"So he starts his own investigation," says Quill.

"Exactly."

"This makes sense, Mac," says Quill. His voice is low, but I can hear the excitement in it. "It all makes so much fucking sense."

"I know," I say. "It explains everything."

"To a point," he says.

"Yeah."

We sit in silence for a few moments, staring at our coffee, trying to work out what happened next.

"So the way I see it," says Quill. "We've got two viable theories. Either Connor discovered the Catalog Killer's identity and paid the price for it, or Connor thought he'd discovered who it was, and someone took advantage of that."

"I feel like the answer is staring us right in the face," I say. "We're so close, but something is still missing."

The elderly couple is gone, and from across the counter the

owner catches my eye and taps on his watch. "Gonna close up soon, guys," he says.

We finish our drinks and drop the mugs on the counter before exiting into the night. The street is empty, and we cross to where I've parked my car in no particular rush. Trying not to appear obvious, I glance into the alleys and darkened corners near the car, wondering if I actually did see something earlier. There's nothing and nobody around.

When I drop Quill at the trailer park, he leans over and kisses me.

"We'll figure it out, Mac," he says. "I promise."

Afterward, I drive back along the deserted roads toward town, trying to make sense of the final pieces of the puzzle. The trees on either side form a tunnel of shadows on the outer edges of the headlights. Somebody killed Connor and the others. Was it one killer or two? How close did Connor get to the truth? What did he see?

What *did* he see?

A light snaps on in my mind. Connor saw something that led him to the caves that night.

And when Connor saw something, he usually drew a picture of it.

TWENTY-SEVEN

I ENTER THE LIBRARY through the back door, making sure there is nobody around to spot me. I keep the lights off as I make my way through the storage area and into the main library, but once my eyes adjust, there's more than enough light for me to find my way to the children's section.

I've brought a flashlight from the car, and I snap it on, shining it slowly over the unfinished mural. Couples strolling, kids playing, elderly men walking dogs; a barbershop quartet in the town square, a lifeguard on her tower, a shopkeeper sweeping his step. I shine the light on our group: me and Connor and Carrie and Doris and Ben. It's clear to me that it's us, but as I peer closer, I begin to understand the problem I'm facing.

The faces, as well done as they are, are unidentifiable. They look specific and generic at the same time. From different angles, they take on different expressions, and even the figures I know, like me and my friends, are only recognizable to me because I know what to look for. Even if Connor had drawn the killer into the mural, which is what I'd been hoping, it would be impossible to know who it was in real life.

After staring endlessly at the mural, I give up and shut off the flashlight.

In the instant the room goes dark, something catches my attention.

It's just the faintest suggestion of a noise, out of place from the rest of the space. I stand perfectly still, aware of a change in the atmosphere in the air of the library. I glance past the children's area into the dimness of the stacks, and the shadows remain completely still. The only noise is the aggressive ticking of the clock. I'm just imagining things.

I step around the tiny, colorful furniture, and this time I'm sure I hear a noise. Quiet and indistinct, but it's there. My stomach turns to jelly.

"Hello?" I call, with trepidation.

The library is dead silent, and after a few moments, I convince myself again that it's all in my head. Still, I'm unsettled, and I want to get out of here as quickly as possible.

The back door to the library is on the other side of the building, at the end of a small hallway that contains the bathrooms. To get there, I have to either walk through or around the stacks and get to the more open, main space with the computers and work tables. I take a deep breath, telling myself that I'm only imagining things, and take a step toward the stacks.

As I approach the tall, book-lined shelves, the shadows they cast seem to lengthen and darken. It would be so easy for someone to hide in them.

I realize, with a sinking feeling in my gut, that I don't remember locking the back door behind me when I came in. I was in such a rush, trying to get a good look at the mural, that I don't know if I took a second to flip the deadbolt.

I stop and stand still again, listening to the stillness of the library. Again, I'm struck by the feeling of something not quite right—an unsettled edge to the air.

The library is empty.

I step briskly into the stacks, my eyes darting back and forth as I reach the first row, the second, and then the third and final row. There's nobody here, and I let out a deep sigh of relief, and a slight chuckle, as I step out into the open main area.

My mind is playing tricks on me, and who could blame it? I've been feeding it a solid diet of murder and conspiracies all summer long.

From this end of the stacks, I turn to take one last look back at the mural. In the dim light, it takes on a new quality, as if the people in it are underwater, stuck in the middle of coming into focus. It's like the shaken image on a Polaroid photograph.

Then one of the figures in the painting moves.

My first instinct is to think that I've imagined it; that it's a trick of the light and the time of day, and after a crazy month, my mind is playing tricks on me. But then the figure steps away from the mural, and I realize that it actually is a person—someone who was standing still against the artwork, camouflaged among the other taller figures in the foreground.

I step back, startled and scared. From somewhere, I hear the sound of shallow, panicked breathing. It takes a moment to realize it's coming from me.

The figure holds both hands up, palms facing me, and I stumble backward into a shelving cart, knocking several books over and ending up on my ass. The figure chuckles.

"I'm not going to hurt you," a man's voice says.

Thinking wildly, I reach into my pocket and grab my phone, sliding on the camera to shoot a picture. The flash goes off, and the man yells in surprise. I fumble wildly with my phone. Frantically, I open the most recent message thread. It's from Quill. I try to select the photo to put it into a message, but before I can press Send, a hand reaches down and grabs me by the arm, yanking me up. My phone drops and slides underneath a table.

"Leave me alone!" I yell.

"Just be quiet, for fuck's sake," he says. He lets me go and I stagger backward, somewhat stupidly grabbing a book off the shelf and holding it up as a weapon. He holds his hands out again and steps back from me, then he pulls his hood back.

It's Christopher Brindle.

He looks disheveled; nothing like the well-arranged town councilor and lawyer that I've seen in newspaper ads and later, in the news stories about his wife's murder. His hair is askew, and he's wearing a pair of shorts and a dark hoodie that I recognize at once.

"I'm not going to hurt you," he says again. "Seriously. I just want to talk to you."

"You've been following me," I say. "You followed me on the day of the parade."

He puts his hands up in mock surrender. "Guilty," he says. "Although I wasn't really following you. Not just you, anyway."

He takes another step forward, and I hold the book up higher, ready to toss it.

"Jesus," he says. "Relax. I'll sit if it will calm you down."

He grabs a plastic chair from the nearest table and spins it around so he's sitting backwards on the chair. He crosses his arms and rests his chin over the back of the chair.

I realize that every muscle in my body is clenched tight, and I force myself to take a deep breath. "What do you mean, 'not *just* me'?"

"I did follow you after the parade," he admits. "I've been watching for something suspicious for the last year. Other than Celeste and Ashleigh, it's the only thing that keeps me sane…trying to find out what happened to my wife. I saw that other kid attack Cubby French."

"Ben," I say.

He nods. "Yeah. Then I saw you trying to calm him down, and right away I recognized you. I started to wonder, 'Where have I seen this kid before?' And then it occurred to me. You were at my house, looking for donations. What a coincidence. So I thought, why does this kid keep popping up?"

"I was friends with Connor," I say. At this point, there's no reason to lie anymore. "I've been trying to learn who did this to him. To all of them."

He looks at me with interest.

"Join the club, kid," he says. "I've spent the past year trying to do the same thing. Not that I've learned anything."

"You don't think it was a drifter?" I ask.

"I don't know," he says. "I don't know what to think. Some days I think that's exactly what happened, so random and awful. Other days, I think it must have…"

"Must have what?" I ask.

He shakes his head, frustrated. "It just all felt too close to home, you know? There were too many coincidences."

"Coincidences?"

He doesn't answer me, but I get the feeling he knows something and wants to talk.

"What coincidences?" I ask again.

He leans his head back so that he's staring at the ceiling and laughs, bitterly. "Maria was having an affair with George Smith."

My mouth drops open. "What?"

He nods, his face grim. "Victim Number One."

"Are you sure?"

He nods again. "I followed her one day, just a couple of weeks before he was murdered. Saw them together. It only lasted a couple of months."

"How do you know that?"

"I asked her," he says. "After he died. I didn't know who the guy was until his face was all over the news. She admitted everything. She was horrified and terrified."

"Do you think she knew who did it?"

He shakes his head. "Definitely not. She was totally blindsided. Then the same thing happened to her." His voice catches and he looks away, wiping a tear from the corner of his eye.

As awful as the past year has been for me, for Quill, and for all the other families and friends of the victims, it must have been a hundred times worse for Christopher Brindle. Not only did he find out his wife was having an affair right before she was murdered, but he was one of the only suspects that the police took seriously, if you believe what was being said in the news.

"You didn't tell the police about this, did you?" I ask, although I already know the answer.

"How could I?" he asks. "How would it have looked if they knew that Maria and George were having an affair, and I knew about it before either of them were murdered?"

"What would she tell you, when she left the house to go see him?" I ask. "Where did they meet?"

He looks up again and glances around the darkened library. "They used to meet here."

My brain starts to spin, gears and cogs and tiny dials and levers snapping into place like an intricate puzzle box finally being solved. The library. All four of them had this library in common. Two secret couples—Connor Williams and Joey Standish, Maria Brindle and George Smith.

On my first day at the library, Libby had told me that the tourists liked to use it, and she wasn't lying. Strange faces came in on a daily basis; unfamiliar, indescribable individuals in khaki shorts and baseball caps, sunglasses and backpacks, all using the washrooms and stealing the Wi-Fi. Eventually they become wallpaper: ignored. How easy would it be for a drifter to blend into this space, to get used to people's comings and goings? To strike up a casual conversation with a potential victim?

It would have been the perfect opportunity for the Catalog Killer to find his victims and then disappear.

Another question occurs to me. "Did you draw an eyeball on the window of my car?"

He looks surprised. "An eyeball?"

"In the dust, on the driver's side window."

He shakes his head. "Not me," he says. "What's that about?"

"It's nothing," I say.

Brindle stands. "Listen," he says. "I'm sorry I scared you like that. I've gone off the deep end a bit lately, and I thought maybe...I don't know. Maybe I thought you knew something. At this point, I'm ready to start talking to fortune tellers, you know what I mean?"

"Yeah," I say. "I do."

He walks over to me, and without meaning to, I flinch. He holds both hands up in surrender.

"I'm going to leave now," he says. "I won't bother you anymore."

I follow him to the back door.

"Will you promise me something?" he asks. "Will you promise that if you learn something, you'll tell me, and I'll do the same thing?"

I nod. "I promise."

He puts his hand on the door, then stops and turns back one more time.

"Celeste tells me we have to put it behind us," he says. "I know she's right, but it's not that easy, is it?"

"No," I say, "it's not."

For a moment, we lock eyes, and then he turns and pushes through the door and into the night. The initial adrenaline rush from my encounter with Brindle is gone, and I'm left feeling deflated. Before locking up, I stand in front of the mural one last time, willing myself to notice something, *anything* in Connor's images that will point me in the right direction. But it's no use; the faces remain indistinct and anonymous.

What makes this extra frustrating is that Connor's portraits were usually extremely lifelike. I think back to that quick sketch he did for our time capsule, each of us rendered perfectly in just a few quick lines. Why couldn't he have carried this skill over to the mural?

The answer comes to me all at once, and it's so obvious I almost laugh. Connor's final product might have been stylized, but his original drawings probably weren't nearly as refined, and they might hold clues that the mural doesn't.

And I know exactly where to find them.

TWENTY-EIGHT

ASTRID BILLINGSLEY'S HOUSE is on a quiet street near the beach. It's not hard to find. It's a brightly painted little cottage, surrounded by a massive, tangled garden. A whimsical fence constructed from driftwood surrounds the house and gardens, and on the gate, a hand-painted sign announces that I've reached "Astrid Billingsley: Artist's Studio."

I'm wondering if I should push open the gate and walk up to knock on the door, when Astrid appears from behind the house. She's wearing gardening gloves, faded blue denim overalls over a bright pink, long sleeved shirt, and a big pair of rubber boots. Her hair flies out in wisps from under the edges of a large straw hat, bedecked with a ribbon. She's awkwardly carrying a large folded tarp in her arms. A cat saunters behind her and then disappears into a thick border of flowers.

I call out, and she turns to me with no hint of recognition.

"I work at the library," I tell her, as she approaches. "I wanted to talk to you about the mural."

"Oh, yes," she says. "Connor's friend."

"I'm wondering if you have a few minutes to talk."

"I wish you'd called first," she says, dropping the tarp next to a large rosebush. "I'm trying to prepare for the storm."

"Storm?" I ask.

She looks at me like I'm completely stupid. "Hurricane Selena," she says. "It's making its way up the eastern seaboard right now, gathering strength. If it stays on target, it will hit land nearby in a couple of days."

"I hadn't heard," I say.

"That figures," she says. "You millennials just float through life like a bunch of clueless, fragile butterflies, don't you?" She sighs and pulls off her gloves. "Well, I suppose if you came all this way, I can't very well send you away. Come along."

I'm not about to explain that I'm not really a millennial, so I just follow her around the house to her back garden, where a little building sits nestled amidst even more flowers. She shoos away her cats, then ushers me inside.

The studio is a riot of color, but despite the initial impression of chaos, it's actually a very well organized space. An old couch covered with multi-colored textiles stretches across one wall, and another wall is taken up by a large wooden cabinet, full of paints and brushes and jars of various paint thinners, with a row of heavy art books running along the top. Every square inch of wall is taken up by paintings and sketches.

She gestures me toward the couch, then perches on a stool next to an easel.

"I'm pleased to see that Libby has sent you to work out the details," she says. "I am already exhausted at the thought of butting heads with that interminable woman throughout this entire process. But I give her credit for sending a diplomat in her place. I can already tell that you're a much more rational person. I've always liked the company of gay men."

My eyes widen, and I'm unsure of how to respond to this, but she's already moved on.

"I have been working on some studies for the mural," she says, pointing at a large drafting table in the corner of the room.

I stand in front of the drawing board, and it is immediately clear to me that despite her ramblings, she is exceptionally talented. A photo of the actual mural, in its current state, is taped to the center of the board. Surrounding it are small sketches, simply but elegantly drawn, that have been neatly cut out of the paper they were drawn on. Clearly, they are intended to fill in the unfinished areas of Connor's mural.

Astrid walks up behind me and points to one of the sketches—a kid on a bike.

"This will go here," she says, lifting the sketch and sitting it over the photo of the mural. It fits perfectly.

"This is great," I say. "I can already imagine it."

"Yes," she says. "It will be a proper completion."

"Did you come up with these ideas on your own?"

"Of course not," she says, as if this is the dumbest question in the world. "These are Connor's ideas. He was always drawing, thinking, planning. He was a natural. In many years of teaching, I have rarely seen anyone so capable of transferring the essence of a person onto paper with such a seamless style. I like to think I had something to do with his aptitude, but teaching really only takes you so far. The talent has to be there to begin with."

She turns back to the board and touches the printed image of the mural with a gentle finger.

"When I was at art school in the sixties," she says, "people were doing all kinds of fabulous public artwork—art wasn't just for walls, it was for the world. Connor was really interested in that idea, but he realized that you can't do anything without the basics: a good eye, and the ability to draw. The mural was a test; an opportunity to bring his skills to the next level. He was willing to start small and work his way up. It's all so very sad. We'll never know what he would have done next."

I try again. "If these are Connor's ideas, how did you get them?"

"From his sketchbook, of course," she says. "He kept a very detailed sketchbook with images of the people and places and scenes that he thought would fit well into the mural."

"So you have it?" I ask, barely willing to hope.

"Absolutely not," she says, her voice stern and scolding. "I have certain facsimiles. Photocopies that we made when Connor and I were working together."

"Do you know where it is?" I ask.

"His parents have it," she says. Something in her tone of voice catches my attention.

"And they won't let you see it?" I guess. I remember the black covered sketchbook that was on Connor's desk when I visited his parents.

"Well," she sniffs, "I can hardly blame them for their short-sightedness. Although it is difficult to understand why they'd hold back information so vital to their son's legacy. No matter. I have plenty to work with, although it would be nice to have had the chance to look through the fullest version of his vision."

You and I both, I think.

"He was spying on people, you know," she says.

My mouth goes dry. "Spying?"

"Of course," she says. "That's what gives his illustrations such vibrancy and immediacy. It's the only way to get a pure view of a person. He wanted to capture the essence of his subjects, and the only way to do that was to observe them without their knowledge, so he would hide and draw them from a distance. He'd even use binoculars."

"This has been very helpful," I say, suddenly desperate to get away from here. "The mural is definitely in great hands with you."

She nods, as if I've just mentioned that the sky is blue.

"Indeed. It isn't right to let it stay like that, unfinished," she says. "It was his final piece. His only legacy. We owe it to him to see that it is finished."

"Absolutely," I say, working my way toward the door. "We really appreciate that you've been so willing to help. You're obviously the only person talented enough to do it in a way that would make Connor proud. It just makes sense."

My flattery pleases her, and she sees me graciously to the door after I promise to check in on her progress within a couple of weeks.

I step into the sunlight, and the brightness almost blinds me. It's clearer to me now, more than ever, that I need to get a look at Connor's sketchbook.

The only problem is how to get to it.

TWENTY-NINE

AFTER NIGHTFALL, I SIT in the dark and watch Connor's house through my bedroom window. At a certain point, the light to his room comes on, and his mother enters from the hallway, sitting on the edge of his bed and staring forward. She leans over and puts her head in her hands, then she stands abruptly and walks to the window, where she stares out.

I hold my breath, wondering if she can see me, if she knows I'm here in the shadows, watching her watch me.

I don't think she does. I don't think she's even looking in my direction; not really. She's trying to be Connor, trying to put herself back into the world where he still existed.

I can understand that. She and I have that much in common.

She turns away and leaves the room, shutting off the light as she exits. On the main floor, Connor's dad sits in his recliner in the glow of the TV. A beer sits on the side table, and he reaches over and picks it up, taking a sip before putting it back down. A few seconds later, he does it again. And again. And again. As steady as a metronome.

Another light comes on upstairs, blocked by blinds, and after a few moments, it turns off again. Connor's mother going to bed.

For the next hour, I watch Connor's father watching TV, waiting for him to call it a night. But other than a few quick trips to the kitchen to grab more beer, he doesn't move. He doesn't even change the channel.

My own breathing slows, and I begin to get drowsy, fighting harder and harder against the sleep that wants to come. Just when I begin to wonder if he's going to sit like that all night, he stands and stretches, turns off the TV, and then leaves the room, turning off the light on his way out. He follows the same ritual as his wife, and the light behind the blinds turns briefly on and off before the house descends into complete darkness.

I wait for fifteen minutes. Twenty. Then I quietly walk downstairs, and with an apologetic pat to Hobo's head, I slip into my backyard, quietly closing the sliding door behind me. I can feel my dog's eyes on me as I move around the side of the house.

The street is empty, and the night is eerily quiet. I stick to the shadows of the trees that the streetlight casts. Then I creep across the street and hug the hedges around the Williamses' backyard until I'm safely hidden under the awning at the back door.

When we were kids, Connor's parents both worked long hours, and he was often left behind to fend for himself. The rest of us spent a lot of time hanging out at his place. All of us knew where the key was hidden. The big question now is whether it's still there.

It is there, hidden underneath a rock at the corner of the back patio. I pull it out and then crouch for a moment, debating whether I can really go through with this. Digging around into the murders has forced me to do some questionable things, but I've never, not for one moment, considered breaking into someone's house. Until now.

I scan the edges of the Williamses' moonlit yard. Unlike the immaculate interior of their house, the outside has been ignored. The flowers that Connor's mother was always so proud of are unkempt and overgrown, and a collection of planters sits clustered together, full of last year's dead annuals. I think about how deflated his mother was when I last came to see her; how his father seemed to be struggling to keep things together. They need closure as much as I do. More than I do.

There's no other option.

The noises of the night seem to drop away as I carefully slide the key into the lock of the side door. The click as the dead bolt slides open is as loud to me as if I'd picked up one of the flowerpots and smashed it against the patio stone. I stop, my hand poised at the key, and hold my breath, but the only sound is the rushing of the wind through the trees. I turn the knob and push the door inward.

The house is dead silent, and I move quietly, taking long pauses between steps, through the kitchen and onto the padded carpet of the family room. Through the room and into the hallway. I stand at the bottom of the stairs for a long time, building courage, listening for any noise that will tell me to leave, but the house just sits in stillness, entirely hushed. I step slowly onto the first tread, then carefully navigate the steps, checking for creaks, until I'm finally on the upstairs landing.

I stop again. To get to Connor's room, I have to walk past the slightly open door to his parents' room. I hear a soft snore, and it gives me the courage to move past them. Then I quickly open the door to Connor's room and let myself inside. Carefully and silently, I close the door and then sink gratefully to the floor, allowing myself to catch a deep, relieved breath.

I look around the room. There are more sketchbooks than I even remember—a whole wide shelf full of them—and another couple stacked neatly on top of his desk.

I don't know how much time I have, so I start pulling out pads, quickly rifling through to get a sense of what's in them.

There are many, many doodles, quick studies, and fanciful designs. Some of the pads—the ones with nicer paper—are full studies of landscapes, townscapes, pictures of the beach, and the cliffs. I stop at a beautiful colored pencil rendering of our neighborhood's bluff, with the tree framing it from the side and a sunset dropping into the ocean.

It doesn't take me long to realize that the books are in chronological order, and I skip ahead to the most recent. They end, to my disappointment, before the studies for the mural.

I sit against the bed, defeated. I'm starting to think about how to best get out of there, when I glance across the room at Connor's dresser and remember his hiding place.

I carefully slide the bottom drawer of the dresser out, trying to keep the wood from squeaking, and place it carefully on the floor.

Underneath, in a space only about four inches deep, is a thick, black, bound sketchbook.

As I draw it out from its hiding place, my arms begin to tingle. I open the front cover and see written in Connor's scrawl, *Mural Studies*.

The book is huge, and I'm beginning to get very nervous. I debate for a moment. Nobody knows that this sketchbook exists.

I shove it into my backpack.

I carefully replace the drawer. When I stand again, it's like my surroundings are real to me for the first time. Have I really broken into Connor's house in the middle of the night? I stand in the window and look across the street to my house, trying to imagine myself in Connor's shoes again.

"What did you know?" I whisper. "Help me, Connor. Help me put this to rest."

I turn, ready to leave, when the door bursts open.

"What the hell is going on?"

Connor's father stands before me, wearing a ragged old T-shirt over pajama bottoms. He's furious.

"I—I—" I lose my train of thought, unable to go any further.

"You come into my house!" he practically yells, although it comes out in an odd, loud rasp, as if he's trying—and failing—to whisper. He strides through the room toward me and grabs me by the shoulder, shaking me. "You come into my house and into his room?!"

My eyes burn, and I'm worried I might cry. I'm terrified and shocked, but most of all, I'm terribly ashamed.

"I'm sorry," I say. "I want to help. Connor wanted me to help him."

"Help him?!" he thunders. He gives me a shove, and I stagger backward against the desk, knocking a jar of pencils onto the floor.

"He left me a note!" I say, trying to get him to listen to me. He is so unhinged I worry that I'm in real trouble.

"Jim?"

We both turn to the door and see Connor's mother standing there, her eyes wide. Her presence seems to deflate Connor's father, and he drops onto the bed, his gaze turning back and forth from his wife to me.

For a long moment, none of us speak. I stand there, clutching the strap of my backpack.

Finally, Connor's mother walks into the room and comes over to me. Unlike the last time I saw her, she seems more present now, and her eyes actually focus on mine when she looks at me. She puts her hand out and touches it to my face, and I find that the tears that have been threatening are now falling down my cheeks.

"Oh, Mac," she says. "You and I have the same problem. We can't let it go."

"He wanted me to help," I say, again. I wipe at my cheek with the back of my hands.

"Why don't you explain what you're talking about, Mac?" says his mother.

I do. I tell them about finding the note in the comic books, about trying to find an answer when nobody else could. The whole time, Mr. Williams sits forward on the bed, his head in his hands, although I can tell that he's listening.

"I still don't understand why you broke into our house in the middle of the night," he says, finally.

"I tried to come before," I say. "You told me not to come back. I didn't know what to do, but I thought there would be a clue in here, somewhere."

Connor's parents exchange a look.

"There are no clues here," Mrs. Williams says gently. "The police went through everything. Even his sketchbooks."

My backpack seems to pulse against my back.

"I guess I should have figured that out," I say.

"It's okay, Mac," says Mrs. Williams. "None of us know how to wrap our heads around things. You were a good friend to him."

It's so strange to be here like this, in the middle of the night, having a normal conversation with them under these circumstances.

Connor's father stands now. "It's late," he says. "And I think we all really need to rest." He goes over and puts his arm around his wife's shoulders, and she sinks into him gratefully. "Mac," he continues. "This is a terrible thing that you did, but I understand why you did it. We can keep this between the three of us. That monster ruined our lives. It's time to start putting it behind us, so the rest of our lives aren't ruined as well."

I nod, agreeing, but I know I can't stop now. I'm too close.

THIRTY

THE SKETCHBOOK is still in my bag when I leave. I am certain that the cops didn't have the chance to see it, otherwise it wouldn't have been put back into its hiding place. Part of me feels like I should take it straight to Parnatsky, but she's been so discouraging every time we've talked. I can't hand this over when it might actually be something, and have her dismiss me yet again.

At home, I pull the book from my bag but realize that I can't face opening it. Not now. Not by myself.

I text Quill. Are you awake?

He responds right away.

Always awake for you.

I need to see you. I found something.

Now? What is it?

Morning. I'll show you then. Can I pick you up first thing? 8 o'clock?

That's early. You can help me wipe the sleep out of my eyes. ;)

I lie in bed, awake, for hours, staring at the ceiling. My thoughts go back and forth.

Quill and Connor. Quill and Connor. Quill and Connor.

I don't know which one of them is still on my mind when I finally fall asleep.

× × ×

"What's the plan?" Quill asks, as he slides into the front seat the next morning. It's raining, and the sky is gray. It feels more like November than the middle of summer—the early signs of Hurricane Selena.

I hand him one of the coffees I picked up, and he groans gratefully as he sips.

"Can we get the hell out of here for a while?" I ask.

"That sounds ideal," he says, with a wide grin.

When we leave Brookfield Estates, I turn in the opposite direction of town. I want to get as far away from Camera Cove as possible. I finally pull into an empty parking lot near a remote beach and park. Then I reach into the back seat and pull the sketchbook out of my bag.

The book is full of sketches of people from town. I see Libby, Mr. Anderson, our teachers. Even Cubby French makes an appearance. Several pages have been devoted to our group: Carrie and Ben and Doris and, off slightly to the side, me. Smaller sketches of our faces, done over and over again—laughing, serious, surprised—fill all the empty space.

I turn the page and take in a small, shuddering breath when I recognize my own house, or the upper half of it anyway. My bedroom window is the focus, and there's a sketch of me sitting at my desk, working at something. Incredulously, I flip through page after page of sketches of me. In the yard with Hobo, standing astride my bike, staring into space...

I guess Connor noticed me after all.

"You sure he wasn't gay?" asks Quill, mischievously.

"I know he wasn't," I say. He doesn't look convinced, but I ignore him.

A few pages later, I stop. I recognize the library right away; the stacks, the shelving cart, the many people who frequent it. Libby, kids in the children's section, old ladies checking out magazines. And clearly drawn together, at a table in the corner, as if watched secretly from a distance, Maria Brindle and George Smith, leaning toward each other, deep in conversation. His hand resting on top of hers.

"Whoa," says Quill.

I don't say anything. Part one of my suspicions has been confirmed. I turn the page and register a sharp intake of breath from Quill.

It's a full-page drawing of a beautiful girl, her head tilted backward and her mouth slightly open, the edges of her lips curled upward, as if she's just finished laughing. Her eyes sparkle, and a stray lock of hair cuts across her forehead like a punctuation mark.

"So I guess this proves it," Quill says, reaching out with a finger to stroke the page. "Joey and Connor were together, and somebody was watching them."

"The killer could have used the opportunity that they were couples to his advantage," I say. "How hard would it have been? Someone gives Joey a fake note from Connor, telling her to meet him at the tree, and that's the end of that."

He leans back into his seat. "That's messed up."

"Yes," I agree. "It's totally messed up."

He grabs the book, suddenly determined.

"There's got to be a picture of the killer in here," he says.

We flip through the book, but nothing stands out. No odd characters; no suspicious figures in the background. I slam the book shut, frustrated, angry that I've come this close, but still there's no clue leading me to the answer.

"Hey," says Quill, recognizing my frustration. "It's okay."

"It's not okay," I say. Tears burn my eyes, and I turn away from him, gritting my teeth. "Everything I've been through, trying to figure this out. If only I hadn't been so stupid, hadn't missed his note for a whole fucking year, maybe we'd be closer to the truth."

Quill's hand reaches out, and he brushes a tear away from my face. "Even if we don't learn anything else," he says. "I'm happy to know that Joey was with someone she really liked. Someone like Connor, who meant so much to you and to so many other people. And if you hadn't started looking into this the way you did, I wouldn't have met someone who makes me feel the same way."

I turn back to him and our eyes lock, and then we're reaching for each other.

Quill's body is like a treasure to be unburied—a hint of ribs pushing against the smooth, taut skin of his abdomen, a soft trail of spine leading my hand up his back to his neck.

I used to look at Connor this way; I know I did. Maybe he knew it. Maybe that was okay to him. I think, probably, it was. But I could only look at Connor, and the closest he would come to touching me was a light punch in the arm, a high five, or his eyes scanning me while he sketched me in one of his books. Connor saw me the way he saw everyone else, trying to catch on paper the way my body moved or the curves and angles of my face. Maybe the way he looked at me was the spark that lit something inside me—a fire that was never able to find fuel.

I know now that being looked at isn't enough. I want to be touched, the way Quill is touching me. I want someone to want me to touch them back.

× × ×

Afterward, we sit in the car, listening to the heavy drum of the rain on the roof, watching whitecaps roll in and out, clawing at sand and rocks and tossing pieces of driftwood about.

It has been nice to forget about everything for a while.

Quill squeezes my arm, and I lean over to rest my head against his shoulder, absentmindedly staring down along the curve of his arm, toward his long fingers. All the smooth pieces of him clicking into place, a perfect machine.

He kisses me on the head. "I'm starving," he says. "You want to grab something to eat?"

We find a small lobster shack on the side of the road. We're the only people in the place. I'm ravenous, and the two of us plow through our food in comfortable silence.

"Man," says Quill. "It's so good to eat something that didn't come out of a frozen package from the grocery store. I miss a lot of things about Joey, but her cooking is high up on the list."

Somewhere deep in the recesses of my brain, a switch is flipped.

"What is it?" asks Quill, noticing my change.

"Oh," I say, faking exasperation, "I just completely forgot that my grandparents are coming to stay with us for the weekend, and my mom is freaking out. She needs me to buy groceries. I'm sorry, but I really have to get home."

"Bummer," he says.

"I'm sorry," I say. "I'll make it up to you."

He laughs and reaches out to stroke my face with the back of his hand. "You don't need to make up for anything," he says.

I smile, but the truth is I barely notice him touching me. My mind is somewhere else. Somewhere I need to go on my own.

THIRTY-ONE

FROM THE WINDOW of our guest room, I can see Anderson Farm.

I told my parents I was going upstairs to have a nap, but instead, I'm sitting on the guest bed, staring out at the little white farmhouse and the old pickup truck beside it. A couple of times, I see Mr. Anderson moving around outside. He's wearing a bright yellow rain slicker and working quickly, no doubt tying things down and preparing for the storm. But the only thing I can think about is whether or not he'll leave at some point.

Finally, he reappears and slides into the pickup. He's soon pulling away, and I watch him as he drives behind the barn, then down Anderson Lane, disappearing into the rain.

This is my chance. I don't know how much time I'll have before he returns, so I hurry downstairs and pull on my raincoat and boots. I whistle for Hobo and hook him to his leash, then call into the kitchen.

"I'm taking the dog for a walk!"

"Wait, what?" My mother comes out and stands in the hallway, wiping her hands on a towel. "The weather is terrible. Just let him into the backyard."

"I need some fresh air," I tell her. "I won't be long."

I don't wait for her reply. I just push through the front door, dragging Hobo behind me.

Instead of taking him onto the road, I duck around the side of the house, through the trees in the backyard, and into the overgrown field that borders our property.

We played hide-and-seek here as kids, hidden by the tall, swaying grasses. Now I'm a head above the grass, and as I hurry across, my jeans get soaked from the wet hay. The wind has really picked up. When I let Hobo off leash, he happily races through the field, exhilarated by the wind, leading me to the other side.

Behind the hayfield, a small copse of trees is clustered around a dip in the hill. At the bottom of the hill is a bunch of rusted out farm equipment and a defeated old pickup truck with a tree growing up through the floorboard filling up the cabin—the collected debris from many generations of families.

We reach the other end of the field. I grab a fence post and swing myself over the sagging metal fencing wire, while Hobo scrambles underneath.

I stop at the Andersons' barn. The huge door is open just a crack, giving me a glimpse of the dark, cavernous space beyond it. I wish Quill were here with me, but this is one theory I need to follow up on by myself, because if I'm wrong, I don't want anyone else to ever know that I suspected this.

I close my eyes and try to imagine that I'm a kid again, playing hide-and-seek. I imagine Connor and Carrie and Doris and Ben are hiding nearby, stifling giggles. I step inside.

The musty smell of old manure and slowly rotting hay isn't unpleasant. It actually brings me back to my childhood, when the Andersons had chickens, pigs, a couple of dairy cows, and of course, Star, the beautiful golden horse that Mrs. Anderson used to ride in the parade every summer.

And Prince. The happiest dog anyone ever knew.

Eventually the Andersons grew old—even when we were in elementary school, they'd seemed ancient—and the animals became too much to take care of. Now even Prince is gone, and the rest of the animals are just memories too.

There's a slam, and then a low, mournful wail runs through the barn. I jump, my heart skipping, and then realize that the wind has just ripped open a shutter in the hayloft. I climb the ladder and walk to the small window on the far end. I can see all the way down to Camera Cove, which looks tiny and vulnerable, nestled up against the huge, churning ocean. A thick black bank of clouds is approaching from the horizon, like horses racing across a field. I reach out and grab the shutter, swinging it inward and securing it.

I scan the interior. Most of the empty work space has been taken up by large folding tables that sit under the narrow, dirty windows, covered with unsorted vegetables. Piles of carrots and turnips and potatoes cover an especially dirty one. Another, covered in black garbage bags, is loaded down with tomatoes. Hobo shuffles about, sniffing into corners.

I head down the ladder and move into the workshop room

in the far corner of the barn. This is where Mr. Anderson always had his tools neatly laid out. It isn't the organized room I remember. The tools are carelessly strewn across the long wooden workbench, and moldering old cardboard boxes are stacked erratically into the corner of the space.

Something catches my attention, and I step closer, examining the pile. I begin opening boxes. Inside one, I find old clothes; in another, stacks of old romance novels; dated country and western cassettes sit in yet another.

Then I open a box and find the thing I have been dreading. The thing I must have expected all along, but didn't want to find.

It's full of old catalogs.

Carefully, heart pounding, I pull catalogs out of the box, one after the other. *Summer Catalog, 1967*, one reads. *Fall Lookbook, 1985*, reads another. I pull the box away and open the one beneath it, then dig behind and pull out a couple of fresh boxes. They're all full of catalogs. Dozens and dozens of catalogs that must stretch back over four or five decades.

Everything starts to come into focus. What was the one thing that all the victims except Connor had in common? They all liked to cook. Took it seriously, in fact. I think of George Smith's mother-in-law telling me to take his cooking stuff. Christopher Brindle's new wife trying to live up to Maria's abilities. Joey, teaching herself how to cook, and learning to do it well. They were all the type of people who would have been inclined to visit a farmer's stand for fresh produce. A stand that was conveniently set up right outside the local library.

George Smith and Maria Brindle and Joey Standish weren't killed by someone inside the library, they were killed by someone outside it.

Mr. Anderson.

The friendly conversations at his market stall; the regular customers; the well-framed inquiries to learn about a victim's habits and whereabouts.

Then there was Connor, who worked at the library and would have stopped to talk to Mr. Anderson every day, after a lifetime of being neighbors. Connor, who was spying on people, trying to see them in their natural habitat, trying to draw them as they were, not as how they presented themselves to the world. What did he see? How long did he know? What happened when Mr. Anderson learned that he knew?

It's all so completely insane, but as I think it through, it makes more and more sense. The murders stopped after Connor died. Maybe Mr. Anderson realized that he'd almost been found out. Maybe the shock of killing a neighbor, someone he'd known as a child, broke some kind of evil spell.

I remember Doris saying that she found Mr. Anderson creepy after his wife died. I'd brushed it off, but was she right? Had she picked up on something I hadn't? Had the death of his wife somehow sent him off the deep end?

Another, more urgent question occurs to me. Was Connor meant to be the final victim, or did he only mess up Mr. Anderson's plans? Did Mr. Anderson have someone else in mind for the role of the teenage boy?

I think about Mr. Anderson's repeated invitations to visit him, and a chill runs down my spine. I don't want to stay here; I don't know when he'll return. I glance at my phone. I've only been here for ten minutes, although it seems much, much longer than that. Moving quickly, I open and close doors and drawers underneath the work bench. Mason jars full of screws and nails, random pieces of scrap wood, and then, stuffed into the back corner of a cupboard, behind an old tobacco tin, a box of rat poison.

I don't touch it. I stare at it for a few moments, trying to remain calm, then I close the cupboard door and begin to pack the catalogs back into the box. I push the box back under the pile, trying to make it look the way it did when I entered the room. I stand up and brush off my hands on my jeans, glancing around for any telltale signs that might let on that I was here.

Finally, more or less satisfied that it looks the same, I turn around and step out of the workroom, and as I do so, I hear a vehicle pull into the driveway. The hair raises on the back of my neck. Instinctively, I step back into the workroom and duck behind the door, standing deadly silent.

"Hobo," I say, keeping my voice low but assertive. "Come here."

He stands in the open main room of the barn, near the door. He looks at me and cocks his head. Beyond the barn doors, I can hear the wind and the heavy swell of the distant ocean. Then, the slam of a truck door.

Hobo barks, and before I can run out and grab him, he takes off out the door.

I freeze.

I hear a voice outside in the driveway and Hobo barking excitedly. I scramble, trying to think about what to do. Should I hide? He knows Hobo is here. Should I run back to the house and pretend he got loose and came over on his own?

I hear footsteps approaching the barn. I stare frantically around the tool room. There's nowhere to hide. I swallow hard and step out into the main barn. A moment later, the door pushes open. Hobo races back in, wagging his tail, delighted to see me, as if he hasn't just totally blown it.

Mr. Anderson steps into the barn. His yellow slicker is soaked. With one hand, he reaches up and pulls back his hood. His other hand, I see right away, is holding a hatchet.

"Hi, Mr. Anderson," I say, trying to sound cheerful and normal. I quickly size up the space between him and the door, in case I have to make a run for it, but he's blocking me in.

"Mac," he says. "What are you doing here?" He's staring directly at me, his face grim and unreadable.

"I—I uh," I stammer, trying to figure out what to say. "I thought I'd come over and see if you needed help getting yourself ready for the storm."

"I feel like you've found me out, Mac," he says.

My blood runs cold.

"I think you've been paying more attention than I gave you credit for." He smiles, but it's not natural. The expression on his face is pained, tight.

"I'm not sure what you mean," I say. Desperately, I scan the room, trying to locate a possible weapon. In the corner, I spy a shovel. It's not perfect, but I can use it to keep him and his hatchet at bay. If I can just get to it.

He just stares at me, and his flat face starts to shift from blankness to a clearer expression. He looks angry.

"What was I supposed to do?" he asks, with a sudden flare of rage. He raises his hands, and the hatchet catches the light and glints. He's staring straight into my eyes, and his expression is fierce, almost panicked.

"What do you mean?" I ask. I step backward, considering whether to make a run for the shovel. Mr. Anderson is older than me, much older, but he's bigger, and he's spent his life working on a farm. He's strong and capable, and I don't know if I could fend him off with my bare hands.

"We didn't even know she was sick," he says.

"What?" I ask, genuinely confused.

The hatchet drops to the floor, and he lifts his hands to his face. I could leave now. I could run, yell for Hobo to follow me, and Mr. Anderson wouldn't get me, I know it. But I'm frozen. What is he talking about?

"All we ever wanted was to live here and raise children," he says from behind his hands. "When that didn't happen, we adjusted our expectations. We loved the farm, the animals, loved the town and the view, all of it. We should have grown old together."

His wife. He's talking about Mrs. Anderson.

"I could have done it with her," he says. "I could have kept it up if we were together. But I'm scrambling. Forgetting things. I have no kindling cut, and the storm will be here in a couple of hours. The crops will be ruined. I should have known. I should have prepared better."

He starts to cry. Not even moving, just standing there with tears flowing from his eyes and down his cheeks, onto the packed dirt floor of the barn.

Overwhelmed by the immensity of my mistake, my own eyes begin to itch, but I pinch the bridge of my nose to stop the tears. Right now, my feelings are irrelevant.

"Mr. Anderson," I say, moving to him and putting my hand on his arm, "why don't we go inside. I'll make you some tea."

He nods and allows me to lead him back to the house. In the kitchen, he slumps into a seat at the table. I let out a breath and move through the kitchen, turning on the kettle, looking for tea.

"Thank you," he says, wiping his eyes. He takes a deep breath and then looks at me, shyly. "I'm sorry, Mac. I haven't cried about Margaret for a good year, I suppose. I wish you hadn't seen that."

"Hey, don't worry about it." I lean against the counter, glance down at the hatchet, and feel a twinge of shame for thinking he was going to hurt me.

"It's been a rough couple of years," he says. "Margaret got sick so quickly, and then things just went to hell. She'd only been dead a couple of weeks before the…events of last summer happened. I'm just so glad to have a friend that noticed I need help, Mac."

I feel a deep wave of shame. How could I have suspected him? How could I have thought sweet old Mr. Anderson could have done something like that, when really he'd been left to deal with his wife's death alone? Everything has been overshadowed by the murders. I think for the first time about how difficult it must have been for him to try to grieve his wife, while all around him his neighbors, the whole town, were preoccupied with their own particular horrors.

"I'm just sorry I didn't notice sooner," I say.

I'm talking about him. But as I think of the boxes of catalogs hiding in the barn, I'm beginning to wonder what else I failed to notice.

THIRTY-TWO

BY THE TIME I LEAVE Mr. Anderson's house, my mind is spinning, trying to shift gears and come up with a new explanation. He stands at the door as I back down the steps.

"I'm sorry to leave you, Mr. Anderson, but I should probably get home before the storm."

He smiles kindly, if a bit confused, and raises a hand at me.

"Don't worry about me, Mac," he says. "I'll be just fine. You get that dog home, and both of you stay warm inside tonight. It won't be fit for man nor beast."

"I will," I say, smiling widely, falsely. "I promise."

I turn on my heels before he has a chance to reply, and I'm racing down his driveway, away from the farm and the barn and the junkyard. As Hobo and I run back home, we're gusted by the wind so furiously that I'm reminded of Dorothy and Toto in *The Wizard of Oz*.

What have I learned? What does it mean? A box of poison. A pile of old catalogs.

Connor's face flashes into my mind, smiling his quirky, sideways smile. He's already a year younger than me. He'll always be that age, and I will never be that age again.

Connor.

Connor, who had more talent in his little finger than most of us have in our whole damn bodies.

Connor, who could convince a girl to fall in love with him just by looking sideways at her, just by being himself. No effort required.

I'm away from the farm, and I turn back onto our street, not even stopping to register the sea and the town below me or the path to our spot—the tree where we buried our childhoods. I have no time to think about these things. Not now. I need to get home.

I think of Joey Standish and Connor together. A connection that they wanted to keep to themselves. A pure secret.

I picture them now: Joey opening the door to the cottage, Connor standing there, smiling his smile, waiting for her. The two of them pushing across the room to each other, pulling together, happy to have found a place to hide.

More pictures are starting to come together in my mind. Somebody jealous and unhinged. Somebody lurking in the shadows, watching things unfold and not liking it. Somebody with an axe to grind. Someone who realized they could use the Catalog Killer as a cover. Somebody with a perfect opportunity and alibi.

At home, I yell to my parents that I need to change out of my wet clothes, and run upstairs to my room. I stand in front of Connor's drawing from the time capsule and stare at it. There's only one possibility now, and it's right in front of my face.

I consider calling Parnatsky and telling her what I think I've figured out, but I know the cops will be busy preparing for the hurricane.

Besides, if I call her now, she's just going to ask me what evidence I've come up with, and I'll have nothing to show her except a few boxes full of catalogs and a hunch. If my theory is true, I'm going to need more proof than that.

I pull my phone out of my pocket and scroll through old texts until I find what I'm looking for. My fingers hover over the message box as I stare at the name at the top of the screen.

Ben.

Ben, who idolized Connor, wished he could be Connor, but could never live up to Connor's pure talent.

Ben, who loved Carrie, only to watch his best friend scoop her up from under his nose.

Ben, who has gone completely off the rails since Connor's death.

I type quickly, then press Send before I lose my nerve.

Ben, I need to talk to you. It's important. Please text me back as soon as you get this.

I drop back onto my bed and wait. After ten minutes, I still haven't heard anything, so I try calling. On the third ring, the phone picks up.

"Ben?"

There's no answer, but I can hear someone breathing on the other end. "Ben," I say. "If you can hear me, I need to see you. Please call or text me back." The phone stays connected for a few more seconds, then hangs up. I try calling again, but there's no answer.

I go downstairs to join my parents for dinner. I need to act calm and let things happen in their own time.

"You're distracted," my mother observes, as I pick at my plate.

"I guess I'm just worried about the storm," I lie. As if responding to me, the wind picks up with a huge gust, and there's a loud crash on the deck.

"Shit," says my father, jumping up and running to check. "I thought I got everything into the shed."

Mom and I follow him to the sliding doors in the family room. A branch has broken off the huge maple tree in the backyard and come crashing down a few feet from the house.

"This is horrible," says my mother. "Hasn't this town suffered enough?"

As if to emphasize this, the lights flicker.

"The power won't stay on long in this weather," my father says. He kneels to reach into the cupboard beneath the sink and begins pulling out flashlights and emergency candles.

"We'll just have to make the most of it," says Mom. "What do you say, Mac? You up for a board game?"

"Not really," I say. "I think I'm going to bed."

"Oh, come on," she says. "You used to love a good storm." She grabs the light from my father and holds it under her chin, so that her eyes turn into dark hollows. "We could tell ghost stories."

"I have a headache," I say. "It's been a long week."

She looks at me with concern. "Are you going to be okay? Do you want some Tylenol?"

"I'll be fine," I tell her. "I just need to lie down."

The lights flicker again on my way upstairs. As I push into my room, my phone vibrates in my pocket, and I almost drop it in my haste to see if Ben has texted me back. It's from Quill.

this storm is going to be insane—wish we could cuddle up together

I text him back.

wish you were here too. I could stand to get my mind off things.

I fall back onto my bed and lay there in the dark, staring at the ceiling, trying to make sense of what I'm beginning to piece together.

My phone rings, and I nearly jump out of my skin. I'm surprised when I see who it is.

"Doris?" I answer. I can't remember the last time Doris and I spoke on the phone.

"Mac?" Her voice sounds static and surrounded, as if she's outside.

"Yes!" I yell. "Doris, it's me!"

The static crackles again, and her voice breaks in and out. "—can—me?—hear me? I—heard—Ben."

"You talked to Ben?" I sit up. "What did he say?"

"Mac, I can't hear you," she yells, and her voice suddenly comes in clearer, alarmed in a way I don't recognize. "Ben left me a crazy message. I couldn't understand him at all. He was frantic. He mentioned you. He told me he was going to the caves. He sounded totally unhinged. He said something about you knowing too much. What does he even mean?"

"Doris, where are you?" I ask.

Her voice begins to break up again.

"—going—meet him."

"Don't go in there without me!" I tell her.

Her voice comes back, clear again, and it's the stubborn and resolved Doris I remember. "I think he's going to hurt himself, Mac."

"Doris," I say, speaking as loud and as clear as I can. "You have to listen to me. I think Ben had something to do with Connor's murder. I think he might be dangerous."

There's no answer. The call has dropped off.

THIRTY-THREE

I COME DOWN THE STAIRS quietly and stop at the bottom. An indirect flicker of candlelight comes from the family room. I can hear my parents talking, and from the way their conversation continues without pause, I know they haven't heard me.

I carefully grab my coat from its hook and my backpack from where I tossed it by the door, then I slip out.

I get my bike out of the shed, and then I pedal wildly, racing down the hill toward town.

The streets are empty. The only sound is the chaos of the storm, wind, and waves. I don't know what to do or where to go.

"Think," I say to myself. "Think."

I bike toward the waterfront. All around me, trees creak heavily. Street signs swing back and forth in wide arcs, and wild, erratic winds buffet against me as I pedal into the storm. I drop my bike in the parking lot at the beach and continue on foot. The surf is so high that there's only a thin strip of sand between the boardwalk and the heavy, churning waves.

As I stand there, wondering if I dare to go on, I get a strange feeling, and when I turn back, I realize that the power has gone out. The streets are now as dark as they are deserted.

I step onto the boardwalk, holding the rail for support as I head toward the cliffs. The wood is slippery, and in a few spots, the surf comes up so high that it shoots spray in a high arc that blankets me in mist. It takes me twice as long as it would normally, but I finally reach the cliffs. At the steps to the cave, I stop and pull my phone from my pocket and scroll through my contacts until I find Trish Parnatsky.

I dial, and it goes straight to voice mail. I find myself yelling just to hear my own voice over the sound of wind and surf.

"Chief Parnatsky? It's Mac Bell. I think I might have learned something about Connor's murder. Can you call me back when you get this?"

I hang up and then step onto the first stair. I can't wait for the cops to arrive. Doris might be in danger.

Besides. Ben is one of my oldest friends. I need to hear what he has to say. I owe him that much.

The rain is falling more steadily now, and I stop at the bottom of the staircase. I close my eyes and try to walk back through the events of the night that Connor died, trying to imagine them playing out the way I've begun to suspect they did.

Somehow, Connor set things up to lure the murderer to the caves. At some point, he decided to reach out to me for backup, leaving a note where he was sure I would find it. I've been asking myself for weeks why he wanted me to help him, and the one thing that never crossed my mind was that he needed the help of someone who knew the killer as well as he did. *Keep this to yourself*, his note said. Was it a plea for secrecy, because the person he suspected was someone we knew? A friend? Someone so close to us that Connor had decided to give him a chance to explain?

Expecting that I would show up to help him with his confrontation, he went to the caves to wait for my help, never anticipating that the killer had plans of his own...

I climb onto the wet granite steps, holding out my hand and gripping onto the rope banister to help me along. At the top, at the entrance, I turn and look back along the beach. With the lights out, the town has completely disappeared, and there's nothing but churning surf and heaving, twisting wind.

I step out of the rain and into the mouth of the cave. Instantly, the sounds of the sea from outside become muffled, as if I've slipped into a seashell.

The tunnel curves slowly inward, away from the entrance. I use the glow from my phone's screen to light the floor, and then I come around into the main chamber. The charred remains of the bonfire from the grad party sit in the middle of the space; empty beer cans and food wrappers radiate outward. A filthy old blanket is wadded up against the wall.

There's nobody here.

"Doris?" I call, and my voice goes completely dead, only to return a moment later as a perfect echo. The acoustics are profoundly creepy. "Ben?"

I strain my ears and hear nothing but the rising tide, the rush of water in and out of the caves. I turn off my light and notice immediately that the entrance to the grotto is eerily lit from within. The light is flickering, and I step cautiously toward the hole and crouch to look through it. It's hard to see anything.

I check my phone. No service. I take a deep breath and get onto my butt, kicking my knees through the hole. I slide awkwardly, scuffing gravel and rocks down into the cavern. When I reach out to the sides to slow my descent, I scratch the palm of my hand on the wall. Finally, I land and ball up my fist; I can feel the stickiness of blood oozing out already.

I get to my feet and immediately see Ben. He's standing on the far edge of the ledge. Below him, water thrusts in and out, slow and rhythmic, like a piston. Ben's head is dropped to his chest, and he doesn't even bother to look at me. His fists are clenched, and he's shaking very slightly. I can see now that the light in the chamber is coming from some small stubs of candles that have been melted onto the walls.

"Ben," I say. "Where's Doris?"

He glances toward the churning channel of water, and I feel my mouth go dry as I watch the water suck out of the cavern with a dramatic pounding.

"Why didn't you leave it all alone, Mac?" he asks. His voice is rough, and I can tell that he's been crying.

"I couldn't," I say. "He was one of my best friends."

"You should have left it alone."

"I know what you did," I say. "You couldn't handle that Connor got with Carrie, and you wanted revenge. When he found someone new, you decided to hurt him, didn't you?"

His face is blank, but I can see his hand clench and his shoulders start to twitch.

"You killed him," I say. "First you killed Joey to get back at him, and then you killed Connor."

"No!" he yells, and the vehemence in his voice causes me to take a step backward, but I keep talking.

"You knew that nobody would suspect you, and you thought the murders would be the perfect cover. You went to Joey's house, and you lured her into the woods, and you killed her with poison from Anderson's barn, and you left a catalog picture that you found there too."

Ben's chin drops to his chest, and he puts his face in his hands. He starts to cry, shaking from the bottom up.

"But Connor knew, didn't he Ben?" I ask. "He knew you did it. He confronted you, and you killed him too. Our best friend. It was the perfect alibi. It didn't matter to you who the murderer might end up going after next, and it turned out you didn't even have to wonder. Because the murderer got spooked by the copycatting and hit the road."

Ben's whole body stops moving, and as he lifts his head, I realize that he hasn't been crying.

He's been laughing.

"You don't have the first idea, do you?" he asks, and a hard, resigned look settles on his face. He looks like someone who has made a decision that nobody is going to like, and now he has to break the bad news.

"Everyone thinks that people are so valuable. Everyone thinks that people are irreplaceable. But they're just puppets. When one puppet breaks, there are a million other puppets waiting in line."

"What are you talking about?" I ask, and I begin to see that this wasn't just revenge. He's truly insane.

The ocean pounds in and out of the cavern, and with every cycle, the water gets closer to the ledge. I stay as far back as I can, ready to turn and scramble up the hole. I gauge my distance from Ben. If I can turn and get my footing quickly, I can get up and out of here before he can grab my leg.

I hope.

Ben steps toward me, and I turn to the entrance.

"That's what he called them," Ben says, and it's almost like he's not talking to me at all. He's just casting his words into the hollow of the cave, willing them to be sucked away by the sea. "He called them puppets."

I freeze, then slowly turn back to face him.

"What do you mean, Ben?" I ask. He doesn't answer. "Ben! What are you talking about?"

The water has lifted over the edge, and the noise in my head is competing with the sound of the waves.

"Ben," I repeat. "What are you talking about? Who called them puppets?"

He turns to look at me, and his face twists into an expression of deep and inconsolable unhappiness. "Connor," he says. "Connor called them puppets."

"What?" I ask, barely able to hear my own voice. But even as I'm asking the question, the picture is revealing itself to me. Ben didn't kill Joey.

The truth hits me with the strength of the storm itself, sudden and powerful and unstoppable. The force of it makes me feel like I'm drowning.

Ben didn't kill Joey; Connor did.

Connor killed them all.

"It didn't make any sense, Mac," says Ben, and he's speaking fast now, pleading, desperate for me to understand. "He was our friend. He was my best friend in the world."

The water rushes in with a dramatic crash, only to be sucked out again with a powerful whoosh. The chamber is like a giant heart, methodically pumping blood in and out of the caves. The water is licking at the rubber soles of Ben's sneakers now, and I edge my way back along the ledge.

"Ben, we need to get out of here," I say. "The tide is going to fill up the chamber. Climb up with me, and you can tell me what's going on in the main cave."

"Nobody's going anywhere," says a familiar voice. Before I turn around, I see Ben's eyes lift to the entrance, and the sadness in his face transforms to a bitter hatred.

Doris climbs through the hole, sliding down into the chamber as if it's a move she's practiced a hundred times before. She lands on her feet and brushes off the seat of her jeans.

"Ben," she says, "Get away from the edge. We need to talk about this."

"I'm done talking to you, Doris," he says.

"Ben, you need to take a breath," she says. "We can't go through all this again."

A chill scrapes lightly down my spine. "What do you mean 'again,' Doris?" I ask.

She ignores me. "Ben," she says again, her voice firm and commanding. "Get the hell away from the edge. You're going to slip."

The water rushes in again, and I realize that Ben is up to his ankles in water, and it's now creeping toward my feet. As if in a daze, he moves away from the edge and gets into a kneeling position in the corner. He crouches with his head hanging between his knees, as if he's trying to pretend that he isn't here.

Doris turns her attention to me. "You just had to start asking questions, didn't you?" she asks. "Everything would have been fine, Mac. We would have gone on with our lives. I would have gone to Cornell, you would have gone to Amherst, and we would have put all of this in the rearview mirror. But instead of focusing on getting out, you had to start poking your nose into the past, where it doesn't belong."

"You both killed him," I say, realization creeping up over me like a fog. "You actually did it. You killed Connor."

"We killed a serial killer," Doris says matter-of-factly.

A low wail comes from the corner, and I turn to see Ben standing up from his crouched position. He steps toward me, and I see that his face is wet with tears.

"I didn't mean to do it, Mac," he says, pleading with me. "It was an accident, I swear to you."

"I don't understand," I say. "I just don't understand."

But I am beginning to.

"I knew something was wrong with Connor for a long time," Doris says. "Maybe I always knew. He was so good at being mean when people weren't looking, and the nicest guy in the world when they turned back to him. If you only knew the things he used to say to me...He made me feel like dirt. I hated him, long before he ever moved beyond using words as weapons. Then Ben found out what Connor was like."

I look at Ben.

"How?" I ask him.

"Prince," he whispers.

"Prince? What do you mean?"

"The Andersons' dog," says Doris, impatiently. "Connor killed him."

"Connor came to me," says Ben. "After Prince died, when we were in eighth grade. He told me he'd done it; he'd killed Prince with rat poison he found in the Andersons' barn. I was so upset, because I loved that dog. We all loved that dog. And Connor was joking around with me about how he fed Prince poison and then watched him die. He made it sound like he thought it was a big, funny practical joke or something. I got really upset, and he told me to relax—that he was making the whole thing up. He ended up making me feel crazy. I never knew what to believe."

"Then he had the gall to put the dog tag in the time capsule," says Doris. "The twisted bastard."

I think back to their reaction when I pulled the tag out of the envelope.

Doris reaches into her large canvas bag and pulls something out. It's a sketchbook. She hands it to me, and I hold it in front of me, afraid of what I'm going to see.

"Open it," she demands.

Hands trembling, I flip open the front page. STUDIES, it says, in large block letters.

I turn the page, and I see right away that it's a collage of small sketches of a man. George Smith. I look up at Doris.

"Keep going," she says.

For three more pages, I see innocuous drawings of Smith, some at the library, but also in various other places. It looks like Connor was drawing him from a distance. Then I turn another page, and my blood runs cold. It's a full page drawing of George Smith, dead in his workshop. The way he would have been found by his family.

"No," I say.

"It's true," she says. "You can probably guess what's in the rest of this book. Maria Brindle, Joey Standish. Both of them dead."

"It can't be true," I say. "It doesn't make any sense. Why would he have asked me for my help? What, was he going to tell me he did it himself?"

Ben's face tightens in on itself, and he turns away from me to look at Doris, questioning, as if he wants her permission for something, but she holds up her hand.

"Look toward the end," she says.

Terrified of what I'm going to find, I flip through the pages to the final drawings.

At the back of the book, filling three pages, are sketches of me.

"He didn't ask you to meet him here because he wanted to confess," says Doris. "He asked you to meet him here because you were supposed to be his big finale."

THIRTY-FOUR

MY EARS BEGIN TO RING, and I feel the blood draining from my head. I step back from them.

"No," I say, shaking my head furiously. "No, it can't be true."

"It is true," Doris says. "You were supposed to be the Catalog Killer's final victim. You don't even know how close you came, Mac."

"You don't know that," I say. "How the hell could you have learned that?"

"I suspected him from the start," she says. "The minute the first body was found and rumors started to spread about a weirdly posed crime scene, a picture found with the body, I started to think maybe it was Connor. He was a psychopath, Mac, but nobody else seemed to notice it. Or at least that's what I thought at first."

"Why didn't you say something?" I ask. "Why didn't you go to the cops?"

"I had no proof," she says. "How would it have looked if I'd just waltzed into the investigation headquarters and accused one of my 'best friends,' based on a hunch? I needed evidence, so I started following him. He was spying on people, always with that stupid sketchbook, as if he were some sort of criminal mastermind. What he didn't know was that I was spying on him the whole time."

"But two more people died," I say.

"You're right. I couldn't get to him. I couldn't find proof, couldn't be a hundred percent *sure*. I tried hard, I promise, but I couldn't follow him every minute of every day. But after Joey died…"

"Ben got involved," I cut in.

She nods. "Everyone likes to talk about how Ben hasn't been the same since Connor died, but really, it started when Joey died."

Realization dawns on me. "Joey was seeing you," I say, turning to Ben. "Not Connor."

He looks pained. "I met her in late spring," he says. "She was outside the library, just lying on the grass, reading. She was so beautiful that I had to talk to her. We didn't tell anyone about it. We wanted it to be a secret. We went to those cottages one day—we were exploring the coastline, being together—and we found the key just hanging there on a nail above the window. It was like the place was destined to be ours. We started meeting there twice a week. It was…" he struggles to find the words. "It was perfect."

"Then Connor found out," I say.

"The day she died," he says, "we were supposed to meet there, at the cottage. She never showed. I didn't find out about her until the next day. I was a mess. I was going to talk to the cops, tell them that we'd been seeing each other. Of course I wanted to help them, to find out who had done this to her. But first, I wanted to go back there one last time, to our spot. When I got there, I saw Connor. He didn't notice me approaching. I saw him through the window. He was busy trying to hide something in the ceiling."

"A backpack full of drugs," I say.

"He stole them from Ant," says Doris. "He was trying to frame Ben."

"Why?"

"Because he was a twisted monster," says Doris. "Why else?"

"I think he got with Carrie because he wanted to mess with me," says Ben, "just like when he told me about Prince. When he realized that I didn't care about her, that I wasn't infatuated with her anymore, he broke up with her. Somehow he learned about Joey. After he killed her, he must have broken into the cottage and planted the drugs, assuming I'd tell the cops about us, and they'd find them."

"He wanted to kill two birds with one stone," says Doris. "He wanted to incriminate Ben and rub salt in the wound."

"After I saw him at the cottage," says Ben, "I knew he'd killed Joey. I knew he was the Catalog Killer. I was going to go to the cops, but…"

"But Doris got to you first," I finish.

"I was following Connor when he went to the cottage," she says, "and that's when I saw Ben. I knew it was just a matter of time before he put two and two together."

"She came to see me that night," says Ben. "We walked

through everything. All the evil things Connor did when we were kids. The murders."

"I don't understand," I say. "The two of you knew what was happening. Why didn't you go immediately to the police?"

They look at each other, and for the first time I see a hint of regret in Doris's face.

"We should have," she admits. "We talked about it endlessly. Instead, we decided to confront him first—to give him a chance to come forward on his own. Against my better judgment."

The look she gives Ben tells me whose idea that was.

"You wanted to hear him out?" I ask Ben.

"I wanted to look him in the eye and tell him I knew what he'd done," says Ben, through gritted teeth. "I wanted him to know that I knew who he really was."

"And that's how we ended up here," says Doris.

The two of them regard each other, a mix of sorrow and anger and resignation in their faces. I know they're both wondering what might have happened, or how different things would be now, if they hadn't made that decision.

"How did it happen?" I ask.

"We'd been watching him," says Doris, "covering him, trying to figure out his next move. It wasn't easy. One of us had to be on him all the time, but we figured out a system."

"I started basically living at my old house," says Ben. "My parents were too concerned with their own bullshit to notice how little I was around. It was the perfect place to watch him."

I think back to Ben's empty house, to the dark windows that seemed to stare sadly down at the street after his family moved out. Had he watched me from that window, sitting inside a ghostly shadow of his old life?

"Connor was following you, Mac," says Doris. "He watched your every move, sketched you obsessively. It was hard to believe that he'd target one of his oldest friends, but eventually we both had to agree that you were his next intended victim. We couldn't let that happen."

"I knew about the comics," says Ben. "I knew that you guys had traded them back and forth forever, so when I saw him drop the bag off at your house, I knew that's what it was. But there was something odd about how carefully he placed the bag; the way he stood and looked at it before he turned and left. I knew something was going to happen, that we couldn't stall any longer, so we followed him that night."

"He was waiting for you, Mac," says Doris. "Right here. Like a spider waiting for its prey to just fly into the web. When we stepped down into the cave, instead of you, he was surprised, but not for long. I could see the wheels spinning, the story forming behind his eyes. I was actually curious to hear what he'd say, but he didn't get the chance."

She looks again at Ben, and his face is tight with the memory.

"His face was so smug, so confident," Ben says. "I couldn't stand it anymore. I attacked him. I didn't want to kill him; I wanted to hurt him. I wanted him to suffer for what he'd done. Killing him would have been too easy."

"But you did kill him," I say.

"It all happened so quickly," Doris explains. "It was chaos. One minute we were standing here, looking at him; the next minute, they were on the ground, wrestling. I was screaming for them to stop. They were rolling around on the ground, trying to get in punches, and then Connor was on top of Ben, pushing him toward the ledge. I didn't think. I just grabbed a rock and—"

She stops speaking, her mouth open as if she's forgotten the words.

"She hit him in the head," Ben finishes. "I felt him go limp on top of me and managed to scramble out from under him. We checked to see if he was breathing, and he was. He wasn't dead; just knocked out."

I wait for them to go on, to finish telling me what happened. But they just stand there, staring at the edge. Remembering.

"Which one of you pushed him?" I ask, finally.

"We both did," says Doris. "We didn't discuss it. We just knelt and pushed him. His watch fell off in the fight, and I took it because I thought I might need it." She looks at me, her face defiant. "I'd do it again if I had to."

"His backpack was here," says Ben. "We found the poison and sprinkled some out to make it look like the killer had been sloppy. Then we found the final catalog picture in the sketchbook and stuck it to the ledge."

In the distance, I'm vaguely aware of the water still rushing into the cavern, but the thrumming, pounding drumbeat of my mind crowds it out. As the reality of Connor's death begins to arrange itself into a horrible, logical chain of events, questions begin to tumble out of me.

"What about the Abernathy house and the killer's lair?" I ask.

"We staged it," says Doris. "I knew there were a bunch of abandoned houses outside of town, so we found one, planted some evidence, and waited for someone to stumble across it. We didn't expect it to happen so soon, but a few days later, some kids playing in the woods found it, and the cops jumped at it. They were dying for a break; we just had to hand one to them. Everything would have worked out, and for a year, it did. Then you found that stupid note and started poking around."

"So when you tried to help me, that was all bullshit?" I say. "Leading me to the house? Finding the watch? Your little show in Parnatsky's office?"

"I wouldn't call it bullshit," says Doris. "I'd call it creative redirection."

"What about the eyeball?" I ask. Ben looks confused, but Doris smiles lightly.

"There was an eyeball drawn on the window of my car," I tell him. I turn to Doris. "It was you?"

She nods, giving me a bemused look. I notice that the more she reveals, the more relaxed she seems to get, while the opposite is true of Ben, who is pressed up against the wall of the grotto, shivering miserably. "When you were in the basement at the Abernathy house, I ran back through the woods to the car, then I got back and started yelling for you. Pretended I found the watch."

"I don't understand," I say. "What possible reason would you have for doing that?"

"It was kind of a gamble," she admits. "I knew it would make you think someone was following you, but I also knew that if I could get you to doubt yourself, you might start thinking that you were going crazy."

"So all that stuff about people in town thinking I was in love with Connor?"

"The only people saying that were me and Ben," she says. "I needed you to stop thinking there was something to all this, and start believing that you were imagining it. Thing is, it worked, didn't it?"

I don't answer her. She knows she's right. Even in the face of such a horrible reality, I feel myself flush at the thought that I was so easy to fool.

"I needed to get you to back off, Mac," she says. "For a while, I thought it worked. Until Ben screwed everything up at the parade."

"So what now?" I ask. "What's the plan moving forward? You going to kill me too?"

"That's not what we want, Mac," she says, and although I believe that she's telling the truth, there's also something else in her voice. Something that tells me my safety will come at a price.

I turn to Ben. His face is twisted in on itself, and tears are running down his cheeks. "Why didn't you just leave it alone, Mac?" he moans.

"We can't get caught, Mac," says Doris, her voice calm and controlled, in marked contrast to Ben's. "Think about this. There's no reason for you to tell anyone anything."

"They'll catch you," I say. "They'll know that you did it. There are texts. Phone logs."

"They'll only catch us if you tell them," she says. "You don't have to tell them."

"You can't expect me to keep this secret, Doris," I say.

"Why not?" she yells, and her composure slips for the first time. "I don't care how much this stupid town loved him; he was evil!"

"We only loved him because we didn't know that side of him," I say.

She laughs bitterly. "Bullshit. Even if you put aside the fact that he was a fucking serial killer, he was pure poison right to the core. Do you have any idea how many girls he screwed over, just for his narcissistic games? How many times he reached inside the minds of his friends and twisted them into knots, for no reason except to prove to himself that he could? But people saw a handsome, charming guy, and they turned a blind eye, because that's what the world has always done for awful, talented men."

Her face is tight and pained, the rage in her eyes difficult to look at. In the corner, Ben sits folded in on himself, unable or unwilling to look at us or to contribute to what Doris is saying.

"I've spent my whole life studying, volunteering, signing up for every extracurricular thing I could think of," she goes on. "I had scholarship offers from each of the four colleges I applied to. All four of them offered me full rides! But who noticed? Who cared? Nobody. So please, let's not give Connor the benefit of the doubt anymore."

My mind feels like it's collapsing in on itself. "I don't know what to do."

"I can't keep this up forever, Doris," says Ben. "I feel like I'm going crazy."

Doris turns to look at him, her face going wide with fear as she realizes the situation is slipping away from her.

"I am not giving up my future for this," she says, her voice full of steel. "I've worked too hard to let it go up in flames because of the two of you."

I realize that she's been slowly, imperceptibly advancing on me, and now she's just a couple of feet away. I'm horribly aware of the rushing channel of water behind me—the mighty suction the storm has churned up.

With a sudden jolt of terror, I understand what she's considering, and I take an instinctive half-step back toward the edge of the chasm.

"Doris," Ben pleads, "you don't have to do this. He won't turn us in. I know he won't. Tell her, Mac. Tell her you understand why we did it."

I turn around to look at him, and his eyes are pleading with me. This is my only chance to save myself.

"Doris," I say. "I understand why you did what you did. I do. But if you take this next step, you'll become as bad as he was."

Her eyes are full of tears. "I'll never be like that monster."

"You're right," I say. "You're not."

"I'm sorry, Mac," she whispers, and she reaches out toward me.

I flinch, expecting her to push, to find myself falling back, but instead, her hand grabs my arm and I find myself pulled into an embrace. Doris's breath is hot on my neck, and her tears are a hot slick between our cheeks.

"I'm sorry," she says again.

"I know," I say.

Above the rushing water and the whistle of wind through the caves, another sound emerges from somewhere in the distance: the echo of a voice calling. Doris and I pull apart and turn toward the entrance to the grotto. As the flicker of flashlights shifts to the cave, a huge wave rushes into the channel beside us, spraying water up onto the ledge. I manage to move away from the edge to the safety of the wall, but Doris stumbles and falls awkwardly onto her side.

Water rushes into the cavity below us with a ferocious roar, and as Doris scrambles to her feet, she slips and loses her balance.

There's a horrible moment that seems to stretch out forever, where she manages to catch herself, one foot standing precariously on the edge of the chasm. She locks eyes with me, and I see a terror so complete that it chills me through to the bone. Instinctively, I push myself away from the wall and reach for her, and just as she's about to fall back and be sucked out to sea, I manage to grab her hand.

Her fingers are wet, and her palm is slippery in my grasp. I'm only barely managing to hang on, and as I look into her eyes, I see the kind of terror that must have run through the eyes of Connor's victims.

Next to me, Ben drops to his knees and reaches out. With one strong hand, he gets a good grasp of Doris's other arm, and together we are able to pull her to safety on the ledge.

The three of us collapse into a heap, shuddering with stilted sobs, our chests heaving as we catch our breath.

I'm vaguely aware of someone sliding into the cavern and a flashlight scanning the room until it finds us.

"What is happening in here?" asks Patricia Parnatsky, the shock evident in her voice. "Is everyone okay?"

Somehow I stand, reaching down to give a hand to Ben, and then the two of us pull Doris to her feet.

"We're okay," I say. "They...they saved me. Ben and Doris knew I was letting my imagination get away from me. They convinced me I was wrong. It's over."

"No it's not," says Doris, and I look at her, surprised. She steps toward Parnatsky and holds out her hands in front of her.

"I learned that Connor Williams was the Catalog Killer, and I killed him."

THIRTY-FIVE

THE BACK DOOR on the moving truck parked outside Christopher and Celeste Brindle's town house is open, and as I pull up behind it, I can see that it's almost completely full. Furniture and lamps jockey for space with boxes and bins, and clear plastic bags stuffed full of blankets and clothes and plush toys have been shoved into every available inch of free space. All the bits and pieces of a life—three lives—are crammed into a cube on wheels, ready to hit the road.

It gives me a small thrill of excitement at my own upcoming move, and I sit for a moment, allowing myself to savor the feeling. It's nice to look forward to something for a change, instead of always looking backward.

I get out of the car and walk around to the sidewalk, just as Chris Brindle steps out the front door of his town house, carrying a suitcase down the walk. He stops when he sees me and puts the suitcase down, then reaches out to shake my hand as I approach.

"I was wondering if I'd run into you again before we left," he says.

"I heard through the grapevine that you guys were moving away," I say. "I wanted to stop and say good-bye. And good luck, I guess."

He grins. "Probably the same grapevine that's convincing us to leave," he says. "Not that it matters. It's just that this town knows too much, if you know what I mean."

"Believe me," I say. "I understand better than anyone."

"I know you do," he says, and his face turns serious. "You're a good kid, Mac. I hope you're able to find a way past things, to get on with your life."

I smile. "You know what? I think I'm going to get there."

He shakes his head in disbelief. "You were friends with him, weren't you?"

I nod. "We grew up together."

"The sick bastard," he says. "You never saw anything in him? Any indication that he was a psychopath?"

"No," I say. "But I think maybe some people did. It's hard to say."

It's been a couple of weeks since the news broke that Connor Williams, the golden boy of Camera Cove, was the Catalog Killer. The story went international in the blink of an eye, and I found my own face spreading across the Internet like a virus. The teen who discovered the truth about his childhood best friend. The kid who cracked the case that stumped the cops.

Of course other stories have since taken over, and things have already started to die down. Still, I've received several offers to give interviews, and even a literary agent was in touch, asking if she could represent my story. So far, I've turned them all down. It's not really a story I want to stay alive.

"I'll tell you one thing," says Chris. "I'm glad that he's gone and that people don't have to worry anymore. I'm glad that I know what happened to Maria, and I'm glad that Celeste and Ashleigh and I can start to move on. But it will piss me off until the day I die that he didn't face justice for what he did. He didn't give us the chance."

I glance at the ground, wishing I could tell him the truth, but I know that's not an option. Instead, I tell him the closest thing to it.

"I don't know why," I say, "but I think that in the end, Connor was forced to face the consequences of his actions." I consider my next words carefully. "I think that's why things ended the way they did."

Brindle looks at me curiously, cocking his head slightly to the side.

"I hope you're right, Mac."

He looks like he wants to ask me more, but the screen door behind him opens and shuts with a slam. We both watch as Celeste walks toward us, Ashleigh balanced on her hip. She squints as she approaches, trying to register who I am, then smiles curiously as she places me.

"Hello," she says, the *What brings you here?* hanging unsaid in the air.

"Hi," I say. "I heard you guys were moving, so I wanted to bring you this." I hold out the small envelope I've been gripping since I got out of the car. Celeste hands Ashleigh to Chris and takes the envelope, opens it, and pulls out a small card.

"It's just a thank-you card from all of us at the library," I say. "We really appreciated your donation to our sale."

"Well aren't you sweet?" she says as she reads the short note I scrawled inside. "I'm just glad we were able to help."

"You helped more than you know," I say. "Anyway, I should be going. I've got some more people to thank. Have a safe trip."

I glance over at them as I climb into my car, and Ashleigh, still in her father's arms, waves at me. I wave back at the three of them as they watch me drive away.

When I pull back into my driveway, I'm surprised to see Quill sitting outside with my parents, sipping on iced tea.

"I didn't expect you this early," I say, as I step up onto the porch.

"We were delighted to have some time to get to know Quill," says my mother, with an enormous smile.

"He's a real catch, Mac," says my dad, reaching over to punch Quill in the arm.

"Thank you!" says Quill. "That's what I've been trying to tell him!"

"Oh my God," I say. "Can we go already?"

"I thought we were early," he says. I shoot him a dirty look, and he stands, laughing. "Okay, let's go." He turns to my parents. "It was nice to get to know you guys."

"You'll have to come for a barbecue sometime in the next few weeks," says my mother. "And we'll be having a going-away dinner for Mac before he leaves for school. You should come to that too! His grandparents will be here."

"Why don't you just invite him to move in?" I ask.

"That's fine with us," says my father. "Separate bedrooms though, at least until you're married."

"If we don't leave right now, I'm going to set this house on fire," I say to Quill.

"Okay, okay," he says, still laughing.

I whistle for Hobo, and we walk down my driveway to the road, turning toward the bluff. As we reach the end of Anderson Lane, I hear someone call my name, and I turn to see Mr. Anderson standing up from his garden patch, walking to the fence with a full basket of tomatoes.

"Hey, Mr. Anderson," I say. "Nice evening to get some work done."

"No rest for the wicked," he says with a wink. He smiles at Quill, pulls off a glove, and reaches out his hand. "John Anderson," he says.

"Quill Daye," says Quill, giving Mr. Anderson the kind of firm handshake that old men like.

"Quill's my boyfriend," I tell Mr. Anderson, who beams.

"Well, you couldn't have done better than Mac, here," he says. "A good guy if ever I met one."

"Thank you!" I say. "That's what I've been trying to tell him."

"You don't need to tell me," says Quill, "I knew that the minute I met you."

A flush runs from my neck up to my face, a combination of embarrassment at the mushy talk in front of Mr. Anderson, and the fact that I couldn't be happier if I tried.

"I'll see you on Tuesday with your parents?" Mr. Anderson asks.

"You bet," I say. "Wouldn't miss it." Over the past couple of weeks, at my suggestion, my family has been having a weekly supper with Mr. Anderson. We swap houses, and so far it's been really nice. Maybe someday I'll ask Quill if he wants to come, but for now, he's invited to enough family gatherings.

It's another beautiful night, and I'm happy we're a bit early getting to the bluff. For a while, we sit and talk, just enjoying each other's company. But before long, Carrie and Ant show up, hands raised in greeting, hopping up to join us on the ledge.

"It's weird being here," says Carrie. "It's been a long time."

"A lot has changed," I say.

She nods, and her face darkens. "I still can't believe it," she says. "I can't believe Connor really did those things. How is it possible, Mac?"

"I guess we'll never really know," I say.

"Well, it's over now," she says. "We can start to move on with our lives. I still can't believe you guys will be gone in less than a month."

I nod. "It's kind of crazy."

"I think it's exciting," she says. "You're going to have a new town, new friends, new everything."

"Not everything," I say, and Quill shimmies back to sit up against me. I wrap my arms around him.

Carrie smiles. "I think it's good. I think moving on is a good thing, after what happened."

I feel a twinge of guilt that what Carrie thinks happened isn't the real story, but just like almost everyone else in the world, she knows enough, and I have to be satisfied with that.

It was Parnatsky who came up with the plan. She'd been tipped off by my message. The sound of my voice, faint and straining to be heard over the sound of the hurricane, had sent her to the caves on a hunch. After Doris's confession, she took us back to her office, letting her battery operated emergency lights dimly illuminate the empty police station. Sitting around her desk, drenched with saltwater, the wind whipping outside the empty police station, we'd told her everything. My contribution to the story was minor, just an explanation of what my investigation had uncovered. It was Doris and Ben who did most of the talking. They held back no details, and it was clear they'd been waiting to unburden themselves all year.

At the end of our story, Parnatsky sat quietly for a few minutes, thinking. Then she started talking. It turned out she'd been suspicious of Doris for a while, ever since her phony breakdown in the police station. "It never sat right with me," she said. "You were hiding something. I could see it in your eyes."

"Are you going to arrest us?" Doris asked.

There was a long, dense pause, and the eerie, distant echo of the storm outside the police station was the only sound.

"No," said Parnatsky finally. "As far as I can see, Connor got what he deserved, and there's nothing to be gained from bringing you two before the courts. He's dead. There's no more punishment to be handed out. The only question I have is, Will the three of you be able to keep the story straight?"

The story was sketched out by the four of us in Parnatsky's office and committed to memory by the time the hurricane had worn itself out and the sun had begun to rise on the storm-battered streets of Camera Cove. Between us, we assembled the pieces of the puzzle into a picture satisfying enough so that nobody would question whether there was a different way to put them together.

According to the account we ultimately gave to the authorities, the three of us had privately suspected Connor, but none of us had been willing to fully believe he was responsible. After Ben's breakdown at the parade, I confronted him, and our suspicions came tumbling out. We approached Doris, hoping she would talk us out of our theory, but she had only confirmed that she'd been wondering the exact same thing. It was at this point that the three of us had decided to join forces and search for evidence of Connor's guilt. It was my break-in to Connor's house, and my discovery of the sketchbook, that gave us enough evidence to go to Parnatsky with our theory.

There was enough truth in our story to make it believable and easy to remember. But it was different enough from what had really happened to keep Doris and Ben safe from suspicion and prosecution…and prison.

Most important of all, it worked. With the drugs removed from the cabin and returned to Junior Merlin, Ben was free to tell the story of his secret relationship with Joey and their meetings at the Wandering Surf Cottages. The watch that Doris had removed from Connor and planted at the Abernathy house was enough to suggest that Connor had used the house as a place to plan his crimes.

The final, most important piece of the puzzle was Connor's own death, and this solution, when Parnatsky suggested it, had made as much sense as anything: Connor had been his own final victim. He'd staged it to look like a murder, to keep the world guessing, to keep Camera Cove frightened and suspicious. In a way, it was true; after all, he'd brought himself to the point of no return.

The feds needed to talk to us, of course, but these interviews were little more than a formality. There was no denying the truth, as Connor himself had presented it: his perfect hand had sketched the murder scenes so clearly, unambiguously. After more than a year without a break in the case, the authorities were happy to finally put it to rest, and the people of Camera Cove were beyond relieved to finally put the case of the Catalog Killer behind them.

I squeeze Quill a bit tighter, and he twists around to kiss me on the cheek. He knows everything. Parnatsky agreed that we needed to tell him as well; he was too deeply invested in our investigation. It's been a huge relief to have someone to talk to about it, and he's just glad that it's over, that I'm safe, and that he finally knows what happened to Joey.

Together, we stare out at the water. It is calm and sparkling, vastly different from the storm-tossed waves on the night of the hurricane. But even today, as serene as it seems, there's a whole unseen world beneath the surface...and somewhere, a shark circles, looking for prey.

"Hello, friends."

We turn as Doris and Ben step down from the path into the clearing. It's been a couple of weeks since the hurricane, since the night the truth cracked open in front of me, and I haven't seen much of them since.

I'd assumed they felt the same way I did, that they'd needed space away from everything we shared, but from the way they've arrived together, the comfortable way they move into the space almost in unison, I wonder if I might have read things wrong. I wonder if they've found comfort and solace in each other, the way Quill and I have.

Ben stops in front of me, more centered and at ease than I remember him looking in a very long time. "How's it going man?" he asks, reaching up to slap my leg.

"I'm good," I tell him. "You?"

He nods, smiling. "I'm okay."

I glance past him and catch Doris looking at me. She doesn't drop her gaze, and we stare at each other like that for a few seconds. She looks as calm as ever, but I have to wonder if it's more authentic now—if the release of her most horrible secret has allowed her the space to breathe, after a year of holding it in.

I'll never really know how far Doris was willing to go to keep her secret. All that matters to me is our embrace in the caves—the moment I forgave her for the awful choice she was forced to make. There might be two versions of this story, but there's only one villain, and he's the same in each one.

"Are we ready?" I ask her.

She nods. "You bet we are."

I reach for my backpack and hop down from the ledge. I reach up to give Carrie a hand, and she jumps down after me. Quill and Ant stay on the ledge. I'm glad that they're here to be witnesses, but this moment is for Ben and Carrie and Doris and me.

We gather at the tree, and I pull the thermos out of my bag.

When we buried it those years ago, I remember feeling like everything about it was epic. A time capsule. I remember all of us, even skeptical Doris, squinting toward the future, trying to imagine how much would change between that day and now.

I'm sure none of us could have imagined it, even if we'd tried.

I unscrew the top and turn it upside down, shaking it to make sure there's nothing inside. I hesitate for a moment, then I spit into the thermos. I hand it to Ben, who does the same and passes it on to Carrie, who follows our lead. The thermos ends with Doris. She holds it for a long time, her eyes closed. Finally she spits and reaches out for the lid. I hand it to her, and she screws it back on.

"Good riddance," she says. "Let's do this."

This time, I've remembered to bring a trowel. I bend down and quickly dig out the hole. The dirt is still loose from a few months ago, so the job is easy. I reach back, and Carrie hands me the time capsule, now empty. I press it down into the hole, then fill it back in.

When I stand, I step on the spot a few times to press the dirt down, and Carrie, Ben, and Doris follow suit.

We stay by the tree for a few moments, each of us staring at the freshly churned ground beneath it. I know we're all thinking the same thing.

This time, the past is going to stay buried.

ACKNOWLEDGMENTS

I could ramble on for a hundred years (and I'm capable of it, just ask my friends and family) and still not find the right words to thank my incredible agent, Eric Smith. You're a true inspiration, Eric—hardworking, enthusiastic, kind, and deeply committed to better representation in publishing. I couldn't ask for a better cheerleader, and I'm so grateful that you took me and this manuscript into your fold. Thanks, also, to the wonderful team at P.S. Literary, and of course, thank you to everyone in Team Rocks, my gang of fabulous agent siblings.

A million thanks to Eliza Swift, who saw something in this manuscript and put so much time and effort into making it the best book it could be. Any writer will tell you that a good editor is worth their weight in gold, and I truly hit the jackpot when she decided to take on this project. Thanks to the entire wonderful Albert Whitman team, especially Wendy McClure, who enthusiastically stepped in with her formidable skillset while Eliza was off finishing up another (very important!) project; Christina Pulles, who helped me take the manuscript across the finish line; Lisa White, Annette Hobbs-Magier, and Tracie Schneider, who have been so much fun to bounce promotional ideas around with; and Aphee Messer and Ellen Kokontis, who designed the cover of my dreams. As soon as I make it to Chicago, I'm heading to the AW office with cupcakes!

I'm so lucky to have such a wonderful family, especially Mom and Dad, who have supported me every step of the way. Many thanks to my amazing friends, especially A1 for his input on comics and superheroes, and Angie and Lora for letting me use their hideout in the dead of winter (I spent my birthday by their fireplace, working through a particularly difficult round of edits).

To my many writer friends who know how difficult and rewarding this game can be—thanks for celebrating and commiserating, and for always reminding me that there is a community beyond the closed door of my office. To the booksellers and librarians who have shoved copies of my books into the right hands, I am so grateful for the work you do—you're the ultimate influencers, and you keep this industry rolling.

To the readers who keep coming back, book after book, and especially to the queer teens who write to tell me that they've found themselves in my stories, thank you. In all honesty, there is no higher compliment.

Finally, thank you to Andrew. I'm living my best life, and it's all because of you (and Wheeler, of course).

100 Years of

Albert Whitman & Company

1919–2019

Albert Whitman & Company encompasses all ages and reading levels, including board books, picture books, early readers, chapter books, middle grade, and YA

Present

2017

The Boxcar Children celebrates its 75th anniversary and the second Boxcar Children movie, *Surprise Island*, is scheduled to be released

2014

The first Boxcar Children movie is released

2008

John Quattrocchi and employee Pat McPartland buy Albert Whitman & Company, continuing the tradition of keeping it independently owned and operated

Losing Uncle Tim, a book about the AIDS crisis, wins the first-ever Lambda Literary Award in the Children's/YA category

1989

1970

The first Albert Whitman issues book, *How Do I Feel?* by Norma Simon, is published

Three states boycott the company after it publishes *Fun for Chris*, a book about integration

1956

1942

The Boxcar Children is published

Pecos Bill: The Greatest Cowboy of All Time wins a Newbery Honor Award

1938

1919

Albert Whitman & Company is started

Albert Whitman begins his career in publishing

Early 1900s

Celebrate with us in 2019!
Find out more at www.albertwhitman.com.